THUNDER
OF EAGLES

THUNDER OF EAGLES

William W. Johnstone
with J. A. Johnstone

PINNACLE BOOKS
Kensington Publishing Corp.
www.kensingtonbooks.com

PINNACLE BOOKS are published by

Kensington Publishing Corp.
119 West 40th Street
New York, NY 10018

PUBLISHER'S NOTE
Following the death of William W. Johnstone, the Johnstone family is working with a carefully selected writer to organize and complete Mr. Johnstone's outlines and many unfinished manuscripts to create additional novels in all of his series like The Last Gunfighter, Mountain Man, and Eagles, among others. This novel was inspired by Mr. Johnstone's superb storytelling.

All Kensington titles, imprints, and distributed lines are available at special quantity discounts for bulk purchases for sales promotions, premiums, fund-raising, educational, or institutional use.

Special book excerpts or customized printings can also be created to fit specific needs. For details, write or phone the office of the Kensington special sales manager: Kensington Publishing Corp., 119 West 40th Street, New York, NY 10018, attn: Special Sales Department; phone 1-800-221-2647.

ISBN-13: 978-0-7860-2847-4
ISBN-10: 0-7860-2847-5

First printing: May 2008

14 13 12 11 10 9 8 7 6

Printed in the United States of America

Chapter One

Jefferson Tyree lay on top of a flat rock, looking back along the trail over which they had just come. He saw the single rider unerringly following them.

"Is he still there?" Luke Bacca asked.

"Yeah, he's still there," Tyree answered. Tyree was a short man, lean as rawhide, with a thin face and a hawklike nose.

Jefferson Tyree and Luke and John Bacca were on the run. Just over a week earlier, they had raided a ranch just outside MacCallister, Colorado. Waiting outside the house until sunup, they surprised the Poindexters at breakfast, killing Sam Poindexter and his sixteen-year-old-son, Mort. They also raped, then killed Poindexter's wife, Edna.

They took particular pleasure in raping Poindexter's fifteen-year-old daughter, Cindy, leaving her alive, though not through any act of compassion. They stabbed her, then rode off, leaving her lying in a pool of her own blood, thinking that she was dead.

Before they left the Poindexter ranch, they stole fifty head of prime beef and moved them up to the railhead at Platte Summit, where the cattle were sold at thirty dollars a head for shipment back East.

"Who'd you say that fella was that's trailin' us?" Luke asked.

"His name is MacCallister. Falcon MacCallister," Tyree said.

"Damn!" John Bacca said, his face showing his fright. "Are you sure it's Falcon MacCallister?"

Tyree got up from the rock, knocked the dust off his pants leg, then worked up a spit before he answered. "Yeah," he said. "I'm sure."

"Son of a bitch! Why did he get involved?"

"Who is Falcon MacCallister?" Luke asked.

"You mean you ain't never heard of him?" John asked.

"No."

"Well, that's 'cause you been in prison for the last ten years. But he's—"

"Nobody," Tyree interrupted. "He ain't nobody."

"The hell he ain't nobody. They write books about him, is all," John Bacca replied. "I don't think they'd be writin' books about nobody."

"They ain't real books," Tyree said. "They're dime novels. Hell, they make near 'bout all that stuff up."

"You ain't never had one wrote about you, have you?" John challenged.

"What are you, some kind of idiot?" Tyree challenged. "Why the hell would I want books wrote about me? I ain't exactly in the kind of business where it's good to have ever'body know who you are."

Luke pointed back down the trail. "This here MacCallister may be nobody, but I'll say this for the son of a bitch. Once he gets his teeth into you, he don't give up. We've tried ever' trick in the book to shake him off our tail and he's still there."

Jefferson Tyree knew who Falcon MacCallister was,

but what he did not realize was that the Poindexters had lived very close to Falcon MacCallister's ranch, which meant that Falcon had considered them friends as well as neighbors. And though Falcon was not a lawman, nor a bounty hunter, he'd taken a personal interest in this case. Having himself deputized, he'd made it his personal mission to track down the perpetrators.

"So, what are we goin' to do about that son of a bitch? We can't shake him off," John Bacca growled.

"We're goin' to kill 'im," Tyree said.

"All right. How are we goin' to do that?"

Tyree looked around. "We're goin' to ambush him," he said. He pointed to a draw that cut through the mountain range. "Let's go up through this draw. It's got two or three good places in there where we can hide. All we got to do is let him follow us in there, then ambush him."

"What if he don't come in?" John asked.

"He's after us, ain't he? He has to come in, or figure we went on out the other side."

"Tyree's right," Luke said. "Seems to me like the thing to do is just kill this MacCallister fella and get it over with."

"He ain't goin' to be that easy to kill," John protested.

"You think if we shoot him, the bullets will just bounce off of him?" Tyree asked.

"Well, no, but—"

"No, but nothin'," Tyree said, interrupting John. "Come on, I know a perfect spot."

The man called Falcon MacCallister stopped at the mouth of the canyon to take a drink from his canteen as he studied the terrain. Falcon had a weathered face and hair the color of dried oak. But it was his eyes that people noticed. Deeply lined from hard years, they opened onto a soul that was stoked by experiences that would fill the lifetimes of three men.

Falcon MacCallister had been here before, and he knew this would be a perfect spot to set up an ambush. The question was, had the outlaws done that, or had they gone on through?

Pulling his long gun out of the saddle holster, Falcon started walking into the canyon, leading his horse. The horse's hooves fell sharply on the stone floor and echoed loudly back from the canyon walls. The canyon made a forty-five-degree turn to the left just in front of him, so he stopped. Right before he got to the turn, he slapped his horse on the rump and sent it on through.

The canyon exploded with the sound of gunfire as the outlaws opened up on what they thought would be their pursuer. Instead, their bullets whizzed harmlessly over the empty saddle of the riderless horse, raised sparks as they hit the rocky ground, then sped off into empty space, echoing and reechoing in a cacophony of whines and shrieks.

Falcon chuckled. "I guess that answers my question," he said aloud.

From his position just around the corner from the turn, Falcon located two of his ambushers. They were about a third of the way up the north wall of the canyon, squeezed in between the wall itself and a rock outcropping that provided them with a natural cover. Or, so they thought.

The firing stopped and, after a few seconds of dying echoes, the canyon grew silent.

"Tyree, do you see him? Where the hell is he?" one of the ambushers yelled, and Falcon could hear the last two words repeated in echo down through the canyon. *". . . is he, is he, is he?"*

Falcon studied the rock face of the wall just behind the spot where he had located two of them; then he began firing. His rifle boomed loudly, the thunder of the detonating cartridges picking up resonance through the canyon and doubling and redoubling in intensity. Falcon wasn't even trying to aim at the two men, but was instead taking advantage of the position in which they had placed themselves. He fired several rounds, knowing that the bullets were splattering against the rock wall behind the two men, fragmenting into whizzing, flying missiles. It had the effect that he wanted, because the two men who had thought they had the perfect cover were exposed. Yelling and cursing, they began firing back at Falcon.

It took but two more shots from Falcon to silence both of them.

For a long moment, the canyon was in silence.

"Luke, John?" Tyree called.

"They're dead, Tyree," Falcon replied. "Both of them."

Tyree's voice had come from the other side of the narrow draw, halfway up on the opposite wall.

"How do you know they're dead?"

"Because I killed them," Falcon said. "Just like I aim to kill you."

"The hell you say," Tyree replied.

Falcon changed positions, then searched the opposite canyon wall. There was silence for a long time. Then, as Falcon knew he would, Tyree popped up to have a look around.

"Tyree," Falcon shouted. And the echo repeated the names. *"Tyree, Tyree, Tyree."*

"What do you want? . . . *want, want, want?"*

"I want you to throw your gun down and give yourself up," Falcon said.

"Why should I do that?"

For his answer, Falcon raised his rifle and shot at the wall just behind Tyree, creating the same effect he had with Luke and John. The only difference was that he'd shot only one round, but he'd placed it accurately enough to give a demonstration of what he could do.

"Son of a bitch!" Tyree shouted.

"I can take you out of there if I need to," Falcon said.

"How the hell did you know who we are?" Tyree asked.

"Hell, the whole country knows who you are!" Falcon replied. "You don't have anywhere to go."

Falcon was bluffing. All the time he had been trailing them, he had not known who they were. The names Tyree, John, and Luke, he had gotten from the men yelling at each other across the canyon.

"Come on down, Tyree," Falcon said. "I don't want to have to kill you."

"You go to hell," Tyree shouted back down. "*. . . hell, hell, hell!*" said the echo.

Falcon waited a few minutes, then he fired a second time. The boom sounded like a cannon blast, and he heard the scream of the bullet, followed once more by a curse.

"By now you've probably figured out that I can make it pretty hot for you up there," Falcon said. "If I shoot again, I'm going to put them where they can do the most damage. You've got five seconds to give yourselves up or die."

Falcon raised his rifle.

"No, wait! . . . *wait, wait, wait!*" the terrified word

echoed through the canyon. "I'm comin' down! . . . *down, down, down!*"

"Throw your weapons down first."

Falcon saw a hand appear; then a pistol and rifle started tumbling down the side of the canyon, rattling and clattering until they reached the canyon floor.

"Put your hands up, then step out where I can see you," Falcon ordered.

Moving hesitantly, Tyree edged out from behind the rocky slab where he had taken cover. He was holding his hands over his head.

"Come on down here," Falcon said.

Stepping gingerly, Tyree came down the wall until, a moment later, he was standing in front of Falcon. Falcon handcuffed him.

"Where are you takin' me?" Tyree asked.

"I'm going to take you back to MacCallister to stand trial," Falcon explained.

Two weeks later

The trial of Jefferson Tyree started at nine in the morning, and by lunchtime was over but for the closing arguments. Court recessed for lunch, but by one o'clock everyone was back in place, awaiting the closing arguments.

There was a constant buzz among the spectators in the gallery, but it stilled when the bailiff came into the room.

"Oyez, oyez, oyez, this court in and for the county of Eagle is now in session, the Honorable Thomas Kuntz presiding," the bailiff called.

Wearing a black robe, Judge Thomas Kuntz entered

the courtroom from a door in front, stood behind the bench for a moment, then sat down.

"Be seated," he said.

Kuntz picked up a gavel and banged it once. "This court is now in session. Mr. Bailiff, if you would, please, bring the jury into the courtroom."

The bailiff left the room for a moment, then returned, leading the twelve men who were serving on the jury. They were a disparate group consisting of cowboys, farmers, store clerks, draymen, and businessmen. Quietly, they took their seats.

"Counsel for defense may now present closing arguments," Kuntz said.

Tony Norton, the court-appointed attorney for Tyree, stood and looked at the jury for a moment before he approached the jury box.

"Gentlemen of the jury," he said. "Mine is a very difficult task. I am duty bound to provide Mr. Tyree with the best defense I possibly can." He looked back at Tyree. "It is difficult because Tyree is not a man whose character I can defend. Therefore, I will make no attempt to defend him by his character, but I can, and I will, defend him by the law.

"In order to find Jefferson Tyree guilty of the heinous crime of murdering the Poindexter family, you must be convinced, beyond the shadow of a doubt, that he did it." Norton looked over at Tyree.

"And while every instinct in your gut may tell you he is guilty, this is the United States of America. And in America we do not find guilt by gut instinct. We find guilt by evidence, and by eyewitness accounts.

"Gentlemen, the only evidence we have that connects Tyree with the Poindexter ranch is the fact that he sold fifty head of Poindexter's cattle. He could have stolen those cattle from some remote corner of the Poindexter ranch without ever setting foot in the house, or even seeing any member of the family. Because the truth is, we have no physical evidence to put him in the Poindexter family home on that fateful day, and we have no witnesses who have testified that they saw him there.

"The prosecution," he said, looking toward the prosecutor's table, "has told us that young Cindy Poindexter lived long enough to give a description of the three men who attacked her family. One of the men she described as being short."

Norton looked over at Tyree. "Mr. Tyree is short. But so are you, Mr. Blanton. And you, Mr. Dempster." He was specifically referring to two of the men who were seated in the jury box. "And so are you, sir," he said to a man in the gallery, "and, if you will excuse me, so is His Honor, the judge.

"She also said that he had a big nose." Norton pointed toward the prosecutor. "So does Mr. Crader. For that matter, so do I." Norton rubbed his own nose.

"Tragically, young Cindy Poindexter died of her wounds, so she is not here to be able to provide direct, eyewitness testimony. And without any physical evidence, and without eyewitness testimony, you cannot, by law, find my client, Mr. Tyree, guilty of murder."

The prosecutor stood up then and stared for a long, pointed moment at Tyree. He stared for so long that the judge cleared his throat.

"Mr. Crader, are you going to honor us with your closing? Or must we somehow discern what you plan to say?" Judge Kuntz asked.

"Sorry, Your Honor," Crader replied. He stepped over

to the jury box, standing exactly where Norton had been standing but a few moments before.

"Tragically, young Cindy Poindexter died of her wounds," Crader began. "These are the exact words that Mr. Norton used in his defense of this murderer. Tragically, she died, so she is not here to provide direct, eye-witness testimony.

"Gentlemen, Cindy may not be here in person, but she is here in spirit. With her dying breath, she gave the sheriff a description of the short, big-nosed man who seemed to be the leader. Tyree is a short, big-nosed man.

"'There were three of them,' Cindy said. And when Mr. MacCallister tracked Tyree down, there were three of them.

"I remind you also that Jefferson Tyree and two other men sold fifty head of cattle that bore the Poindexter brand. Perhaps this is circumstantial, and not direct physical evidence, but if you put the circumstantial evidence with the gut feeling that you know Tyree is guilty, you will not let young Cindy Poindexter's last desperate attempt to bring about justice be unrewarded. Bring in the verdict that will allow the souls of Cindy and her family to rest in peace. Bring in the verdict that will allow us to hang this monster."

"Damn right!" someone said from the gallery.

"Hang the son of a bitch!" another added.

Judge Kuntz brought his gavel down sharply. "Order," he said.

Having finished his closing, and with the case now presented, the judge released the jury for their deliberation.

They were back within an hour.

"Mr. Foreman, has the jury reached a verdict?" Judge Kuntz asked the foreman.

"We have, Your Honor."

Kuntz turned toward the defense table. "Would the defendant and attorney please stand?"

Norton and Tyree stood.

Kuntz turned back toward the foreman of the jury.

"Publish the verdict, Mr. Foreman."

"Your Honor, on the first charge, the murder of the Poindexters in the first degree, we, the jury, find the defendant, Jefferson Tyree"—the foreman made a long, direct pause before he finished—"not guilty."

"What?" someone in the courtroom shouted.

"No! This is a travesty!" another yelled.

The entire courtroom broke out into shouts of derision and disapproval.

"Order!" Kuntz said as he repeatedly banged his gavel. "Order!"

He banged the gavel repeatedly.

"I will have order now, or I will clear this court!" he said.

Finally, the court grew quiet, and Kuntz looked toward the foreman.

"As to the second charge of cattle rustling, how do you find?"

"Your Honor, on the charge of cattle rustling, we find the defendant, Jefferson Tyree, guilty as charged."

"Thank you, Mr. Foreman."

He turned to the defendant.

"Mr. Tyree. I can understand the jury's inability to find you guilty of murder due to lack of evidence, or the sworn testimony of an eyewitness. Therefore, I cannot sentence you to hang."

Tyree smiled broadly.

"Before you get too happy, Mr. Tryee, let me tell you what I am going to do. I am going to sentence you to life in prison."

"What? For stealing a few cows? You can't do that," Tyree complained.

"That's where you are quite wrong, Mr. Tyree. I can, and I just did," Judge Kuntz said.

Chapter Two

One year later

When Kyle Pollard came on duty as a guard at the maximum security blockhouse of the State Prison at Cañon City, Colorado, he settled back in his chair, tipped it against the wall, and picked up the notes that had been left by the previous guard.

"Jefferson Tyree is to go to the dispensary at two-thirty today."

Pollard drummed his fingers on the desk for a moment, then let out a long breath.

"Hey, you, Pollard," one of the prisoners called.

"What do you want?" Pollard called back.

"Is it true Tyree is gettin' out of here?"

"What?"

"Tyree is saying that his sentence has been commuted by the governor. He says he's gettin' out of here today."

"Tyree is full of it," Pollard said. "He's not getting out of here today, or any day, until the day he dies."

"Yeah, well, I didn't think so. But I just thought you'd like to know what he's tellin' everyone."

"So, you've told me."

"Is that worth a chaw of terbaccy?"

Pollard chuckled. "Simmons, you sure you didn't make all this up just to get a little tobacco?"

"No, sir, I didn't make none of it up," Simmons said. "He tole me that he's gettin' out of prison today. He says that's why he's goin' to the dispensary. He says the state needs to show that he wasn't sick or nothin' when they let him go."

"It's nothing of the kind," Pollard replied. "He's goin' to the dispensary to be checked out for cooties, same as ever'one else in the prison."

"I'm just tellin' you what he's tellin' ever'one is all," Simmons said.

"Well, that's not worth anything," Pollard said. "But I do like you keeping me up with what's goin' on, so I guess it's worth a chew."

Pollard opened the outer gate, then stepped up to Simmons's cell to pass a twist of chewing tobacco through the bars.

"Thanks," Simmons said.

Pollard then walked up and down the length of the corridor looking into all the cells. When he reached Tyree's cell at about five minutes before he was due at the dispensary, he saw that the prisoner was lying on his bunk with his hands laced behind his head.

"Are you ready to go?" he asked.

"What's there to getting ready?" Tyree replied. "What am I supposed to do, get all the cooties lined up for the doc?" Tyree laughed at his own joke.

"What's this I hear about you telling people you're going to be getting out today?"

Tyree chuckled. "Some folks will believe anything," he

said. "Don't tell me. Simmons reported it to you and you paid him off with some tobacco. Am I right?"

Pollard chuckled as well. "Yeah, I gave him a small twist."

Tyree shook his head. "I can't believe you were dumb enough to fall for that. But then, you are dumb enough to have a job like this, so, I guess it isn't all that hard to believe."

"I'm dumb?" Pollard said. "In a couple of hours, I'll be home with the wife and kids. You'll still be here." Pollard sniggered. "In fact, you'll be here for the rest of your life."

The smile left Tyree's face. "So they say," he said.

"So they say," Pollard said with a snort. "You damn right, so they say." He started to unlock the cell, then stopped and looked over at Tyree. "Get up. You know the procedure," he said.

Tyree was well acquainted with the procedure. He had already been in prison for a year, and this wasn't the first time he had ever been incarcerated.

"Come on, Tyree, I'm waiting," Pollard said again, more impatiently than before.

"Yeah, keep your shirt on. I'm movin' as fast as I can," Tyree grunted.

Tyree got out of his bunk, then leaned against the wall. Pollard stepped into the cell then, and cuffed Tyree's hands behind his back. The cuffs were held together with a twelve-inch length of chain.

"All right, Tyree, let's go," Pollard said. "You lead the way; you know where the dispensary is." He pushed Tyree roughly to get him started.

"I'm goin', I'm goin', ain't no need to be a'pushin' me like that."

"Come on, let's go." He jabbed Tyree with his nightstick

again, this time in the small of the back, hard enough to make the killer gasp. "That hurt."

"Did it now?" Pollard taunted.

They left the cell block and stepped out into the yard. This being the heat of the day, the yard was empty, and as Tyree checked each of the guard towers, he noticed that none of the guards were looking inward; they were all looking out, away from the prison. Just in front of him, Tyree saw a wagon sitting outside the prison commissary. It had just made the two-thirty delivery. Tyree was expecting to see it—in fact, that was why he'd arranged to have his nine o'clock appointment traded with one of the other prisoners.

Suddenly, Tyree stopped and stooped down.

"What are you doing?" Pollard asked. "Stand up."

"I've got a rock in my shoe," Pollard said.

"Just leave it, you don't have far to go."

"It hurts," Tyree complained. "It'll just take a second to get it out."

"All right, but hurry it up," Pollard said.

"Look up there at the wall. What the hell is Cooper doing, pissing off the wall like that?" Tyree said. "This may be a prison, but we have to live here, and I don't like it when a guard steps out of the tower and pisses in our yard like that."

"What are you talking about?" Pollard asked, looking toward the wall. "I don't see anybody—unnhg!"

While squatted down on the ground, Tyree had stepped back over the length of chain in order to get his hand-cuffed hands in front of him. Then, before Pollard knew what was happening, Tyree had used the length of chain as a club to knock the guard down.

Tyree fell upon Pollard, hitting him with the chain several more times, until he was sure the man was dead. Quickly, he got the keys and released the handcuffs. Then he dragged Pollard's body over to the well and dropped him down into it. After that, he climbed into the delivery wagon and hid himself under a roll of canvas.

A moment later, the driver and one of the cooks came out of the prison commissary.

"I won't be makin' the delivery next week," the driver said. "I'm goin' down to Yorkville to visit my daughter. She just had a baby."

"Just had a baby, did she? Was it a boy or a girl?" the cook asked.

"Boy."

"Ha! Knowin' you, you'll have him out huntin' with you in a couple of years."

"I may not wait that long," the wagon driver said, and both laughed.

Tyree felt the wagon sag as the driver climbed into the scat, then pulled away from the commissary. The driver stopped at the gate, and Tyree grew tense. This was the critical moment.

"Open up!" the driver shouted. "I just came to deliver groceries. I don't plan to stay here all day."

"Make you nervous, does it, Zeb?" one of the guards called down from the tower. "'Fraid we might keep you in here for a while?"

"Just open the damn door, will you? This place gives me the willies."

"What do you think, Paul? You think we should go down and check it out?" the guard who had been talking to Zeb asked the other.

"Nah, no need to do that," Paul replied. "I can see the

wagon from up here. Ain't nothin' in it but a tarp roll. Let 'im out, Clay."

Clay pulled the lever to unlock the gate. "See you on Friday, Zeb," Clay shouted down to him.

Zeb gave the guards a little wave, then drove on through.

Tyree lay very still as the wagon passed through the gate, then proceeded up the road. He counted to one hundred, then very carefully lifted the tarp and looked around. They were on First Street, having just crossed over the railroad. Tyree slipped out from under the tarp, and without being noticed, let himself down from the back of the wagon. He moved quickly off the road into a little stand of trees, and down to the banks of the Arkansas River. He continued along the river, following it west, eventually breaking into an easy, ground-covering lope.

Many escapees, Tyree knew, were recaptured almost immediately, because they really didn't know where they were going. Tyree was different; he knew exactly where he was going. He had planned it all out well in advance. He knew that there was a ranch house just over three miles from the prison. Tyree had seen it when the barred wagon that transported prisoners had brought him to the prison. When Tyree and five other prisoners were transferred to the State Penitentiary, they were sitting in the back of the wagon, chained to a steel rod that ran the length of the floor. The others were badly dispirited, and they kept their heads down in defeat and disgrace.

Tyree was still defiant, and he studied the area around the prison, already making plans for an opportunity like the one he had seized upon today. Even then he had noticed the small ranch and the stable of horses.

And yet, a horse and freedom wouldn't satisfy Tyree's

most burning need. That need wouldn't be completely satisfied until he settled a score with the man who sent him up in the first place.

"Mr. Falcon MacCallister," Tyree said quietly. "I'm comin' after you."

Ten miles west of Cañon City, Jefferson Tyree saw a rambling, unpainted wooden structure that stretched and leaned and bulged and sagged until it looked as if the slightest puff of wind might blow it down. A crudely lettered sign nailed to one of the porch supports read: FOOD, DRINK, GOODS.

There were no horses tied up outside, which was good. Tyree planned to pick up a few dollars here, and the fewer people in the building, the better it would be.

The interior of the store was a study in shadow and light. Some of the light came through the door, and some came through windows that were nearly opaque with dirt. Most of it, however, was in the form of gleaming dust motes that hung suspended in the still air, illuminated by the bars of sunbeams that stabbed through the cracks between the boards.

There were only two people in the building, a man and woman. The man was behind a counter, the woman was sweeping the floor.

"This your store?" Tyree asked.

"Yes, sir, it is," the man behind the counter replied. "It may not look like much, but it keeps the wife and me workin'. Don't it, dear?"

"Keeps one of us workin' anyway," the woman replied as she continued to sweep the floor.

The man laughed. "The wife has a good sense of

humor," he said to Tyree. "Yes, sir, if you can't find a woman that's rich or pretty, then the next best thing is to find one with a sense of humor." He laughed out loud at his own joke. "Now, what can I do for you?"

"You got any pistols?"

"Yes, sir, I do," the clerk said. "I've got a dandy collection of pistols—Smith and Wessons, Colts, Remingtons. Just take a look here."

"I'll need ammunition as well," Tyree said.

The proprietor laughed. "My, you aren't prepared at all, are you?" he said. "Well, before I can sell you any ammunition, I'll need to know what sort of pistol you are going to be buying."

"Tell me about this one," Tyree said, picking up one of the pistols.

"Yes, sir, that's one of our finest," the proprietor said. "It is a Colt, single-action, six-shot, solid-frame revolver."

"Solid-frame? What does that mean?"

"It means that the frame doesn't break down to load it. The cylinder is loaded by single rounds. See, you've got a loading gate, located at the right side of the frame. Then, the empty cases are ejected one by one, through the opened loading gate, by pulling back on the ejector rod, located under the barrel and to the right."

"What is this, a .45?"

"It's a .44, sir."

Tyree shook his head. "I'm not very good with a gun, I don't know much about them. You'll have to show me how to load it."

"It's very simple, sir," the proprietor said. He took a couple of cartridges from the box and handed them to Tyree. "Open the side gate there."

"It won't open," Tyree said.

"Oh, I forgot to tell you. The gun can be loaded and unloaded only when the hammer is set to half-cock position, like so."

The proprietor set the hammer, then watched as Tyree slipped two rounds into the cylinder.

"Very good, sir," the proprietor said. "Now, will there be anything else?"

Tyree pointed to the black metal cash drawer that set on the counter. "Yes. You can open that cash drawer for me," he said.

"I beg your pardon?" the proprietor said, shocked by the unexpected turn of events.

"I said, open the cash drawer for me," Tyree repeated. "And give me all your money."

Suddenly, and unexpectedly, Tyree felt a blow on the back of his head. The blow knocked him down, but not out, and looking up, he saw the proprietor's wife holding the broom handle.

"You crazy bitch!" Tyree shouted. He shot her, and saw the look of surprise on her face as the bullet plunged into her heart.

"Suzie!" the proprietor shouted.

Tyree shot him as well, then got up from the floor and dusted himself off. Almost casually, he finished loading the pistol, then, moving around the store, he began collecting supplies: a belt and holster, a couple of new shirts, some coffee, bacon, beans, and a hat. After that, he cleaned out the cash drawer, finding a total of sixty-two dollars and fifty-one cents.

Turning southwest, Tyree rode hard for two days, avoiding towns until he reached Badito. Badito was little more than a flyblown speck on the wide-open range. He chose it because it had no railroad and he saw no telegraph wires leading into it, which meant they had probably not heard of his escape yet. Stopping in front of the Bull's Head Saloon, Tyree went inside and ordered a beer. It was his first beer in over a year.

Shortly after Tyree arrived, a young man stopped in front of the Bull's Head. Going inside, he stepped up to the bar. The saloon was relatively quiet, with only four men at one table, and a fifth standing down at the far end of the bar. The four at the table were playing cards; the one at the end of the bar was nursing a drink. The man nursing the drink was a fairly small man with dark hair, dark, beady eyes, a narrow mouth, and a nose shaped somewhat like a hawk's beak. He looked up as the young man entered, but turned his attention back to the beer in front of him.

"What'll it be?" the bartender asked.

"Beer."

"A beer it is," the bartender replied. He turned to draw the beer.

"Make it two beers."

The bartender laughed. "You sound like you've worked yourself up quite a thirst."

"Yes, sir, I reckon I have. I went down into New Mexico to have a look around."

"Did you now?" the bartender replied as he put the beers on the bar before the young man. "See anything interesting down there?"

"A lot of desert. It's good to be back to land that can be farmed."

"You like farmin', do you?" the bartender asked.

"Yes, sir, I do. My pa's a farmer, and I was raised on a farm."

"I know some farmers. What's you pa's name?"

"My pa's name is Carter Manning."

"Hmm, I don't know think I know him."

"We live up in a place called Hancock," Manning said. "Well, we don't actually live there. Like I say, we live on a farm outside Hancock. But we get our mail at the Hancock post office."

"I was wonderin' why you smelled like pig shit," Tyree said without looking up from his beer.

"I beg your pardon, sir," Manning said. "What did you just say?"

"I said you smelled like pig shit," Tyree said. "You and your old man. As far as I'm concerned, all farmers smell like pig shit."

"I won't hold that against you, 'cause I reckon you are just trying to make a joke," Manning said. "But I don't mind tellin' you, mister, I don't see anything funny about it."

"Well, that's good, 'cause I don't mean it as a joke. You smell like pig shit, just like all the rest of the farmers in the world."

"Mister, looks to me like we're getting off on the wrong foot here. Let me see if I can't change your mind. My name's Manning, John Nathan Manning, and here's to you, Mr.—"

"My name is MacCallister, Falcon MacCallister," Tyree said. "And I'd sooner drink horse piss than drink with a farmer."

"Falcon MacCallister? You're Falcon MacCallister?"

"That's what I said."

"I—I've never met Falcon MacCallister, but I've certainly heard a lot about him. If you are MacCallister, you are very different from anything I've ever heard."

"Boy, that sounds like you're callin' me a liar," Tyree said.

Using the back of his hand, Manning wiped beer foam from his mouth. It was obvious that Tyree had irritated him, and for the briefest of moments, that irritation was reflected in his face. But he put it aside, then forced a smile.

"Hell, Mr. MacCallister, if you don't want to drink to me, that's fine. You're the one that butted into this conversation, so why don't we just each one of us mind our own business? I'll keep quiet, and you do the same."

"So now, you not only call me a liar, you tell me to shut up," Tyree said.

"What's the matter with you, mister?" Manning asked, bristling now at the man's comment. "Are you aching for a fight or something? Because, if you are, I'll be happy to oblige."

"Easy, son," the bartender said, reaching across the bar to put his hand on Manning's arm. "There's something about this that ain't goin' down right."

Manning continued to stare at Tyree, his anger showing clearly in his face. By contrast, the expression on Tyree's face had not changed.

"I just don't like being insulted by some sawed-off runt of a man who doesn't know when to keep his mouth shut," Manning said. "And I don't care if he's the famous Falcon MacCallister or not."

"Let it go," the bartender said.

"Yeah, sonny, let it go, before you get so scared you piss in your pants," Tyree taunted.

"That's it, mister! I'm going to mop the floor with your sorry hide!" Manning said. He put up his fists.

Tyree smiled, a smile without mirth. "If we're going to fight, why don't we make it permanent?" he asked. He stepped away from the bar, then turned, exposing a pistol that he wore low and kicked out, in the way of a gunfighter.

"Hold on there, mister," the bartender said to Tyree. "There's no need to carry this any further."

"Yeah, there is," Tyree said. "This young fella here has brought me to the ball and now I reckon he owes me a dance."

Manning suddenly realized that he had been suckered into this, and he stopped, then opened his fists and held his hands palm out in front of him.

"Why are you pushing this?" he asked. "What do you want?"

"I want to settle this little dispute between us permanently," Tyree said.

"No, there's no need for all this. This little disagreement isn't worth either one of us dying over."

"Oh, it won't be *either* of us, sonny. It'll just be you dyin'," Tyree said.

"I'm not a gunfighter, mister. I don't have any intention of drawing on you. If you shoot me, you are going to have to shoot me in cold blood, and in front of these witnesses."

"What witnesses?" Tyree asked, looking toward the table where the cardplayers had interrupted their game to watch the unfolding drama. "I don't see any witnesses."

Taking their cue, all four men got up from the table, two of them standing so quickly that their chairs fell over. The chairs struck the floor with two pops, as loud as gunshots, and Manning jumped. The four cardplayers hurried out the front door.

Tyree turned toward the bartender. "You plannin' on takin' part in this?" he asked.

"Don't do this, mister," the bartender said. "The boy didn't mean nothin'."

"Either get a gun and take part in this, or go outside with the others," Tyree ordered.

A line of perspiration beads broke out on the bartender's upper lip. He looked over at Manning with an expression of pity in his face.

"I'm sorry, boy," he said. "I—I—" He couldn't finish.

"Go ahead, Mr. Bartender," Manning said, his voice tight with fear. "I'm just sorry I got you into this. I know this ain't your fight."

The bartender remained a second longer, then, with a sigh, headed for the door.

The saloon was now empty except for Manning and Tyree. Manning's knees grew so weak that he could barely stand, and he felt nauseous.

"Anytime, sonny," Tyree said with an evil smile.

Suddenly, Manning made a ragged, desperate grab for his pistol. He cleared the holster with it. Then, as if changing his mind in the middle, he turned and tried to run, doing so just as Tyree fired. As a result, Tyree's bullet struck Manning in the back. Manning went down, took a few ragged gasps, and then died.

Tyree finished his drink, then walked over to look down at Manning's body.

"Son of a bitch, boy," he said. "You made Falcon Mac-Callister shoot you in the back. Wonder what your pa will think of that."

Tyree was laughing as he walked by the saloon patrons and bartender, who were gathered just outside.

"I've heard of Falcon MacCallister," someone said as

they watched Tyree ride off. "Never knew he was an evil son of a bitch."

"That wasn't Falcon MacCallister, you damn fool," the bartender said. "That was Jefferson Tyree."

A few days later, and from another town, Tyree posted a letter.

Carter Manning
General Delivery
Hancock, Colorado

Dear Mr. Manning,
I don't know if nobody has told you this yet but your boy has been kilt. I seen it happen and can tell you that it was Falcon MacCallister what shot him in the back.

Jefferson Tyree

Chapter Three

Pueblo, Colorado

Rachael Kirby played the opening bars of the music as the curtain opened on stage. There, on stage, were Hugh and Mary Buffington, members of the troupe from the J. Garon production of the play *Squatter Sovereignty.*

When they first appeared on stage, the audience saw nothing unusual. The two moved around from one side of the stage to the other, as if searching for something, and Rachael played the music to accompany their movement.

Then, with a crashing piano crescendo, Hugh turned, so that the audience could see his back.

Hanging from his back was a fish.

The audience roared with laughter.

Hugh reacted as if he had no idea what the audience was laughing at, and he kept whirling about, looking behind him, but of course, as the fish was attached to his back, he never saw it.

Rachael kept time with the antics on stage, the piano music adding to the comedy.

Finally, Hugh reached over his shoulder and, finding the fish, unhooked it, and brought it around so he could see it. He gasped, and opened his mouth and eyes wide as he looked at the fish.

Again, the piano music reflected his reaction.

HUGH: By heavens, that's a *haddock*.
MARY: 'Tis, and was hanging to a *sucker*.

The crowd exploded with laughter.

HUGH: You're only *codding* me.

More laughter.

MARY: What *eels* you?

By now, the laughter was nonstop.

HUGH: I've *smelt* that before.

The crowd's laughter was so loud that for the moment, Rachael had to quit playing the piano.

Throwing the fish into the wings of the stage, Hugh and Mary looped their arms together and marched about singing:

> If you want for information
> Or in need of merriment,
> Come over with me socially
> To Murphy's tenement.
> He owns a row of houses
> In the first ward, near the dock,
> Where Ireland's represented
> By the babies on our block.

Rachael accompanied every act and every song, even playing while the curtain was drawn between acts. Most of her music was light, but as a finale to each show, she would play a piece from one of the well-known established composers, such as Bach, Beethoven, Vivaldi, or Chopin.

Such music was not foreign to Rachael, who was a classically trained pianist. She had performed on concert stages in New York, Boston, and Philadelphia, as well as in opera houses in London, Paris, and Berlin.

The conclusion of her number was met with thunderous applause, which intensified, and was accompanied by shouts of "Huzzah!" when the curtains parted for the final bows of the theater group.

Rachael continued to play until the theater emptied. Then, as a couple of theater employees went around extinguishing the gas lanterns, Rachael gathered her music and went backstage to join the others.

It was always an exciting time after a show, with the energy high and the performers teasing each other over the slightest gaff. Also, after every evening performance, the troupe would go out for a late dinner.

But when Rachael went backstage she found, not the merriment and excitement she expected, but angry expressions and harsh words.

"What is it?" she asked, puzzled by the reaction of the others. "What's going on?"

"J. Garon, that's what's going on," Hugh said.

"What about Mr. Garon? Where is he?"

"That's what we'd like to know," Mary said.

"The son of a bitch has absconded with the money," Hugh said.

"You mean tonight's take?"

Hugh shook his head. "No. I mean *all* the money. Everything we've taken in since we started this tour."

"What's worse, he has stuck us with the bill that is due for this theater this week," Mary said.

"Yes, we owe the theater owner two hundred fifty dollars," Hugh explained.

"We owe it? How could we owe it? Garon is the troupe manager."

"Garon's not here and we are," Hugh explained. "The theater manager has already let us know that either we pay what we owe, or he'll take legal action against us."

"Can we come up with two hundred fifty dollars?"

"How much money do you have?" Hugh asked.

"About fifty dollars," Rachael said.

"We can come close."

"But that fifty is all I have. If Garon is gone and we are on our own, I'll need money to live."

"We're all in the same boat, my dear," one of the other players said.

"Maybe we can do another performance tomorrow night," Rachael suggested. "Surely, one more performance will make enough money to get us out of this."

Hugh shook his head. "We've already approached the theater manager with that proposal," he said. "But he has the theater all booked. There's nothing we can do."

"At least, our hotel bill is paid for one more night," Mary said.

"And we have train tickets that will take us back to New York," Hugh said.

"But not enough money to eat on the train," another added. "It's going to be a long, hungry trip."

"The way I see it, we have no choice," Hugh said. "We have to go back to New York."

"I'm not going back," Rachael said, surprising the others.

"What do you mean, you aren't going back?" Hugh asked, surprised by her statement. "Surely you don't intend to stay out here in this—this godforsaken West, do you? Don't you want to go back to New York?"

"No, why should I go back?" Rachael replied. "There's nothing for me back there."

"Rachael, it is ridiculous for you to let Edwin Mathias ruin your whole life," Hugh said.

"Hugh," Mary scolded.

"Oh," Hugh said. "Look, I'm sorry, I shouldn't have—"

"Don't worry about it," Rachael said. "I know you are just trying to be helpful."

They debated as to whether they should have dinner at their usual place that night, or save what little money they had in order to get back home. In the end, they decided they would have dinner.

"We may as well have one last dinner together," Hugh said. "For who knows when we will eat again?"

"That's Hugh for you," one of the others said. "Laughing as we pass through the graveyard."

The others laughed.

Although the dinner could have been a somber affair, the members of the stranded troupe laughed, and exchanged stories in spite of—or perhaps because of—their situation.

Afterward, Rachael went up to her room at the hotel, then lay in bed, staring up at the darkness. She had very little money, no job, no prospects, and no contacts in the West. But she also had no intention of going back East. Her situation was bleak at best, and a lesser person might have cried.

Rachael refused to let herself cry. She had been through

a worse situation than this. She had been through Edwin Mathias.

New York, six months earlier

Unable to sleep after her first performance of the season, Rachael Kirby waited until she was sure that the morning paper was out. Getting out of bed, she went downstairs, and out onto Fourth Avenue to wait by the newsstand until the vendor arrived with a large packet of the day's newspapers.

"Good morning, miss," the vendor said.

"Is that today's paper?" Rachael asked.

The vendor chuckled. "It is indeed. Hot off the press, miss," he said. "It's five o'clock in the morning. There must be a story you really want to see."

"The reviews," Rachael said.

"Ahh, the reviews, yes, I understand. You are an actress, are you?"

"I am a musician, and I did my opening show of the season last night," Rachael said, handing the vendor two cents.

"I hope it is a good review for you then, miss," the vendor said as he gave her a folded issue of the paper.

Rachael took the paper over to the corner and stood under the greenish cast from the gaslight in order to read the review.

Beautiful Chamber Music

Mr. Mathias and Miss Kirby Thrill
Audience at Stuyvesant Theater

The opportunities to hear chamber music under satisfying conditions in New York are not frequent, and

> therefore it is a pleasure to record that Mr. Edwin Mathias and Miss Rachael Kirby gave a violin and piano sonata recital, in the first of what is planned to be many performances for the season.
>
> If last night's performance is any indication, they are assured of a very successful season. The performance was in the Stuyvesant Theater, a perfectly excellent auditorium for chamber music. The feeling is the same as if one is in a drawing room.
>
> The additional fact that Mr. Mathias and Miss Kirby are engaged to be married gave the occasion even more of an air of intimacy.
>
> The program included Brahms' Sonata in A major, Beethoven's Sonata in G minor, and a delightful piece by Chopin. Never was music more beautifully played than by these two wonderful musicians.

"Oh, this is wonderful!" Rachael said aloud.

"I beg your pardon?" the vendor said.

Rachael chuckled. "I'm sorry," she said. "I didn't realize that I had spoken aloud."

Clutching the newspaper tightly, Rachael hurried to Edwin's apartment.

Should she wake him up to share the news? They were both worried about how their concert would be received, being as they were only two people, playing music that normally was performed by full orchestras. In fact, some of their closest friends told them they were taking an enormous risk.

But Rachael and Edwin had put together a schedule hoping for a successful season that would then give them the opportunity to be married. Then, they would go to Europe to play there.

They had each played in Europe before, but always as part of some larger ensemble, never as individuals, and never together. The idea that they could go to Europe as man and wife would be a dream come true. In fact, there were some who said that a marriage between Rachael and Edwin was ordained in heaven.

Rachael went up the stairs to Edwin's third-floor apartment. She started to knock on the door, but feared that if she knocked loudly enough to awaken Edwin, she might also awaken his neighbors. She not only did not want to be rude enough to awaken his neighbors, she also didn't want his neighbors knowing that she was here at this hour, as it might cause talk.

Suddenly, she got an idea. She would cook breakfast for him. She knew where he hid the extra key and, taking it, she went inside to Edwin's small kitchen. She opened the door to the icebox and took out a slab of bacon and some eggs.

The bacon was snapping and twitching in the pan, permeating the apartment with its rich aroma, when she heard Edwin behind her.

"Rachael, what are you doing here?" Edwin asked.

"Isn't it obvious, silly? I'm cooking breakfast," Rachael said, stepping over to kiss him. She intended to kiss him on the lips, but at the last minute, he turned his head so that she wound up kissing him on the cheek, feeling the stubble of a morning beard against her lips.

"But this is my apartment," Edwin said. "What are you doing here?"

"I told you, I'm cooking breakfast. I couldn't wait. Look!" she said, holding up the newspaper opened to the review page. "We got a wonderful write-up! Our season is made, Edwin! It's made! Why, we may not even have to wait until the end of the season to get married. Isn't that wonderful?"

"Edwin, what's going on? Who are you talking to?" a woman's voice asked. The voice was followed by the appearance of a very pretty, and very scantily clad, woman. "Oh, I know you," she said, smiling as she saw Rachael. "You were on the stage with Edwin last night. You were wonderful!"

Rachael was too struck to respond. Instead, she just stared at the young woman.

"Of course you wouldn't remember me, but I was sitting in the front row," she said. "Afterward, I just had to come back and say how much I enjoyed the concert. Then, as Edwin and I began talking, one thing led to another and, somehow, I wound up spending the night here."

"Yes," Rachael said in a quiet, strained voice. "I can see that."

"I know, being in show business, this is probably nothing unusual to you. But I must confess, it's all very new to me, and very exciting."

Rachael turned to go.

"Rachael, wait," Edwin called.

Rachael stopped. "Wait for what?" she asked.

"This—this." He made a gesture with his hands. "I don't know how to explain this, it just happened," he said. He forced a smile. "But you are right, it's wonderful news about the review."

"Good-bye, Edwin."

"Rachael, no, don't go. We can work this out."

"There is nothing to work out," Rachael said. Stepping outside, she forced herself not to cry.

Now, two years later, Rachael lay in bed in a hotel room in Pueblo, Colorado, staring up into the darkness. She had not cried over Edwin, and she was not going to cry now.

She had given twenty-five dollars of her money to help pay for the theater. The troupe had managed to come up with only two hundred eighteen of the two hundred fifty dollars needed, but Joel Montgomery, owner of the theater, had agreed to accept that.

When Rachael went downstairs to prepare to leave the hotel the next morning, the clerk gave her two envelopes.

"What is this?" she asked.

"You must be quite a popular young lady," the clerk said. "They are letters to be delivered to you."

"Thank you," Rachael said. Paying her bill, she walked out into the lobby and sat on one of the circular couches to read her mail. The first was from Mary Buffington.

Rachael opened the envelope and began to read:

Dear Rachael,

We learned of a train leaving at three o'clock this morning, so we decided to take it. I thought about waking you, and telling you good-bye, but given the blow we all received yesterday, I thought that sleep might be better for you.

Hugh said he is not going to let J. Garon get away with stealing our money, and he intends to recover it. I don't know how he plans to do this, but you know that Hugh is a very determined man, once he sets his mind to it.

If he is successful in recovering the money, I will try to see that you receive what is due you, but in order to do that, you must keep in touch with me, so I will know where you are.

You will always be able to reach us at the Players' Guild in New York. Good luck to you in your Western adventure.

> *Love,*
> *Your friends, Mary and Hugh*

P.S. The rest of the troupe sends their love as well.

Putting that letter aside, Rachael opened the other one.

Dear Miss Kirby,

My name is Corey Hampton. My brother Prentiss and I own a saloon in Higbee, Colorado. Let me assure you, it is a saloon of the highest repute.

Last night I attended the performance you and the others gave, and I enjoyed it very much. But what I enjoyed most was your piano playing. It was beautiful, and it held me spellbound for the entire evening.

Then, later, I enjoyed a late dinner, only to discover that you and the other players were at a table very near mine. I intended to come introduce myself to you, but I overheard your conversation, and realized that you had been stranded by an unscrupulous thief who took all your money.

As I understood the conversation (and I beg you to forgive me for my eavesdropping), you and the others are now without employment. Also, if I understood correctly, the others are returning, but you plan to say out here.

I would be very pleased to offer you a job playing the piano in the Golden Nugget. If you are interested in such a position, please meet me for breakfast at Two Tonys Restaurant on Santa Fe Avenue. I will stay there until ten o'clock, at which time I must catch a train to return to Higbee.

Sincerely,
Corey Hampton

When Rachael stepped into the restaurant a few minutes later, the maitre d' came up to her.

"Yes, madam, are you alone?"

"No, Mr. Deckert, the lady is with me," a man said, getting up from a nearby table.

"You are Mr. Hampton?" Rachael asked.

"I am."

Rachael smiled. "I am a pianist," she said.

"I beg your pardon?"

"In your letter, you said you wanted to hire me as a piano player. I am not a piano player, I am a pianist. Do you still want to hire me?"

Corey Hampton smiled, and nodded. "Oh, yes, ma'am, I want to hire you, Miss Kirby," he said. "I think Higbee is ready for a pianist,"

Chapter Four

As Falcon rode down the street in Boulder, Colorado, the hollow clumping sound of his horse's hooves was interrupted by a clang, then a cheer.

"You're goin' to be workin' against a leaner there, Jimmy," someone said. "Better be careful you don't knock it down so that it becomes a ringer."

"You boys don't be worryin' none about that," Jimmy said. "I'm goin' to knock that one off and drop mine in, clean as a whistle."

By then, Falcon was even with the contest, and he heard the sound of the shoe hitting the steel stob, then shouts and laughter.

"I told you, you was goin' to knock that into a ringer," someone said.

"You jinxed me. If you hadn't said nothin', I would'a knocked that horseshoe plumb away from there."

"Yeah, and if a frog had wings, he wouldn't bump 'is ass ever'time he jumps," someone else said, and everyone laughed.

Falcon continued on until he pulled up in front of the

saloon. Dismounting, he went inside, stepped up to the bar, and slapped a silver coin down in front of him.

Looking around, the bartender broke into a wide grin.

"Well, I'll be damned, if it isn't Falcon MacCallister," the bartender said, smiling at him. "You're a sight for sore eyes."

"Hello, Ed," Falcon said. "How cold is your beer?"

"I'm running a little low on ice," Ed said. "But I can promise you that it's colder than horse piss."

Falcon laughed and slid his coin across the bar. "That's good enough," he said.

The bartender shoved the coin back to Falcon. "Your money's no good here, Falcon. The first one is on me."

"Thanks," Falcon said.

"By the way, did you hear that the son of a bitch who kilt the Poindexter family escaped prison?"

"Yeah, I heard," Falcon replied without elaboration.

"I still don't see how it is that they didn't find him guilty of murder. If they had just gone ahead and hung the bastard, he wouldn't be loose now."

"There's no arguing with that," Falcon replied.

"I hope they find the bastard, that's all I can say," the bartender said. "I heard you are the one who brought him in."

"I am."

"Too bad you didn't kill him."

Falcon took a swallow of his beer to keep from answering. He had killed his share of men—more than his share, if truth be known. He had never backed down from a fight and never would, but he didn't have a lust for killing.

The bartender, realizing Falcon didn't want to talk about it anymore, slid on down to the far end of the bar and began polishing glasses.

* * *

"MacCallister, you are a no-count, back-shooting son of a bitch!"

The loud, angry words silenced all conversation in the saloon, and the piano player halted his song in mid-bar, the last few notes hanging discordantly in the air. Except for the loud tick-tock of the Regulator Clock that hung from the back wall, a deathly quiet came over the room.

Falcon looked into the mirror behind the bar. The mirror was distorted so that, although he saw his challenger, he could not see him clearly enough to make out his features.

"Turn around, real slow," the man said. "I ain't a back-shooter like you. When I kill you, I want you to be lookin' right into my eyes."

Falcon took another drink of his beer, doing so slowly and deliberately.

"I said turn around, you son of a bitch!" the man repeated, his anger reaching a fever pitch.

When Falcon turned around, he saw an older man with graying red hair and a scraggily red beard. The man was pointing a Remington rolling-block .45-70 at him.

"I've never shot a man with one of these before," the man said. "But seein' as it'll leave a hole in a bear big enough to stick your fist into, well, I've got me a pretty good idee what it'll do to a low-assed polecat like you."

Falcon noticed that the hammer was not pulled back on the rifle. "Mister, you seem to have something stuck in your craw," he said calmly.

"You killed my boy," the man said. "You shot him in the back. And now I'm going to kill you."

"What was your boy's name?" Falcon asked.

"What the hell?" the old man sputtered. "Have you done kilt so many men that you can't even keep track of 'em?"

"What was his name?" Falcon repeated.

"His name was Manning. John Nathan Manning. I'm Carter Manning. That boy's mama died when he was just a pup and I raised him all alone." Tears welled up in the man's eyes. "And I didn't raise him up just so someone like you could come along and shoot him in the back."

"Well, Mr. Manning, I hope I don't have to kill you, I hope you'll give me a chance to explain something to you."

"What do you mean, you don't want to have to kill me? I'm the one that's holdin' the gun, or ain't you noticed? And what is there to explain about shootin' someone in the back?"

"That's just the point, Mr. Manning," Falcon continued in a calm, quite voice, "I've never killed anyone named Manning, and I've never shot anyone in the back."

"Oh, no?" Manning said, shaking his head. "I may be nothin' but a dirt farmer, but I ain't so far out of it that I'm goin' to let you lie your way out of this. I got me a letter from a man named Tyree. He said he seen the whole thing."

"Would that be Jefferson Tyree?" Falcon asked.

"Ah-hah! So, you know him, do you? Then I reckon that proves he was tellin' the truth."

Manning raised his rifle, but before he even got it to his shoulder, Falcon had his own pistol out and cocked. He stuck his arm out with his pistol pointed right at Manning.

"Don't make me do it, Manning!" Falcon said sharply.

Manning stopped midway through raising his rifle and stared in shock and fear at the big hole in the end of Falcon's pistol. Nervously, he lowered the rifle. "How'd you do that?" he asked in an awestruck voice. "How'd you get your gun out so fast?"

"Mr. Manning, Jefferson Tyree is an escaped convict. He has killed dozens of people, including an entire family," Falcon said. "He killed more than half of them by shooting them in the back. If he says he saw your son shot, then it's better than even odds that Tyree is the one who shot him."

"MacCallister is right, Manning," the bartender said. "Jefferson Tyree is a murderer."

Manning stared at Falcon, but said nothing.

"You have a cartridge in that piece?" Falcon asked.

Manning nodded.

"Take it out."

Slowly and deliberately, Manning rolled open the block and removed the cartridge.

"Have you had your dinner?" Falcon asked.

"What?"

"Dinner," Falcon repeated. "Have you had your dinner tonight?"

"Uh, no. I had me some deer jerky while I was ridin' down here," Manning replied.

"Deer jerky's not much of a dinner."

"It's all I had."

"How about having dinner with me? I'll buy."

"Mister, what kind of man are you?" Manning asked. "I come here to kill you. You could'a kilt me, but instead, you're askin' me to have dinner with you."

"I want you to get to know me," Falcon said. "I want you to know, beyond a shadow of doubt, that I didn't have anything to do with killing your boy. I don't want to be looking over my shoulder to see if you are trailing me somewhere."

"You don't have to worry about that," Manning said.

"You could'a kilt me fair and square, and you would'a been in the right, but you didn't do it. I don't reckon whoever back-shot my boy would be doin' that."

"Then you will have dinner with me?"

Manning smiled for the first time since coming into the saloon. "You reckon I could get me a piece of apple pie with that dinner?"

Falcon returned the smile. "I know a place that serves the best apple pie in Colorado," he said. "Come on, I'll show you."

"Well, I thank you," Manning said. "I thank you right kindly."

The saloon remained quiet as a tomb until Falcon and Manning were gone. Then one of the cowboys said aloud what most of the others were only thinking.

"Damn! In all my borned days, I ain't never seen nothin' like that, no way, no how." Dozens of loud and excited conversations broke out throughout the saloon then, while at the back of the saloon the piano player resumed his music.

"Why is it, you reckon, that Tyree wanted me to think you was the one that kilt my boy?" Manning asked as he forked a piece of apple pie into his mouth.

"Tyree wants me dead," Falcon said. "And if he can get someone else to kill me, all the better for him. And if that person gets himself killed trying to kill me, well, that's no loss to Tyree. I wouldn't be surprised if he didn't pick a fight with your son just to set this up."

"It takes one evil son of a bitch to do somethin' like that," Manning said.

"You just described Jefferson Tyree."

"You know, I should'a known better than to think you

was the one who shot my boy," Manning said as he forked a piece of apple pie into his mouth. "I've heard tell of you, and I ain't never heard nothin' bad about you before. I reckon I was just so heartbroke over losin' my boy that I wasn't thinkin' straight. I hope you don't hold that a'gin me."

"I understand," Falcon said. He chuckled. "By the way, Mr. Manning, if you ever decide to actually use that rifle on someone, may I give you a little advice?"

"A man's a fool that ain't willin' to listen to a little advice," Manning replied.

"Make sure you have the hammer pulled back," Falcon said.

Manning laughed as well. "I'll be damned," he said. "Yes, sir, I'll remember that."

"And, don't go after Tyree. Believe me, he has made enough enemies in his life. Someone is going to take care of him for you. That is, unless you're just burning to do it yourself."

"I ain't necessarily burnin' to do it myself," Manning answered. "I don't care who kills him. As far as I'm concerned, dead is dead."

Higbee, Colorado

Marshal Titus Calhoun was sitting at the desk in his office, going through wanted posters, when his brothers Travis and Troy came in.

"Titus, we got us a problem down at Maggie's place," Travis said.

Titus didn't look up from his posters. "I told Maggie that if some cowboy doesn't pay for his whore, that's her problem, not mine. I can't be wastin' the city's time or money collecting for her."

"This ain't nothin' like that, Titus," Troy said. "It's the Clintons. The Clintons and a couple of their cowboys."

"I thought Maggie said she wasn't goin' to let them in anymore."

"That's just it. She met them at the door and told them they couldn't come in, but one of 'em cut her face pretty good; then they went in anyway. All the girls ran upstairs and have locked themselves in one of the rooms, and the Clintons are raisin' hell down in the parlor."

"How do you know all this?" Titus asked as he stood up and reached for his hat.

"There was three or four customers in there when this all started," Travis said. "They come runnin' out into the street. I seen 'em and asked what was goin' on, and they told me."

"How long ago?"

"Hell, not more'n a minute or two ago," Travis said. "I yelled over at Troy, then we came down here."

"All right," Titus said. "Let's get down there."

Maggie's place was at the opposite end of the street from the city marshal's office, but by the time Titus and his two brothers, both of whom were his deputies, were halfway there, they could hear what was going on.

They could hear the angry exchange of shouts between men and women.

"Go away!" a woman called.

"What do you mean go away? Our money's as good as anybody else's money!"

"I wouldn't split the sheets with any of you if you paid five times as much as the others."

"You whores better get down here now! You got one minute to get down here," another man's voice shouted. "We got Maggie. We'll start cuttin' her up if one of you don't come down."

"Go away!" the woman's voice shouted again.

"We'll go away after we've had our fun."

There was a crowd gathered around outside Maggie's place, and Titus had to push them aside to open up a path so he and his brothers could get inside. When the three of them were on the porch, Titus placed his finger over his lips in a signal to his brothers to be quiet. Then he looked in through one of the windows.

He saw Ray Clinton sitting on the parlor sofa. Ray was a very big man, at least six feet four inches tall, and weighing well over two hundred pounds. Cletus Clinton was standing at the foot of the stairs, yelling up at the women. Ray and Cletus Clinton were sons of Ike Clinton, whose La Soga Larga ranch was the largest spread in Bent County. Titus also recognized Deke Mathers and Lou Reeder, who were two of the cowboys who rode for the Clintons.

Cletus was holding a bottle and he turned it up for a long, Adams' apple-bobbing drink before he shouted again.

"I'm not teasin'," he said. "If one of you whores don't get down here in the next minute, we're goin' to start carvin' Maggie into little pieces."

Titus looked around the parlor for Maggie, but didn't see her.

"Any of you see Maggie?" he asked the other two, speaking quietly enough not to be heard. "I don't want them to start cuttin' on her when we go in."

"I'm down here, Marshal," a woman's voice said.

Turning, Titus saw a heavyset, bleached-blond woman standing just behind the hydrangea bush. She was holding a handkerchief to a cut on her face, though there was very little blood on the handkerchief, and, when she pulled it down, he saw that the face wound was light.

"They're so drunk they think I'm still in there," she said. "They didn't see me leave."

Titus looked in through the window one more time, just to make certain none of them was holding a gun.

"All right," he said to Travis and Troy. "Are you boys ready?"

"Ready," Troy said, pulling his pistol.

"Say when," Travis said. He was also holding a pistol.

"On the count of three," Titus said. Then he counted aloud. "One, two, three!"

Titus pushed the door open quickly; then he and his two brothers rushed into the parlor.

"What the hell?" Cletus said, turning toward the front door as the three lawmen burst in. "What are you—"

For a moment, it looked as if he was going to reach for his gun, but before he could do so, Titus Calhoun stepped up to him and brought his pistol down sharply on Cletus's head. Cletus went down.

"What did you do to my brother?" Ray shouted angrily, getting up from the couch.

"Easy, there, big man!" Calhoun said, swinging his pistol toward Ray. "You're too damn big for me to pistol-whip. I'd have to shoot you."

"No," Ray said, sitting back down and putting his hands up. "No, there ain't no need for you to be doin' anything like that."

"Get Maggie in here," Titus ordered.

Travis stepped out on the front porch to call out to

Maggie. When she came inside, she was no longer holding the handkerchief to her face and the cut, such as it was, was no longer bleeding.

"Did they do any damage to your place?" Marshal Calhoun asked.

Maggie looked around the parlor, then shook her head. "Nothin' that I can see," she said.

"Which one of them cut you?"

"I'm not sure which one it was," Maggie said. "But I think it was him." She pointed to Deke Mathers.

"I didn't do no such thing!" Mathers said.

"Or it could've been him," she said, pointing to Reeder, "Or him," she added, pointing to Cletus, who was just now beginning to get up.

"Damn, Maggie, you've pointed to everyone but Ray. Are you sure it wasn't Ray?"

"I'm sure it wasn't him," Maggie said. "I would have remembered if it was him."

By now, the five other women had come downstairs. Even if Titus did not know what kind of an establishment this was, he would have been able to tell by the makeup and dress, or more accurately the undress, of the women.

"Were any of you women hurt?" Titus asked.

"No," one of them answered. "We were scared, but we weren't hurt."

"Did any of you see which one of them cut Maggie?"

The women all looked at each other, then shrugged.

"None of us seen it," the oldest of the bunch said. She looked nearly forty, though Titus knew for a fact that she was not yet thirty. The dissipation of her occupation had taken a severe toll on what had once been a very pretty young girl.

"Well, pick one of them," Titus said. "I can't make an arrest unless you press charges."

"Oh, I'm not going to do that," Maggie said.

"You aren't going to do what?"

"I'm not going to press charges," she said.

"Why the hell not?"

"I'm trying to run a business here, Marshal," Maggie said. "If I pressed charges every time someone got a little rowdy, I wouldn't have any customers."

"Ha!" Cletus said. "I reckon that means you ain't got nothin' on us. So, why don't you just go on back to marshalin' and leave us alone."

"Get out of here," Calhoun said.

"We're goin', we're goin'," Cletus said. "Come on, boys, let's go over to the Hog Waller. The girls over there ain't as pretty, but they're a hell of a lot more friendly."

"No," Titus said.

"No? What do you mean, no? No what?"

"No, you aren't goin' over to the Hog Waller," Titus said. "When I told you to get out of here, I mean go on back to your ranch. I don't want you in my town tonight."

"You got no right to run us out of town," Cletus complained.

"You'll either leave town, or spend the night in jail," Titus said.

"On what charges?" Cletus asked. "You already heard Maggie say she wasn't going to press no charges."

"I'll press charges myself."

"Oh, yeah? And just what would those charges be?"

"I would charge you with pissing me off," Titus said. "Now, go on, get!"

"I ain't goin' nowhere."

Titus looked over at Ray. "There ain't neither one of

you got as much sense as your youngest brother. But Billy isn't here, and you seem to be a little smarter than Cletus. Get him out of here, Ray. Get him out of here, or I'll throw his ass in jail, then shoot him in the middle of the night for trying to escape."

"What?" Cletus shouted. "Ray, did you hear what that son of a bitch just said?"

"Yeah, I heard," Ray replied. "Come on, let's go."

"I ain't goin' nowhere, I—"

That was as far as Cletus got before Titus pointed his pistol at Cletus, then pulled back the hammer. The clicking sound of the pistol being cocked stopped Cletus in mid-sentence.

"Come on, Cletus," Ray said. "Let's go."

With his eyes glaring hatred at Marshal Calhoun and his two brothers, Cletus reluctantly followed his own brother outside.

Titus, Travis, and Troy went out on the front porch with them, then watched them mount up and ride away, amidst the cheers and catcalls of the crowd gathered there.

"Troy, Travis, get yourselves a rifle," Titus said. "If any one of those men come back into town tonight, shoot them on sight."

"Gladly," Travis said.

"Thank you, Marshal," Maggie said. She smiled. "I thank all three of you. In fact, you three have one free visit coming," she added. "You can choose any girl you want."

Overhearing Maggie's offer, the men in the crowd laughed out loud.

"What about us, Maggie?" one of the men called. "Don't we get a free visit?"

"Sure," Maggie said.

"Great!"

"When pigs fly," Maggie added, and her comment was met with good-natured laughter. "Come on in, boys," she said. "We're open for business again."

Titus watched several of the men go back inside, but there were still several milling about on the street outside the whorehouse.

"All right, boys, the show's over," Titus said. "Let's break it up. Go on back about your business, unless going to see one of Maggie's whores is your business."

When the crowd broke up, Titus, Travis, and Troy started back down toward the marshal's office, where Travis and Troy could get a long gun for the rest of the night's patrol.

"Hey, Troy, did you give Maggie's offer a thought?" Travis asked.

"Are you kidding? Lucy would kill me. If fact, if she even hears the offer was made, she'll be on me like a duck on a june bug."

"Damn," Travis said, laughing. "What do you think, Titus? Is our brother henpecked or what?"

"He doesn't have to worry about Lucy," Titus said. "If I caught him taking Maggie up on her offer, cheatin' on a good woman like Lucy, I'd bust his head myself."

The three brothers laughed and joked as they walked down the middle of the street. The sounds of merriment from the two saloons, loud and raucous from the Hog Waller, and a bit more reserved from the Golden Nugget, told them that the town was having another normal night.

Chapter Five

Over the last twenty-five years, Ike Clinton had bought, stolen, and bullied his way onto one hundred thousand acres of good grazing land. He did this by the sweat of his own brow, and with the blood of the Mexicans and Indians who got in his way. With a sense of irony, he named his ranch La Soga Larga, or "The Long Rope," a tacit admission that he wasn't always too careful about whose calves he rounded up for branding.

His wife, Martha, had been appalled by her husband's ruthlessness and greed, but she was a good woman who would never think to leave her husband, or to tell anyone else of his misdeeds. Adhering to the Biblical injunction to honor and obey her husband, she lived her short married life without complaint, no more than a shadow within the shadows. Martha died when the youngest of her three children, Billy, was five years old.

She didn't live to see any of her sons grow up, and they, especially Ray and Cletus, were the worse for it. Perhaps the ameliorating influence of a good mother would have made Ray and Cletus good men instead of the pompous bullies they became. Billy, everyone agreed, was made of better stuff.

Having invited all the neighboring ranchers over for a meeting, Ike was now standing by the liquor cabinet, leaning back against the wall, looking out over the gathering. His arms were folded across his chest, and his hat was pushed back on his head. He was smoking a thin cheroot as he watched the others arrive.

"Ike, what's all the secrecy? I mean, why are we meeting here, instead of at the Morning Star at our usual time?" one of the ranchers asked.

"I reckon enough of you came to take care of what we need to take care of," Ike said. "So, if you'll all get settled, we'll get started."

While waiting for the meeting to start, the visiting ranchers had gathered into conversational groupings to exchange pleasantries and information. With Ike's call to them, the little groups broke up and everyone started looking for a place to sit. Ike waited until all were settled and quiet before he continued.

"I'm sure that by now nearly all of you have met a fella in town by the name of Wade Garrison," Ike started.

"Garrison, yeah, I know who he is," one of the other ranchers said. "He's a pretty nice fella."

"Yeah, he's a real nice fella," one of the other ranchers put in.

"Got hisself a real pretty daughter, too."

"Tell you what, George, you keep that up and Louise is likely to use a frying pan to knock out what few teeth you got left," one of the others said, and all laughed.

Ike, perceiving that the meeting was getting out of control, held up his hands to call for quiet.

"We ain't here to talk about Garrison's pretty daughter," he said.

"Well, what are we here to talk about?"

"The railroad."

"The railroad? What railroad?"

"The one that Wade Garrison is plannin' on buildin' between Higbee and La Junta," Ike said.

A couple of the ranchers let out a whoop of joy.

"No kiddin'?" one of them said. "We're gettin' us a railroad? Why, that's wonderful news!"

"No, it ain't good," Ike said. "It ain't no good a'tall. We got to stop this from ever happening."

The other ranchers looked confused.

"Now, why in the Sam Hill would this be a bad thing?" a rancher named Phillips asked. "If we could take our cows into Higbee, instead of La Junta or Benton, think how much easier that would be."

"And think how much money it'll cost us," Ike said. "Don't you see? If Garrison gets control of the railroad, he can hold us up for any amount he wants."

"What makes you think he would do that?" a rancher named Warren asked. "The other railroads don't do such a thing."

"All the other railroads already have the tracks laid and their routes formed. They make enough money they don't need to hold us up. It's different with Garrison. He's tryin' to do all this on his own. It's costin' him a ton of money and trust me, he's goin' to be wantin' to get it all back from us. He'll hold us up for as much as he can get from us."

"Yeah, I hadn't thought about that," Warren said. "It could be you are right."

"You say we have to stop him?" Phillips asked.

"Yes."

"Well, my question is, how do you plan to do that?"

"Shouldn't be too hard," Ike said. "He is going to have to have cattle to ship, in order to make a profit. All we have to do is deny him cattle to ship. If we don't ship any of our cattle—if we don't use the railroad for freight, he'll be done for. A railroad can't make it on just passengers."

"Sounds reasonable to me," Warren said.

"Mr. Clinton, I have to ask this. Suppose he goes ahead and builds the railroad," a man named Lassiter said. "How far are you willin' to go to stop it?"

"If he finds out that we are all determined not to use it, he won't build it. He's not going to just throw his money away."

"But what if he does start buildin' it, how far are we goin' to go to stop it?"

"We'll cross that bridge when it happens," Ike said.

Higbee

Wade Garrison was a former general in the Army of the Confederacy. Before the war, he had been a major in the United States Army, a graduate of West Point with a degree in engineering. He had built railroads for the army; now he was planning to build a railroad for himself.

"These are damn good doughnuts, General," Simon Durant said. Durant was a banker from Denver, one of four bankers who were gathered in Garrison's Higbee office.

"You'll have to thank my daughter for that," Garrison replied. "She made them."

"All right, General, you got us all here," one of the other bankers said. "What do you want to talk about?"

"This," Garrison said, pointing to a large map that was

tacked up on the wall of his office. The map covered Colorado, New Mexico, and Texas, and it was criss-crossed with blue lines, and one red line.

"Gentlemen, on this map, you see the railroads that serve our fair state, and in fact, connect our state with both coasts. Those railroads are represented by the blue lines. I propose to add to that network by building the CNM&T from La Junta, Colorado, to Big Spring, Texas," Garrison said. "On the map, the CNM&T is represented by this red line."

"The CNM&T?" one of the bankers asked.

"The Colorado, New Mexico, and Texas," Garrison said. He stepped up to the map. "As you can see, that will open up all of Southeast Colorado, Northeast New Mexico, and Northwest Texas. That would provide service to several thousand miles of country not now served by rail. And the connections at either end, with existing railroads, will mean that we can ship our cattle from here to Chicago, we can import fruit from Florida, or we can buy a ticket to San Francisco or New York and be there within a matter of a few days."

"If I might ask a dumb question," one of the bankers said.

"Greg, as I used to tell my junior officers, there are no dumb questions," Garrison replied. He paused for a second, then added, "Just the dumb-assed people who ask them."

For a second, the four bankers looked surprised. Then, realizing that it was a joke, they laughed appreciatively.

"Go ahead, ask," Garrison said.

"If you look at that map, you will see that there are very few towns or even settlements along the proposed route. Where will the business come from?"

"Ah, the railroad will generate its own business," Garrison said. He pointed to the state of Nebraska. "Gentlemen, when Nebraska was admitted to the Union in 1867, it had a population of just over one hundred thousand people. Today, it boasts over one million. That is a tenfold increase in two decades' time, and that increase is due to the railroad." Again, Garrison pointed to the route of the CNM&T Railroad. "Our railroad is covering twice the area of the Nebraska railroads, which should mean at least twice as many people."

"You are painting a rosy picture, General," one of the bankers said. "But let's get right down to it, shall we? You are going to need financing."

"Yes."

"How much do you need?"

"I've worked it out very carefully," Garrison said, "taking into account right-of-way that must be purchased, as well as right of way that will be provided by grants from the federal and state governments. I have also considered the cost of supplies and labor."

"How much?" the banker asked again.

"Twenty thousand dollars per mile, which means ten million dollars," Garrison said without blinking an eye.

"Ten million dollars?" one of the bankers replied, blanching at the prospect. "That's a lot of money."

"Yes, it is," Garrison said. He smiled. "That's why I have brought four of you here. I'm not asking you to compete for the loan, I'm asking you to share it. This way, you would only have to come up with two and a half million dollars each."

One of the bankers laughed. "I don't believe I've ever heard the words 'only' and 'two and a half million' mentioned in the same sentence."

The other bankers laughed as well.

"Gentlemen, I've done an economic analysis of ten Western railroads. I had Mr. Denham, publisher of the *Higbee Journal*, print out the report for me." He passed out four printed packets, then pointed to a stack of them on the table. "When you go back home, you can take several of these with you to present to your boards. You will see that, in every case, the railroads recouped their investment within the first eighteen months after construction."

The bankers began examining the booklets.

"To secure your cooperation, I am prepared to issue stock, equal to forty-nine-percent ownership of the railroad, to be divided among those who contribute financing, in accordance with the amount of their investment. Gentlemen, within four years, you will double your investment."

"I'm in," one of the bankers said, dropping the booklet on the table. This was C. D. Matthews, of the First Colorado Bank and Trust.

"Thank you, C.D.," Garrison said. "For how much?"

"If nobody else comes in, I'll take all of it," C.D. said.

"Not so fast," Dan Michaels said. "I'm in as well."

"So am I," Durant said.

"That leaves you, Percy. Are you in or out?"

"You think I could have another doughnut?" he asked.

"Sure," Garrison said, handing him one of the confections.

Percy took a bite, then licked the end of his finger. "These sure are good," he said. "Yes, I'm in."

"I'll be damned," C.D. said, laughing. "Boys, we've just seen a two-and-a-half-million-dollar doughnut."

From the Higbee Journal

NEW RAILROAD TO BE BUILT.

*Financing Already in Place to Connect
Higbee with Rest of the Nation.*

Wade Garrison, a former general in the Army of the Confederacy, is a man who is used to getting things done. He has applied the skill and leadership that served him so ably in the great War Between the States to a more peaceful pursuit, and all will benefit from it.

General Garrison has put into motion the plans to build a railroad that will connect Higbee to La Junta to the north, and Big Spring, Texas, to the south. Such a railroad will mean that Higbee can take its place among the major cities of the nation, and indeed, phenomenal growth is predicted as a result.

General Garrison has chosen Higbee as the headquarters of the new railroad, to be called the Colorado, New Mexico, and Texas line, though it shall be quickly recognized by the initials CNM&T.

Signs of the new railroad will be evident within days, as General Garrison intends to build the Higbee Depot immediately. According to the general, the construction material has already been ordered, and will arrive within the week. The office of the CNM&T, currently housed in a small building on Front Street, will be moved to the depot once construction is completed.

Between La Junta and Higbee

Taking on a load from the depot warehouse, three freight wagons belonging to the Bob Thompson Wagon Freight Company left La Junta at ten o'clock in the morning with the expectation of arriving in Higbee by noon. Norman True was the lead driver. True was the oldest of the three, and had been driving for Mr. Thompson from the day Thompson started the operation ten years earlier. The other two drivers were much younger, one a mere boy of sixteen.

The wooden seat of the wagon gave off the familiar scent of weathered wood when heated by the sun that beat down upon it, and while some complained that it was a somewhat stale smell, True liked it. To him, it was as familiar, and comfortable, as a pair of old shoes.

Loaded with lumber and building supplies, the three wagons belonging to the Thompson Wagon Freight Company rolled slowly across the southeast Colorado Plateau.

"You holding up all right, Mickey?" True called to the boy, who was in the wagon directly behind him.

"Yes, sir," Mickey called back. "I'm gettin' a mite hungry, though."

True laughed. "You was born hungry, Mickey," he said. "But if we don't get no rain, I expect we'll be there by noon."

True had teased the boy for being hungry, but the truth was, he was hungry as well. Sometimes he brought a lunch to work, but today he would go home for lunch. His wife had put on beans to soak last night, and began cooking them with a ham bone this morning. He figured on having beans and cornbread for lunch, and the thought of it caused his stomach to growl.

He snapped the reins against the back of the mule team that was pulling the wagon, not to increase their speed, since they were already walking at a good five miles per hour, but just to let them know he was still here. In response, one of the mules lifted its tail and farted.

"Damn, Rhoda!" True said. "You got the smelliest farts of any critter on God's green earth."

Less than a quarter of a mile ahead of the three wagons, four men waited in a stand of trees. One of the trees near the road had been chopped and notched out.

"How much more before you can fall the tree?" Ray Clinton asked.

"Three, four, maybe five chops ought to do it. I don't expect it'll take any more than that."

"All right, get ready. I'll give you the sign."

Ray watched the wagons approach. Then, as they drew even with the western edge of the little thicket, he brought his hand down.

"Now!" he shouted.

Behind him he heard three more blows of the ax, then the creaking snapping sound of a large tree coming down. It fell through branches of neighboring trees, then hit the ground with a loud crashing noise, sending up a cloud of dust as it did so. The tree fell in such a way as to completely block the road.

True heard the tree coming down before he saw it, and having once worked as a lumberjack, he recognized the sound immediately. He hauled back on the team, stopping the wagon just as the tree crashed across the road in front of him.

"Hey!" he called. "Are you a fool, falling a tree across the road like that? Don't you know that could kill someone? Besides which, how are we supposed to get through here?"

Four men came riding out of the woods then, and they approached the wagons as calmly as if they were about to ask for directions.

"You ain't," one of the riders said.

"I know you," True said. "You're one of the Clintons, ain't you?"

Cletus pulled his pistol and shot True at point-blank range.

"Mr. True!" Mickey called, but before he could say another word, he was also shot.

The driver of the third wagon jumped down and started to run.

"Run him down," Ray Clinton shouted, and the other two riders spurred their horses into a gallop. Catching up with him, they shot him as well.

"Burn the wagons."

Cletus Clinton had a can of kerosene tied to his saddle, and he began pouring it on the three wagons. Then, going back to each one, he struck a match and dropped it on the little wet spot of kerosene, and the flames leapt up. In less than a minute, all three wagons were burning.

"Let's go," Ray said.

Higbee

Kathleen Garrison was waiting in the freight office for Mr. Thompson to come back in from the wagon yard. She was an exceptionally pretty girl, tall and willowy, with high cheekbones, bright blue eyes, and long, chestnut hair that hung down her back.

Thompson came back inside. "I checked with the others," he said. "I don't reckon True has come in yet. Ain't nobody seen him, and the wagons is still gone."

"I thought they would be here by noon," Kathleen said. "That's what we were told."

"Yes, ma'am, I know that's what we told you," Thompson agreed. "I don't know what's keepin' him. He should'a been in a couple of hours ago. Could be one of the wagons broke an axle or something. If so, they would have all stayed back until it got fixed."

"My father really needs those supplies, Mr. Thompson," Kathleen said. "Would you please send someone over to let us know the moment they arrive?"

"Yes, ma'am, I'll do that," Thompson replied. He chuckled. "Even though I'm sort of diggin' my own grave, so to speak. I mean, if your pa gets that railroad built, then who'll be usin' my freight wagons?"

"Why, Mr. Thompson," Kathleen said. "When the railroad is built, your business is likely to double."

"Double? How do you see that?"

"How do you suppose people who have things to ship by rail are going to get them here to the railhead?" Kathleen asked. "They'll have to use your wagons. And with the railroad will come more people, which means more business."

Thompson stroked his chin for a moment, then nodded in agreement.

"Yeah," he said, smiling broadly. "Yeah, now that I think about it, you might just be right at that."

"Of course, I'm right," Kathleen said.

"You tell the general I'll let him know the moment the shipment gets here."

"I'll do that, Mr. Thompson, and thank you."

Leaving the freight office, Kathleen walked down to the opposite end of town to a small building that was attached to the side of the hardware store. A sign in front of the building advertised this to be the office of the Colorado, New Mexico, and Texas Railroad Company, though as Garrison was quick to point out, this was only temporary.

A little bell rang when Kathleen pushed open the door of the office. Her father was leaning over a table, examining a map. He looked up as Kathleen came into the office.

"Kathleen, the county commissioners just gave us final clearance for passage all the way to La Junta. There's nothing can stop us now," he said.

"Oh, Papa, that's wonderful!"

"What about the building materials?" Garrison asked. "I'd like to get the depot built right away."

"The shipment hasn't arrived yet."

"It hasn't?" he asked, the expression on his face registering his surprise. "I received a telegram that they left La Junta at ten o'clock this morning." Garrison glanced at the clock. "It's two o'clock in the afternoon. They should have been here two hours ago."

"That's what Mr. Thompson said, too," Kathleen said. "He said one of the wagons may have broken an axle or something. Anyway, I asked him to let us know the moment they arrive."

"Good, good, I'd really like to get started on the depot right away. I think seeing a depot go up in town would have a great effect on the townspeople and—"

Garrison's comment was interrupted by shouting from outside. The shouts were loud and angry.

"What is it?" Garrison asked. "What's going on outside?"

"I don't have any idea," Kathleen replied. "It was quiet when I came in a moment ago."

Garrison put a paperweight on the map he had been studying, then walked over to the door and stepped outside. Kathleen followed him.

"They're dead! All three of 'em are dead!" someone shouted.

"Marshal Calhoun should get a posse together," another called.

"What good would that do? He ain't got no jurisdiction outside of town."

"What about Sheriff Belmond?"

"Lots of luck getting Belmond to do anything."

"Well, we need to do something! We should go after the sons of bitches who did this. We can't just let them get away with it."

"Don't nobody know who it was."

"Abner!" Garrison called to one of the men.

"Yes, sir, General?"

"What are you men talking about? Who is dead?"

"You mean you ain't heard?"

"If I had heard, would I be asking you?"

"No, I'm sorry, General, I guess you wouldn't be," Abner said. "It's Norman True, Josey Hale, and Mickey Wells is who it is."

"Wait a minute, Norman True you say? He drives for Thompson Wagon Freight, doesn't he?"

"Yes, sir."

"Where was he found?"

"They was found out on the road 'bout halfway between

here and La Junta. All three was shot dead and their wagons burnt."

"The wagons were burned?"

"Yes, sir, all three of 'em, burnt to the ground."

"Papa, that's—"

"Yes, Kathleen, I know," Garrison replied. "That's our shipment."

"But why would anyone do such a thing? Mr. True is as nice a man as you would ever want to meet," Kathleen said.

"They weren't after Mr. True, darlin'," Garrison said. "They were after our shipment."

Chapter Six

Ike Clinton, owner of La Soga Larga Ranch, and his three boys were riding into the town of La Junta.

As they came into town, a dog ran out into the road to yap and snap at the heels of the horses. Cletus, the middle of the three, pulled his gun and shot at the dog. He hit the dog in one of its legs, and the dog ran from the street, yelping in pain. A young Mexican boy ran out to grab the dog.

"Ha! Did you see that?" Cletus asked. "I think I took his foot off."

"You ought not to have done that," Billy said. Billy was the youngest. "That dog wasn't bothering you."

"Yeah, well, he was botherin' my horse," Cletus said. "That's damn near the same thing as botherin' me. Anyway, I did the dog a favor."

Ray laughed. "How did you do that dog a favor by shootin' off his foot?" Ray was the oldest, and by far the largest of the three.

"Well, he won't be runnin' out after horses no more now, will he?" Cletus replied. "Like as not some horse would'a kicked him in the head and kilt him one of these days."

"Yeah," Billy growled. "You were just real good to him."

"Hey, Ray, what do you think? Billy is just all broke up 'cause I shot that dog's foot off."

"Yeah," Ray said. "Billy worries about things like that—being good to dogs, little kids, and old folks."

"Billy, how the hell did you get to be so different from us?" Cletus asked.

"You boys quit pickin' on your brother," Ike said.

"I can't help pickin' on him," Cletus said. "He's so damn easy to pick on."

Ray laughed.

"Pa, you sure they didn't somebody else crawl into bed with Ma before this pup was borned?" Ray asked.

"If there had'a been somebody crawled in bed with Martha, whatever he whelped would'a never been born," Ike said. "I'd'a kilt 'em both."

"So, what you are sayin' is, Billy is our kith an' kin."

"That's what I'm sayin'."

"Well, maybe so, but he sure is different," Ray said. "Always worryin' 'bout the other fella, and puttin' ever'-body else's good a'fore his own blood."

"Hey, Pa, what time does the train get in?" Cletus asked.

"I make it about another hour," Ike replied.

"Then what do you say we stop by the Bull's Head and have us a couple of drinks?" Cletus suggested.

Ike shook his head. "I intend that you boys get on that train. There's a cattle buyer will be in Pueblo, and I aim for you to get us the best offer for our cows I can get."

"We ain't goin' to miss the train, Pa," Ray said. "And it was a long ride over here from the ranch. Don't tell me you ain't got no dust in your mouth that a couple of beers and a whiskey or two wouldn't do for you?"

"All right, we'll stop for a drink," Ike replied. "But I'm goin' to stay with you till I see you are all three on the train."

Dismounting in front of the saloon, the four riders looped the reins of their horses over the hitching rail, then went inside. There wasn't quite room for all four of them to stand at the bar, but Cletus and Ray made room by pushing a couple of men apart to open up a big enough space for them.

"Hey, what the hell do you think you're doin', mister?" one of the men said angrily.

"Larry, that's the Clintons," a man next to him whispered.

"I don't care who it is. There don't nobody—"

Before he could finish his statement, Cletus pulled his pistol and shoved it into the man's face.

"You complainin' about somethin' are you, mister?" Cletus asked menacingly.

The complainer was a good-sized man who was perfectly willing to use his fists to defend his position at the bar. But he wasn't willing to die for it. He stared at the gun for a moment.

"Sure, mister," he said. "You want to stand up here that bad, you are welcome to it." Turning away from the bar, he walked out of the saloon.

"Ha!" Cletus said with a barking laugh. "I sure made him back down, didn't I?"

Turning around to lean against the bar, Ray looked out over the saloon at the bar girls who were working the customers.

"Hey, Cletus, think we got time to go upstairs with one of these here whores?" Ray asked.

"You ain't got time to be messin' with no whores," Ike said.

"If we don't go with no whores here, where can we go?" Cletus asked. "The only whores in Higbee that will go with us is the ones in the Hog Waller. None of Maggie's whores will have anything to do with us."

Billy laughed.

"What are you laughin' at?" Cletus asked.

"I've heard about men who couldn't get themselves a woman," Billy said. "But when you can't even get a whore, that's pretty bad."

"Yeah? Well, I don't see you havin' all that much luck with that Garrison girl, now, do I?" Cletus asked.

"What Garrison girl?" Ike asked quickly. "What are you talking about?"

"Nothin', Pa," Billy said. "We aren't talkin' about anything."

"The hell we ain't," said Cletus. "You been sniffin' round the general's daughter like a male dog around a bitch in heat."

"Boy, tell me that ain't so," Ike said. "After what's goin' on between Garrison and me?"

"Pa, this is between Kathleen and me," Billy said. "It doesn't have anything to do with her pa, or with you."

"The hell it don't," Ike said. He pointed a long, bony finger at Billy. "I don't want you to be havin' anything to do with that girl. Do you hear me?"

Billy didn't answer. Fortunately, he wasn't required to because Cletus started laughing.

"What are you laughin' at?" Ike asked.

"I was just thinkin' about Little Billy here. As far as you're concerned, he can do no wrong. Only, that ain't the case no more, is it?"

The sound of a train whistle could be heard in the distance, and Ike tossed down the rest of his drink, then wiped his mouth with the back of his hand.

"Finish your drinks, boys," he said. "The train's a'comin'."

Relieved that the whistle of the train had interrupted a conversation that was growing increasingly more uncomfortable, Billy finished his beer, then followed his father and brothers out of the saloon.

"Looks like you just lost four of your customers there, Hank," one of the men standing at the bar said.

Hank, the barkeep, wiped the bar in front of where the Clintons had been standing. "Wouldn't bother me if they didn't never come back in here," he said. "There ain't a one of 'em worth the powder it would take to blow 'em to hell."

"Oh, I don't know. Billy's all right," the customer said.

"Yeah, he's not bad if he's by himself. Trouble is, he ain't ever by himself," George said.

Down at the depot, Ike, Ray, Cletus, and Billy stood on the wooden platform as the train pulled into the station with hissing steam, squeaking brakes, and a clanging bell.

"Ray, I'm countin' on you to see to it that we get top dollar for our cows," Ike said to his oldest son.

"All right, Pa," Ray said.

"And Billy, you seem to have the most sense, so I'm countin' on you to keep the other two out of trouble long enough to close the deal."

"I'll do what I can," Billy said.

"What about me, Pa?" Cletus said. "What do you want me to do?"

"You're the worst of the lot," Ike said without regard as to how Cletus would take that comment.

"What do you mean I'm the worst of the lot?" Cletus asked. He seemed genuinely hurt by Ike's words.

"You are good with a gun, you've got a temper, and you can't stay away from whiskey or women," Ike said. He shook his head. "Boy, that ain't a good combination. I want you to keep your mouth shut when Ray is doin' business, and listen to what Billy is sayin' when you're drinkin' or messin' with the whores," Ike said.

Cletus glared at his father. "You don't think much of me, do you, Pa?" he asked.

"Not all that much," Ike replied, again oblivious as to how the words may have sounded to Cletus. "Get on the train now," he ordered.

Ray laughed. "Pa, you goin' to get on the train with us to see if we get the seats we're supposed to?"

Ike shook his head. "I'm hopin' you got enough sense to do that on your own."

Higbee

The warm afternoon, the rocking motion of the stage, and the rhythmic sound of horses' hooves and rolling wheels had combined to put Rachael asleep. She didn't wake up until the coach came to a stop.

"Higbee, folks!" the driver called down. "This is Higbee."

"Oh," Rachael said. "I must've fallen asleep."

"Yes, ma'am, you did," her fellow passenger said. He was a traveling preacher. "Ordinarily, I get into a good conversation with whoever is riding with me when I make this trip. But you were sleeping so soundly that I didn't want to disturb you."

"I'm sorry I was so rude as to fall asleep," Rachael said.

"Oh, no need to apologize, ma'am," he said. He pulled out his pocket watch and checked it. "I guess I had better get on down to the church," he said. "Reverend Owen and the board of deacons are having a meeting and they asked me to come."

The preacher stepped out of the coach, then reached his hand back to help Rachael down.

"Thank you," Rachael said.

Rachael stepped up onto the porch of the depot and looked around.

"Can I help you with somethin', ma'am?" the driver asked. He was standing at the boot, unloading packages as well as Rachael's suitcase.

"No, I suppose not," Rachael said. "Someone was supposed to meet me and I was just looking around to see if I could see him."

At that moment, there was the crash of glass, then a burst of loud raucous laughter from a building across the street.

"What is that building?" Rachael asked.

"Oh, that's the saloon," the driver said.

"The saloon?" Rachael replied in a weak voice.

"Yes, ma'am. Here's your luggage, ma'am."

"Driver, do you suppose I could keep my grip in the depot for a while?"

"I reckon they'd let you do that," the driver said. "How long would you think it might be?"

"I don't know," Rachael said. "Perhaps only until the next stage returns to La Junta."

"That would be tomorrow," the driver said. "Would you really come all the way out here just to spend one night?"

"That might be the case," Rachael said. "If you would, please, put it in the depot."

"Yes, ma'am," the driver replied.

Taking a deep breath, and squaring her shoulders, Rachael walked across the street, then up onto the front porch of the saloon. She paused for just a moment, then pushed open the doors and stepped inside.

The first thing she noticed was the odor, a combination of stale beer, sour whiskey, and unwashed bodies. The floor was covered with expectorated tobacco quids, and the towels, hanging from hooks on the bar, were filthy. At least ten men were standing at the bar, and that many or more were sitting at tables.

Rachael looked around for a piano and finally saw it, sitting against the wall just under the staircase. It was an upright piano, and half of the cover was missing so she could look in and see the soundboard. Several of the wires were broken, and two of them were even lying out on the keyboard itself.

Rachael felt a hollowness in the pit of her stomach. Her knees grew weak, and her head began to spin.

There were three women in the saloon, though Rachael had never seen any women dressed as these were. All three had very low-cut blouses and they were wearing what looked to be bloomers. One of them came over to her.

"Honey, are you sure you are in the right place?" she asked.

"No, she isn't in the right place," a man's voice said. Recognizing the voice, Rachael turned to see Corey Hampton standing just inside the door.

"Mr. Hampton?" she asked in a weak voice.

"Miss Kirby, what are you doing in here?" Corey asked.

Rachael held her hand out. "I—I was told this was the saloon," she said.

"It is a saloon," Corey replied. He smiled at her. "But it isn't the right saloon."

"Oh," Rachael said. "I'm terribly sorry. I suppose I just didn't think a town this small would have more than one saloon."

"No, I'm the one who should apologize," Corey said. "The stage is always late. Wouldn't you know it would pick today to be early? Shall we go?" He offered Rachael his arm.

"Yes, thank you," Rachael said.

"Higbee has two saloons," Corey explained once they were out in the street. "The Golden Nugget, which belongs to my brother and me. And the one you were just in. It is called the Hog Waller."

"I beg your pardon? What did you call it?" Rachael asked.

"I called it by its name. The Hog Waller," Corey said.

Rachael laughed out loud. "Oh, what a perfect name for it," she said.

After stopping by the stage depot to retrieve her luggage, they walked down to the Golden Nugget. By any standards, the Golden Nugget was an attractive saloon, with a long, highly polished mahogany bar; glistening brass rings hanging every four feet along the front of the bar, each ring holding a crisp white towel; an exceptionally clean and varnished hardwood floor; gleaming tables; and a large mirror behind the bar that reflected back a shelf filled with liquors and brightly colored liqueurs. A huge, sparkling chandelier hung from a ceiling that was itself covered with textured brass.

Looking around, she saw the piano, not an upright, but a Haynes Square piano, rosewood, with octagon curved legs and mother-of-pearl inlay on the name board. She walked over to it.

"May I?" she asked.

"By all means, please do," Corey replied.

Standing by the piano, Rachael depressed a few of the keys, and was rewarded with a rich, resonant sound. She sat down and began to play. She played a passage from a Bach Toccata and Fugue, then from Vivaldi's *Four Seasons*, and finally from Beethoven's Ninth Symphony.

"My God," Prentiss Hampton said, the words more a prayer than an oath. "I have never heard anything so beautiful."

"Do you see what I was talking about?" Corey asked.

"Yes. What I can't see is why she would choose to work here."

"Well, she did accept on condition," Corey said. "I guess now we'll have to ask her if the condition has been met."

Rachael continued to play. It was just before noon, and there were very few customers in the place to hear the music, but those few who were in the saloon interrupted their conversations to listen. Even the bar girls who lived upstairs, and who never made an appearance until around seven P.M., were drawn to the music, and they moved halfway down the stairs, then sat on the steps as they listened, spellbound by the sound.

In a strange way, even Rachael was spellbound by her own music, enjoying the beautiful tone of the piano as well as the ambiance of this place. Finally, when the last note hung quivering in the air, she sat there for a long second, letting the strings continue to vibrate with the last harmonic resonance of the music.

Her contemplation of the moment was disturbed by the clapping of those present, and because Rachael was lost in the moment, the applause startled her. Then, standing up to see the source of the applause, she saw that the four customers as well as the young women, Corey, and the man standing with Corey were all applauding.

"Thank you," she said self-consciously.

"Miss Kirby, this is my brother, Prentiss," Cory said by way of introducing the man at his side. "He is my partner in this saloon."

Rachael extended her hand. "It is nice to meet you, Mr. Hampton."

"How do you like the piano?" Corey asked.

"It's beautiful."

"The tone quality is all right?"

"Yes, it is excellent, thank you."

"What about the saloon itself? Does it meet with your approval?"

"Oh, yes," Rachael said. "I've seen concert halls in New York that had less to offer."

Smiling, Prentiss and Corey stared at each other for a moment. Then Prentiss cleared his throat.

"Miss Kirby, I'm not as, uh, subtle as my brother, so you will forgive me, I hope, if we dispense with the small talk and I get right to the point."

"I'm always ready to get right to the point," Rachael replied.

"Good. Then the question is, will you agree to stay and play piano for us?"

"I would love to stay and play for you," Rachael said.

The bar girls on the steps cheered out loud.

Chapter Seven

Falcon was standing on the depot platform at MacCallister, Colorado, when the train pulled into the station, a symphony of hissing steam and rolling steel. It was a beautiful engine, painted a forest green, with shining brass trim. The lettering was yellow, and the huge driver wheels were red.

The engineer was hanging out the window looking at the track ahead, in order to find where to stop. He held a pipe clenched tightly in his teeth. The cars slowed and squeaked as they came to a stop. The conductor, who was standing on the boarding step of the first car, was the first to get off the train.

"MacCallister!" he called. "This here is MacCallister!"

The conductor was followed off the train by a dozen or so others: cowboys, miners, drummers, as well as a woman who may have been pretty at one time and was trying, unsuccessfully, to restore with makeup what nature had taken away. In addition, there were a couple of women who were tending to children.

"Grandma!" one little girl shouted as soon as she stepped down from the train. Falcon watched her run into the arms of an older woman who had come to meet the train.

From time to time when Falcon saw such displays, he thought of what he had lost in his own life. His mother and father had both been murdered, as had his wife and children. The twins, a boy and a girl, would have been about twelve years old today. By now, the boy would know how to ride, shoot, hunt, and track, and the girl would just be showing some of the beauty that so characterized her mother. Not one to dwell on such things, however, Falcon turned his attention back to the train.

When all the arriving passengers were off the train, the conductor pulled out his pocket watch and examined it.

"Board!" the conductor called.

Falcon watched the other departing passengers exchange good-byes, then board the train. He waited until everyone else had boarded before he stepped up into the car.

"Good afternoon, Mr. MacCallister," the conductor said. "It's good to have you traveling with us today. But then it's always good to have you."

"Hello, Syl," Falcon replied. "How is the family?"

"They are doing well. Oh, and my boy is at West Point now thanks to the letter you sent."

"I was glad to do it, Syl. Charley is a fine young man," Falcon said.

Once on board, Falcon moved halfway down the car, then chose a seat on the opposite side from the depot. He watched the other passengers get settled. Then, with a jerk, the train started forward.

It would be an overnight run to La Junta, but as the train was primarily a local, there was no sleeper car. It didn't bother Falcon that there was no sleeper car. During the war, he had slept in holes, filled with mud by drenching rainstorms, while undergoing artillery barrages. Since that time, he had slept in desert heat, mountain blizzards, and even in the saddle, so the prospect of spending a night in a padded seat in a train car was not in the least daunting.

Shortly after the train got under way, Falcon took a letter from his pocket. The return address indicated the letter was from Wade Garrison. Falcon had known a Brigadier General Wade Garrison during the war. The letter had come as a surprise, because he had not seen Garrison in over fifteen years. But any question as to whether or not this was the same Wade Garrison had been answered when he saw the address the letter was mailed to:

Major Falcon MacCallister
General Delivery
MacCallister, Colorado

Dear Major MacCallister,

I reckon I'm about the last person on earth you ever expected to get a letter from. But it's me, the same man you junior officers used to salute to my face and cuss to my back.

I've settled in a place called Higbee, Colorado. It's a fine little town, and I have plans to build a railroad that will connect Higbee with the rest of the country, which means the town will grow and prosper. Unfortunately, though most all the citizens of the town and the surrounding ranchers support my plan, there is one rancher who is opposed, and in fact, is rallying other ranchers to his cause.

Now, a little business opposition I could handle, but this gentleman—and I do use the term gentleman with some reservation—is opposing it in a way that is causing me some concern. Recently, three wagons which were carrying supplies I needed were attacked. The drivers, good men all, were killed, and the wagons burned. I can replace the supplies, but the drivers are irreplaceable.

There have been no charges made; indeed, nobody has even made any accusations because the operation was too clean to have left any physical clues as to who did it. However, there is no doubt in my mind as to who did it. I just need the proof.

I've kept up with you since the war, Falcon. I know that you have gained quite a reputation for what the dime novels call "derring-do." I would like to call upon you to come to Higbee for a visit. While you are here, I can apprise you of the situation and if you can see your way to lend a hand, I would be eternally grateful.

> *Sincerely,*
> *Wade Garrison*

"Eternally grateful," Falcon said, whispering the words. Folding the letter, he put it in his pocket, then pulled his hat down over his eyes and folded his arms across his chest, and in that state of half-awake, half-asleep, he recalled a place named Palmetto Hill in Southern Texas.

It was in late May of 1865, and elements of the Texas 15th had boarded a train for its run south over the bucking strap-iron and rotted cross-ties of the railroad.

The regiment that boarded the train was less than

thirty percent of the mustering-in strength. Of the thirty-five officers who had taken to the field with the brigade when the war started, all had been killed except for Dooley Perkins and Falcon MacCallister. Both were majors now, though they had started the war as second lieutenants.

Lieutenant Colonel Matthew Freeman was now in command of the regiment, having been put in that position by General Wade Garrison.

"Major MacCallister, I gave Freeman the command because he outranks you," Garrison told Falcon when the regiment received the assignment to proceed to Palmetto Hill. "But in truth, you have more experience, and a better knowledge of the regiment than anyone else. So, even though Freeman is in command, I'm going to be counting on you to keep an eye on him. And to be honest, at this point, it doesn't really make that much difference who is in command. I just got word this morning that General Lee surrendered back in Virginia, in a place called Appomattox. For all intents and purposes, the war is over."

"I beg your pardon, General?" Falcon said. "Did you just say that the war was over?"

"Yes."

"Then would you mind tellin' me why we are going to Palmetto Hill?"

"Duty, honor, country," Garrison said.

"General, if we've surrendered, we don't have a country," Falcon said. "And if we don't have a country, then we have no duty."

Garrison held up his index finger. "You may be right, my boy," he said. "But we still have honor. We'll always have honor."

Falcon was quiet for a long moment, then, with a sigh, he nodded.

"You're right, General. We still have our honor," he said.

"Look, Falcon, I know your soldiers are tired, hungry, and dispirited, and I doubt that many of them could understand the concept of fighting, and perhaps dying, for something as abstract as honor.

"But tell them this. Some of the Yankee commanders are not paroling the men they capture. They are putting them in prison. Especially those of us out here in Texas. They consider all of us to be irregulars, not covered by the rules of civilized warfare. They've even hung a few. If we make a good showing at Palmetto, we can at lest sue for better terms."

Falcon chuckled.

"What is it? Why are you laughing?"

"General, the terms don't have to be all that good to be better than hanging," Falcon said.

General Garrison laughed as well.

"I guess you're right at that," he said. He sighed. "I am sorry about having to put Colonel Freeman over you."

"Don't worry about it, General. Colonel Freeman is a good man. I'm fine with him in command," Falcon replied

"God go with you, Major. I'm eternally grateful for all that you have done for the South. It would pain me greatly to see you killed now."

They were less than a mile from their final destination when the train came to a sudden and catastrophic halt. Though neither Falcon nor anyone else in the train knew exactly what had happened, an accurately placed cannonball had burst the boiler and knocked the engine off the track. As a result of the sudden stop, the first three cars of the train telescoped in on themselves, causing a tremendous number of casualties, killing Colonel Freeman and five other regimental officers.

Falcon was riding in one of the rear cars, and his only indication that something had happened was in the fact that the train came to an almost immediate stop, throwing men onto the floor. Even as some of the men were swearing about the incompetence of the engineer, Falcon realized that something drastic had happened, and he started urging the men to get off the cars.

The same soldiers who had attacked the train were now waiting in ambush, and they opened fire as soon as the men of the regiment began pouring off the train.

Falcon and Major Perkins rallied the regiment.

"Take cover in the train wreckage!" Falcon shouted, and the men scrambled to do so.

The Yankees had one artillery piece, the same cannon that had destroyed the engine. And now they were using it to devastating effect, sending the heavy balls crashing through the remaining cars, sometimes using solid shot to further break up the wreckage, other times using shells to burst overhead and spray the soldiers with flaming bits of hot metal.

In addition to the effective artillery piece, the Yankee solders were bold and well led. Three times they came across the field, and three times they were repulsed, but not without casualties on both sides. Falcon was hit in the left arm and left leg. Fortunately, the bullets only creased him, rather than remaining buried in his flesh, but the creases were deep, bloody, and painful.

"Perkins, how are we holding out?" Falcon asked.

"It's that damn gun, Falcon," Perkins said. "It's not only killing and maiming our men, it's got them so rattled that some of the men aren't even shooting back."

Before Falcon could answer, another cannon round came screaming in. This one was fused, and as it hit, it burst with a loud bang, followed by whistling bits of shrapnel. Some of the men cried out in pain and fear.

"What do you mean they aren't shooting back?" Falcon asked. "Hell, some of these boys have been with us from the beginning."

"That's just it," Perkins said. "They're tired, they don't have anything left."

"That's a hell of a note," Falcon said.

"I'm going to take that gun out," Perkins declared.

"Are you sure you want to do this? They can't have an unlimited amount of powder and ball for that thing. Seems to me like the smarter thing to do would be to wait until they run out of ammunition."

Perkins shook his head. "I don't know that our boys can wait that long," Perkins said. "I'm goin' after the gun," he said.

Falcon sighed. "We're equal in rank," he said, "so I don't have the authority to stop you. And the truth is, you may be right. So let me know when you are ready and we'll give you as much cover as we can."

Perkins shook his head. "Yeah," he said. "Yeah, all right, I'll give you the word when I'm ready."

A few minutes later, Perkins had three volunteers prepared to go with him. He gave the signal to Falcon that he was ready.

"All right men, keep Major Perkins covered!" Falcon shouted to the others.

Rifles, carbines, and pistols roared and gun smoke billowed up from the Confederate soldiers in the wrecked train. As he had hoped it would be, the Confederate line was answered by the Union soldiers who were firing back just as vigorously. The reason Falcon wanted the Yankees to match his own troops in the intensity of their firing was because it enabled Perkins and his three volunteers to disappear quickly into the clouds of billowing smoke.

For the next thirty minutes, the gunfire continued at such a pace that Falcon was afraid they would soon run out of ammunition. Then he noticed that the artillery fire had stopped.

"The cannon has stopped!" Captain Thomas said, putting to words what Falcon had only thought. "Major Perkins must've gotten through."

"Yes," Falcon agreed. "Let's just pray that he and his men get back all right."

Then, out of the cloud of gun smoke that obscured the field, they saw the volunteers returning. Only this time, one of the men was being carried. Even from where he was, Falcon could tell that the wounded man was Major Perkins.

"Captain Thomas," Falcon shouted.

"Yes, sir?"

"Set fire to the grass. As soon as the smoke has built up, order the men to pull back. Major Perkins bought us some time . . . let's take advantage of it."

"Yes, sir," Captain Thomas replied.

Within moments, the smoke from a dozen grass fires mixed with the gun smoke to completely blot out the field. Then, outnumbered and outgunned, Falcon withdrew his men, thus avoiding the necessity of surrender.

Some five miles away from the point of the ambush, Falcon called a halt to the retreat. Looking around, he counted thirty-six men. Just thirty-six from a regiment that was once six hundred strong.

"Major MacCallister," Captain Thomas said. Like Falcon, Thomas had a bloody bandage around his left arm.

"Yes, Captain?"

"I thought I ought to tell you, sir. Major Perkins just died."

"Damn."

"What do you want to do now?" Thomas asked.

"Nothing," Falcon said.

"Nothing, sir?" Thomas asked, surprised by the response.

"That's right, Captain, I want to do absolutely nothing. Yesterday, General Garrison told me that General Lee had already surrendered and all we were doing now was trying to reposition ourselves to get better terms. As far as I'm concerned, we'll make our own terms, right here, right now. You knew Major Perkins from before the war, didn't you?"

"Yes sir," Thomas said. "The major's pa lived on the farm next to my pa. He and I grew up together. I reckon I've known him longer than I've known anyone."

"I would like for you to take Major Perkin's body back to his family. I don't know how you are going to manage that, with no wagon or horses, but I'd like to see it done."

Captain Thomas nodded. "I'll get it done. But I'll be coming back. I wouldn't feel right abandoning the regiment."

"What regiment?" Falcon replied.

"I beg your pardon, sir?"

"Look around you, Jerry," Falcon said. He took in the thirty-six men with a wave of his hand. They were sitting, or lying, on the grass, some asleep, others just staring morosely off into space. Nearly all were sporting bloody bandages around arms, legs, or heads. "Do you see a regiment?"

"I guess I see what you mean," Captain Thomas said.

"Men," Falcon called, and everyone looked up at him. "Men, it has been my honor and privilege to serve with you throughout this long war. But as many of you may have heard, Robert E. Lee surrendered all the military in his command to the Yankees at a place called Appomattox. That means the war is over."

"Hell, Major, we ain't in Lee's command," one of the men said. "We're in your command."

"Yeah," one of the others said. "What do you say we should do?"

"What if I told you I wanted to go back and attack the men who attacked us back there?" Falcon asked.

"Major, give the word and we'd soak our britches in coal oil and attack the devil in hell," a sergeant said.

Falcon chuckled and nodded. "I know you would," he said. "But it's over for us. General Garrison said we were fighting this one last battle for honor. As far as I'm concerned, honor was achieved. This regiment is hereby officially disbanded. I want you to all go home and try to put your lives together again."

"Regiment, attention!" the one remaining NCO shouted, and slowly, painfully, but determinedly, every soldier in the regiment stood up. Then they aligned themselves into a military formation.

"Present, arms!" the sergeant said, and every soldier brought his rifle up into a salute.

Both Falcon and Thomas, the only two officers remaining, returned the salute.

"Regiment, dismissed," Falcon said.

"Hoohrah!" the soldiers replied as one. Then, forming little groups of twos and threes, the soldiers left, starting their long walks back home.

"What about you, Major?" Thomas asked.

"I'm no longer a major," Falcon said.

"Yes, sir," Thomas said. Then he chuckled. "I mean, yes. But what are you going to do? Where are you going to go?"

"I had a pa and brothers who fought on both sides of this war," Falcon said. "I reckon I'll be going back home to Colorado and hope they all show up."

"Some of your family was fightin' for the Yankees?" Thomas asked.

"Yes."

"How do you think that's all going to work out when you get back together again?"

"Pa made us feel free to choose whichever side we thought was right. The war's over now, and we've all done our duty as we saw fit. I don't know about the rest of the country, but for the MacCallisters, the war will be behind us once and for all."

At that moment, the train passed over a rough section of railroad, jarring Falcon from his memories and bringing him back to the present. He sat in his seat for just a second, only slowly becoming aware that the war was long behind him. He had been recalling the last battle in which he had been engaged, and wounded. And though he did not know it at the time, his brother Matthew MacCallister had commanded the troops across from him in that very battle. And, like Falcon, Matthew had also been wounded.

Once more, Falcon pulled the letter out to look at it. This was the first time he had heard from General Garrison since that time in Texas so long ago.

Pueblo

"Hey, boys, watch this," Ray said. "I'm going to do me the fandango."

Ray, Cletus, and Billy Clinton were at the Four Aces Saloon in Pueblo. Their meeting with the cattle buyer wasn't until the next day, and though Billy suggested they might just have a good dinner and go to bed, neither Ray nor Cletus would hear of it. They were determined to go to a saloon, and Billy had no choice but to go with them. Billy, in keeping with the promise he had made to keep an eye on his brothers, had nursed a single beer for most of the night.

"Ha!" Cletus said. "What makes you think you can get your big ass to do a fandango?"

"Just watch," Ray said.

Ray, who was so drunk he could barely stand, hauled his big frame up and began stomping around in what he assumed was a fandango dance. Cletus started clapping his hands in accompaniment. Ray got his feet tangled and fell hard to the floor.

"Haw!" Cletus said, laughing out loud. "If you are a fandango dancer, I'm a Injun chief."

As Ray tried to get to his feet, he fell again, only this time he fell into a table where four other men were sitting.

"What the hell?" one of the men asked angrily. Roughly, he shoved Ray off the table and onto the floor. "If you can't hold your liquor, mister, you got no business drinkin'."

Getting pushed to the floor had a temporary sobering effect, and Ray got up slowly, then started toward the man who had pushed him. The man, noticing then how large Ray was, held up his hands and tried to back away from him.

"I don't want no trouble now," he said.

Ray smiled, then picked the man up and threw him. He landed on another table, crashing through it. Several others rushed Ray then, and grinning broadly with pure enjoyment, Ray began taking them on, singly and in pairs.

Finally, someone drew a gun and, pointing it toward the ceiling, fired it. The noise of the gunshot got everyone's attention, including Ray's.

"Stop it, you big ape! Stop it now!" he shouted.

"Friend, that's my brother you are pointing your gun at, and if you don't put it down now, I'm going to kill you," Cletus said in a low, menacing tone.

"Your brother, huh? Well, unless you want your brother killed, you'll lower your gun," the armed saloon patron said.

Cletus cocked his pistol. "I don't care what you do to him. I think I'll just kill you anyway," he said.

"What?" the armed patron shouted, his anger turning to fear. He threw his gun down. "No! My God, no!"

The others at the table scattered, and all the rest of the saloon patrons moved quickly to get out of the way.

Suddenly, Cletus collapsed to the floor, having gone down because Billy had stepped up behind him and hit him over the head with the butt of his pistol.

"What the hell, little brother?" Ray said. "Whose side are you on?"

"Think about it, Ray," Billy said. "If Cletus kills that fella, he'll wind up hangin'."

Ray nodded. "Yeah," he said. "Yeah, I guess you are right."

"Gentlemen, I would like to apologize for both of my brothers," Billy said to the men at the table, though his apology extended to everyone else in the saloon at the moment. "I'm afraid they are both a little drunk."

"They are both a lot of drunk," one of the men who had been sitting at the table said. "Seems to me like the best thing for them would be to sleep it off in a jail cell tonight."

Billy shook his head. "No, sir," he said. "No, sir, I'm not going to let that happen."

"Then will you at least get them out of here?"

Billy nodded. "Yes," he said. "That, I will do. Ray, pick up our brother."

With little effort, Ray picked Cletus up and threw him over his shoulder. The three brothers left the saloon, then walked across the street to the hotel where, earlier, they had taken a room.

"Is your friend all right?" the hotel clerk asked when he saw Cletus draped over Ray's shoulder.

"He's fine," Billy said. "He's just drunk."

Billy shepherded both his brothers upstairs to the single room they had rented. Ray and Cletus fell into the one bed and, almost immediately, began snoring. Billy threw a couple of blankets out on the floor, intending to sleep there, but after tossing and turning for several minutes, it became obvious to him that sleep wasn't coming.

Billy got up. Then, shaking his head in frustration, he sat down in a chair beside a lamp table. Turning up the lamp, Billy took out a tablet and pencil and began writing.

To Kathleen

Like a blooming flower to behold,
Your beauty shines through.
If only I were so bold
To declare my love for you.

But cruel is the fate
That keeps us apart.
Divided by families that hate,
I cannot speak what is in my heart.

Billy had never shared his love of writing poetry with anyone in his family. More importantly, he had not shared with anyone his feelings for Kathleen Garrison.

Chapter Eight

Falcon MacCallister had been on the train for the better part of sixteen hours. With his knees jammed up against the seat in front, his arms folded across his chest, and his hat down over his eyes, he'd tried to sleep, but sleep had been sporadic at best.

It was just after eight o'clock the next morning when the train stopped in Pueblo. There, three young cowboys got on. It was obvious they had been drinking all night long, and in fact they were still drinking because one of them was carrying a bottle.

As Falcon examined them more closely, though, he decided that they weren't cowboys after all. At least, they weren't cowboys working for twenty dollars and found, for these young men were all wearing clothes that were well cut and well sewn. All three had fine Stetson hats encircled by silver hatbands, and one of them was wearing a gunbelt with two pearl-handled pistols.

"Well now, lookie here," the one with a bottle said. "All these folks are asleep. What do you say we wake them up and invite them to a little party?"

"Shhh," the youngest one said. "Cletus, let's just find a seat and settle down somewhere."

"Listen to Billy, will you, Ray?" Cletus said. "You know, I'm worried about that boy. He don't know how to have fun."

"Ray, Pa sent us over here to get a price on our cows, not to get drunk and raise hell."

Playfully, Cletus knocked the hat off Billy and ran his hand through his hair. "Billy, if I didn't know you was only twenty-one, I would swear you was seventy years old."

"Gentlemen, please, some of us are trying to sleep," one of the passengers said. The passenger had white hair and a white beard.

"If I was you, mister, I wouldn't be worryin' none about sleepin'," Cletus said. "Old as you are, you'll be gettin' plenty of sleep before too much longer." Cletus laughed, then poked the other two. "You get that?" he asked. "I said this old codger will be gettin' plenty of sleep before too much longer. That's 'cause he'll be dead," Cletus added. Then he laughed again.

"We got it," Billy said. "Come on, let's find a seat."

The engineer blew the whistle, and the train jerked forward. When it did so, Cletus, who was obviously the drunkest of the three, fell against a young woman.

"Pardon me, miss," Cletus said. As he got up, he let his hands wander across her body, taking the time to squeeze one of her breasts.

"Oh!" the young woman gasped.

"Sorry," Cletus said. "I didn't mean to squeeze your tittie there. I was just tryin' to stand up, is all." Cletus giggled, and the young woman flushed red with embarrassment.

As Cletus stood up, he saw Falcon staring disapprovingly at him.

"What are you lookin' at?" he asked.

Falcon shook his head. "I'm not really sure," he said. "But if I were to guess, I'd say I was lookin' at a pile of cow manure."

"Mister! Do you know who you are talkin' to?" Cletus asked, his eyes flashing with anger.

"I suppose I'm talking to that pile of cow manure," Falcon answered, his calm, low-key voice contrasting with Cletus's increasing hysteria.

"By God, I'm going to teach you a lesson," Cletus shouted. He reached for his gun, only to discover that the holster was empty.

"What the hell! Where's my gun?" he shouted.

"I have it," Billy said.

"What the hell are you doing with it?"

"I'm trying to keep you from being killed," Billy said. "Now get back here."

Cletus pointed at Billy. "Look, you may be my brother, but I don't let nobody order me around, do you understand? Nobody."

Billy walked over to the open window of the train, and stuck his hand through, holding Cletus's gun just above the ground that was moving swiftly beneath.

"Get over here and sit down, or say good-bye to your gun," Billy ordered.

Cletus turned to Falcon. "Mister, I don't know who you are," he said. "But this here ain't over between us."

"Cletus?" Billy called again.

Grumbling, Cletus returned to the end of the car, then sat down in the seat beside Ray, who was already asleep. Within moments, Cletus was also in alcohol induced slumber. Billy waited until both brothers were snoring before he got up. He stopped at the seat of the woman Cletus had groped.

"Miss, I'm sorry about my brother. He don't really mean nothin', he's just drunk," Billy said.

The young woman nodded, but said nothing. Billy then walked back to Falcon. "Mister, I hope you don't hold no grudges," he said.

"Your brother has a mean streak about him," Falcon said.

"Yes, sir, he does," Billy said. "I try and look out for him, but I can't always be there."

"Why do you even try?"

"Because he's my brother," Billy said, as if that explained everything.

By now, the train was fully under way and the excitement was forgotten as nearly everyone on the car went back to sleep.

About an hour later, Falcon walked to the water barrel at the front of the car. As he did so, he passed the three brothers. Cletus and Ray were asleep, or passed out, in the back-facing seat. Billy, who was sitting across from them in the front-facing seat, was awake and looking through the window at the passing desert. Falcon took down a tin cup and held it under the spigot, then filled the cup with water.

"Mister?" Billy called quietly.

Falcon drank the water before he replied.

"Yes."

"I want to apologize again for my two brothers. They ain't like this all the time. They just got drunk back there in Pueblo, that's all."

"Looks to me like you have your hands full just keeping up with them," Falcon said.

"Yes, sir, I reckon I do. But they're sleepin' it off now.

Chances are, when they wake up, there won't neither one of them even remember seein' you."

Falcon hung the cup back on the hook, then started back to his seat. Before he left, though, he turned back toward Billy. "You're a good brother to them," he said. "You're a hell of a lot better than either one of them deserves."

By mid-morning it was very hot in the train car, and though the raised windows did allow air to come in, the air felt as if it were coming off a blast furnace. In addition, smoke and cinders often flew in, and one cinder, which was still white-hot, set fire to a seat and the fire had to be patted out.

By now, both Ray and Cletus were awake. It was obvious that they were suffering the effects of a hangover, because they both sat very quietly, staring morosely at the rest of the car. It also appeared that Billy had been correct in his assessment, because neither one of them showed any recognition of Falcon.

"La Junta!" the conductor called, passing through all the cars of the train. "Next stop is La Junta!"

Stepping down from the train, Falcon took in the sun-baked town with a slow, all-encompassing sweep of his eyes. Behind Falcon, the locomotive relief valve vented steam in loud, rhythmic puffs, while wheel bearings and journals popped and snapped as they cooled. The wheels of a utility cart squeaked as an old Mexican man pushed it up to the baggage car to receive the luggage that had been checked through. A team and carriage waited alongside the station, the horses standing in harness with their heads lowered to escape the sun. A Mexican man sat in the shade near the carriage, apparently waiting to meet one of the passengers. The railroad dispatcher was just outside the door of the depot, wiping the sweat from his face as he looked on at the few departing passengers. The train conductor was standing at the foot of the boarding steps examining his pocket watch as the three cowboys left the train.

"Señor Billy!" the Mexican said, standing then to call out.

"Manuel, thanks for meeting us," Billy answered.

"What do you mean, thanks?" Cletus asked with a low growl. "We pay the son of a bitch, don't we? Don't seem to me like thanks is needed."

Falcon scratched a match on a post and held it to his quirley, squinting through the smoke as he watched two of the young men climb into the carriage. Billy walked over to the baggage cart with Manuel to help him retrieve the luggage.

"Hey, Manuel, how about stopping by the saloon for a bit?" Cletus asked as the Mexican climbed back onto the driver's seat and picked up the reins.

"I'm sorry, señor, I no can do," Manuel said. "Señor Clinton say I must bring you back to La Soga Larga."

"The ranch can get along for half an hour without us," Cletus said.

"I'm sorry, señor. You pa will fire me if I do this."

"And I'll fire you if you don't," Cletus said angrily.

"You cannot fire me," Manuel said. "Only Señor Ike Clinton can fire me."

"Yeah? Well the ole man ain't goin' to live forever, you know," Cletus said. "And when he dies, I'll fire you."

"Cletus, enough," Billy said. "Manuel is only doing his job."

"All right, if we're going home, then let's go home," Cletus said. "I'll drive."

Cletus crawled into the front seat, took the reins from Manuel, and removed the whip from its stand.

"Hyyaah!" he yelled as he lashed out at the team. The horses broke into a gallop from a standing start and, with Cletus shouting warnings and curses, the carriage raced down the main street, scattering pedestrians as it did so.

La Junta had not changed since the last time Falcon was here. The little town was built along the Atchison, Topeka, and Santa Fe Railroad, the steel ribbons that gave it life. By horseback, it would have taken Falcon at least four days to ride to La Junta from his ranch just outside MacCallister. But by rail, it took only sixteen hours.

A stagecoach was drawn up on the street behind the railroad depot and, retrieving his luggage, Falcon walked over to it. The driver of the stage was stretched out on top of the coach. His hands were folded across his chest, and his hat was pulled down over his eyes. Because Falcon once had had a business investment in Higbee, he had made this trip a few times before, and he recognized the driver.

"Wake up, Sam," Falcon called up to him.

"Yeah, I'm awake," the driver said, sitting up and stretching. Then, recognizing Falcon, he smiled. "Well, Mr. MacCallister," he said. "It's good to see you again."

Falcon held up his bag. Attached to the bag was a Winchester rifle.

"Where do you want this, Sam? On top, or in the boot?" he asked.

"The boot'll be fine," Sam replied. He climbed down from the coach, then undid the straps and buckles in order to open the boot.

Other passengers arrived then, a woman with a young boy of about twelve and a short, very rotund, bald man who was carrying a case of samples.

"Billings is the name, and notions is my game," the man said, extending his hand to Falcon.

"Notions?" Falcon asked, taking the drummer's hand.

"Thimbles, needles, thread, lace, and yard goods," Billings explained.

Seeing the woman struggling with her bag, Falcon moved toward her and, with a smile, relieved her of the burden. He put it in the boot alongside his own bag. The drummer kept his case with him.

The woman and her son sat on the back seat, facing forward. Falcon and the drummer took the front seat, facing the rear.

The coach tilted slightly as the driver climbed into his seat up top. "You folks ready down there?" he called.

"We're ready, Sam!" the drummer replied. "You may wonder why I called the driver by his first name, but I take this trip at least once every two weeks," Billings explained to the others. "Why, Sam and I are old friends by now."

The coach started forward with a lurch then, and within a few minutes was out of town and moving at a faster-than-a-walk clip on the road leading to Higbee.

The twelve-year-old boy took a book from his back pocket and began reading. On the cover of the book, a man held blazing guns in each hand and had a knife clenched between his teeth.

Falcon MacCallister and the Polecat Bandits was the title of the book.

Falcon shook his head slightly, then looked out the window at the passing countryside.

"Say, young man," Billings said. "I see that you are reading about Falcon MacCallister."

"Yes," the boy replied.

"Jimmy," his mother said.

"I mean, yes, sir," Jimmy said.

"Jimmy, huh?" the drummer said. "What's your last name?"

"Ellis, sir," Jimmy replied. "Jimmy Ellis."

"Well, Jimmy Ellis, you can read about Falcon MacCallister if you want to. Or you can listen to a story about him from someone who knows him well."

Jimmy's eyes grew wide. "You know Falcon MacCallister?"

Falcon looked over at Billings, but Billings didn't notice it.

"Do I know him?" Billings replied. "Why, Jimmy, I used to ride with him."

"You did?"

"Yes, sir, I did. In fact, most of the adventures me 'n' him had were so big and so dangerous that they ain't even been wrote about yet, 'cause truth to tell, I don't think folks would believe them."

Smiling, Falcon resumed his study of the passing countryside.

"Wow," Jimmy said. He put the book back in his pocket. "Would you tell me about one of them adventures?"

"It's one of 'those' adventures," Jimmy's mother corrected. "And don't bother the gentleman by asking him to tell you stories."

"Oh, it's no bother, ma'am," Billings said. "Believe me,

it's no bother. And I'd love to tell the story. That is, if you'd like to hear it, Jimmy."

"Yes, sir! I would love to hear it!" Jimmy said.

Mrs. Ellis sighed, then, like Falcon, turned her attention outside the coach.

"Well, sir, this here story happened down on the Pecos," the drummer began. "That's a river," he explained.

"Anyway, me 'n' Falcon—I call him that and he calls me Fred, bein' as we're good friends'n all—we was down on the Pecos, lookin' for some men that robbed a bank in Santa Fe. Next thing you know, we was jumped by more'n twenty bandits."

"What did you do?" Jimmy asked.

"Well, sir, that's exactly what Falcon asked. 'What do we do now, Fred?' he asked. So, I put the horse's reins in my teeth, pulled both my guns, then turned my horse toward the outlaws and fed him some spur. 'Follow me!' I yelled."

"Wow!" Jimmy said. "And did he?"

"Oh, yes, Falcon held up his end just real good that day," Billings said. "I didn't get no more'n fourteen or fifteen of 'em myself, and Falcon got all the rest of 'em."

"How come they ain't never wrote no books about you, like they do about Falcon MacCallister?" Jimmy asked.

"Well, Jimmy, it's like this. Some folks sort of crave publicity, and I reckon Falcon, for all that he is a good man, sort of likes all the fame and such. But then there's also folks like me. I figure it's best to just do your duty when you see it, then be quiet about it."

"Would you autograph my book for me?" Jimmy asked.

"Why, I'd be proud to do it," Billings said, taking out a pencil and signing his name to Jimmy's book.

"Whoa, hold it up there!" they heard the driver call.

Sam pulled back on the reins and put his foot on the brakes, bringing the coach to a halt.

"What is it, Sam? What's going on?" Billings called up to the driver.

"There's some folks in front of us, wantin' us to stop," Sam called back.

"Well, that's ridiculous. Just drive on through."

"I don't think I can do that," Sam said.

"You folks in the coach, climb outta there now!" a gruff voice called from outside.

"What? My word, what is going on?"

There was the sound of a gunshot, followed by a sharp cry of alarm from Mrs. Ellis. The bullet penetrated the coach, but it was obvious that it was meant to be a warning shot only.

"I guess we'd better do as they say," Falcon said, opening the door.

"Mr. Billings, do something," Jimmy whispered.

"Do something? What do you mean do something?"

"You know, like when you was down on the Pecos with Falcon MacCallister," Jimmy said.

"That was—uh—a long time ago," Billings said. "I think this gentleman is right. We should do what they say."

The four passengers stepped out of the coach, then stood on the road.

"Driver, throw down your pouch," one of the bandits ordered.

"What do you want the pouch for? There ain't no money in it," Sam called back. "Can't you see that I ain't even got a shotgun guard with me? I ain't got nothin' for you to steal."

"Then climb down from there. We'll take what we can from the passengers."

"Mr. Billings, there's just two of them," said Jimmy.

"They have guns," Billings answered, his voice shaking with fear. "I think the smartest thing to do is to do just what they say."

"If you robbers know what's good for you, you'll leave before it's too late," Jimmy said. "Mr. Billings used to ride with Falcon MacCallister."

One of the two stagecoach robbers laughed out loud. "Ha! You been tellin' the boy tall tales, have you, Billings?"

"Please, don't hurt us," Billings said. "Just take what you need and go."

"I think you boys are going to find that this wasn't a very good idea," Falcon said.

"Not a good idea, huh?" one of the bandits said. "And why do you think that?"

"First of all, it's like the driver told you, he isn't carrying a money pouch. Secondly, you aren't going to get one cent from any of us, and third, if you don't do what I tell you to do, you could get killed," Falcon said.

"Mister, maybe you ain't noticed, but we're both holdin' guns, and you ain't."

In a draw that was so fast as to be a blur, a gun suddenly appeared in Falcon's hand.

"Now I'm holding a gun as well," Falcon said.

"What the hell?"

"Bring your guns over here and put them in the boot of the stage," Falcon said.

"Mister, this here gun cost me twelve bucks, I ain't goin' to—"

The protest was interrupted by the sound of a gunshot. A little spray of red mist flew from the earlobe of one of the bandits.

"Ow!" the bandit shouted, slapping his hand to his ear. "You shot my ear off!"

"No, I just clipped your earlobe," Falcon said. "If I had wanted to take your ear, I would have done so. Now I'm only going to say this one more time. Bring your guns over here and put then in the stage boot."

Meekly, both bandits complied with Falcon's request.

"Take your boots off," Falcon said.

"Why do you want us to do that?"

Falcon didn't answer. Instead, he just made a motion with his pistol.

Reluctantly, the men sat on the road, then took off their boots. The socks of both men were full of holes.

"Bring them over here and put them with your guns."

"Mister, I only got me them one pair of boots," one of the would-be robbers said. "Without them boots, I ain't hardly goin' to be able to get around none a'tall."

"You should've thought of it before you came up with a plan to hold up the stage," Falcon said. "Be thankful that I'm planning on letting you go instead of taking you in town to jail or, better yet, killing you. Now, get, both of you."

"Get? Get to where?" one of the robbers asked.

"I don't care where," Falcon said. "Just don't try to sneak back, because if I see you on this road again, I'll shoot you."

"Yes, sir, yes, sir," the smaller of the two said. "Come on, let's get out of here. This was a dumb fool thing to do in the first place."

The driver laughed as they watched the two bandits limp away on stocking feet.

"I tell you the truth, Mr. MacCallister," he said. "That's 'bout the funniest thing I ever seen."

Billings looked sharply at the driver. "What—what did you call him?"

"I called him MacCallister. Falcon MacCallister," Sam said. "You mean you folks ain't introduced yourselves yet?"

"Y—you're Falcon MacCallister?" Billings asked in a weak, choked voice.

"Yes," Falcon said. He chuckled. "I guess I've changed a lot since that time we were together down on the Pecos."

Billings saw Jimmy and Mrs. Ellis looking at him with challenging eyes.

"Uh, yes," Billings mumbled. "Yes, I expect we have all changed."

"Better get back in the coach, folks," Sam said. "We aren't making any time sitting here."

The passengers reboarded, but for the rest of the trip, Billings, who had been so talkative earlier, now stared morosely out the window, unwilling to meet the gaze of anyone else in the coach.

As the coach approached the edge of town, they passed a welcoming sign.

WELCOME TO HIGBEE
Come Grow With Us

Population 257.

But as the coach rolled further into town, the population number on the welcome sign was put into question by the number of people on the street. The boardwalks on both sides of the street were filled with pedestrians, and the street itself was active with traffic: wagons, buckboards, surreys, and horses. From Falcon's perspective, it looked as if more than two hundred people were moving around. He suspected that the population figure on the sign was from a time before word got out of an impending railroad. Falcon had seen enough "End of Track" towns grow overnight from sleepy little settlements to booming communities, sometimes only to wither and die as the railroad crews moved onward. But if Garrison made this his headquarters, then the rapid growth of the town would be sustainable.

The coach stopped in front of a leather goods store that also bore a small, hand-painted sign that read, STAGECOACH DEPOT.

"Here we are, folks!" the driver called down. "The big city of Higbee."

"Can I give you a hand?" Falcon asked Mrs. Ellis. "Carry your luggage somewhere?"

"Thank you, no," Mrs. Ellis said. "My husband is here to meet me." She nodded toward a man sitting in a buckboard. Even as she was speaking, the man climbed down from the buckboard and ambled over.

"Pa, this is Falcon MacCallister!" Jimmy said excitedly.

"And I'm Buffalo Bill," Ellis said, picking up his wife's suitcase and starting back toward the buckboard. Jimmy and his mother followed, and Jimmy looked back over his shoulder once, staring at Falcon as if trying to determine whether he really was Falcon MacCallister.

"Are you really Falcon MacCallister?" Billings asked in a tight voice.

"Why, Fred, you mean you don't remember me?" Falcon teased.

"I'm sorry, Mr. MacCallister," Billings said. "I'm truly sorry. I didn't mean nothin' by all that. I was just spoofin' the kid, is all."

"Don't worry about it," Falcon said. "Kids have had lot worse done to them."

"Yes, sir, they have," Billings replied. "They truly have. I tell you what—seein' as I been caught in a lie, I think I owe a penance. So the first thing I'm goin' to do soon's I get back to Denver, is donate to the orphanage."

Falcon nodded. "I think that would be a good thing," he said. Then he dropped the subject altogether.

Chapter Nine

After getting a room in the hotel, Falcon walked down to the office of the Colorado, New Mexico, and Texas Railroad Company. When he pushed open the door, a little tinkling bell caused a young woman to look up.

"Yes, sir?" she said. "May I help you?"

"I'm Falcon MacCallister," Falcon said.

"Yes, sir, Mr. MacCallister, what can I do for you?"

"You aren't expecting me?"

The young woman looked confused. "Should I be?"

"Not necessarily you personally, but I believe Wade Garrison is. I received a letter from the general, asking me to come see him," Falcon said.

"That would be my father, but I had no idea he had invited anyone to come stay with us."

"It wasn't exactly that kind of invitation," Falcon replied with a smile. "So, you are Miss Garrison," he said. "I heard the general had a daughter. I must say you are every bit as pretty as your reputation."

Kathleen blushed. "Well, I, uh, appreciate that, Mr. Mac-Callister," she said. "My father is down at Mr. Thompson's freight office right now, but I expect he'll be back very soon."

As if on cue, the bell rang and a tall, ramrod-straight man with a full head of silver hair stepped through the door and into the room.

"Falcon! You old horse thief, you!" Wade Garrison said exuberantly. He stuck out his hand. "It is good to see you. Thanks for coming."

Falcon smiled. "Well, General, you asked me to come. And after all these years, there's still enough of the soldier in me to respond."

Garrison chuckled. "Good, good, I was counting on just that," he said. "So, I see you've met my daughter, Kathleen."

"Yes, I have."

"Kathleen is my right hand," Garrison said. "I couldn't do any of this without her."

"By any of this, you mean build a railroad?"

"Come back here, take a look at this map, and let me show you what I plan to do," Garrison said.

Falcon followed Garrison to the back of the room where there were several maps laid out on a table. Most of the maps were simple line maps that Falcon could read and understand. But a lot of the maps were filled with lines and numbers denoting such things as grade and slant, and with other markings intelligible only to the construction engineers.

"I intend to start by building the railroad to La Junta," Garrison said, pointing it out on the map. "But we have a branch of the Las Animas River to cross here, a gulley here, and another here. Also, the elevation from here to La Junta increases by seven hundred and fifty-three feet. Fortunately, that is one long, continuous grade. But it is something we must take into consideration."

"Have you started yet?"

"We haven't laid any track yet, but as you can see, we do have most of the surveying done." Garrison pointed to another part of the map. "I'll be going to La Junta first. That will open up rail service right away."

"It's smart going to La Junta first," Falcon said. "That should win the support of everyone in town, by connecting them with the rest of the country."

"It also enables me to use rail shipments to bring in all of my needed supplies," Garrison pointed out. "And, yes, you would think that all the people of the town would support that."

"But your letter said not everyone is supporting you," Falcon said.

"You've got that right," Garrison said. He stroked his chin. "There is a rancher by the name of Clinton. Ike Clinton. He opposes the entire operation, and he's talked some of the other ranchers into backing him."

"I don't understand," Falcon said. "What do the ranchers have to lose by having a railroad built? I would think they would among your biggest supporters."

"You would think so, wouldn't you?" Garrison said. "But that would be underestimating the evilness of Ike Clinton. And, of course, he has three sons who are just as bad as he is."

"Billy isn't," Kathleen said.

Falcon looked up at the young woman in surprise.

"Just because young Billy seems to have more manners than the other two, doesn't mean he is any different than his two older brothers."

"No, I agree with your daughter. Billy is different," Falcon said, his comment surprising Garrison.

"He is different? How do you know? Do you know the Clintons?"

"I met the three boys on the train," Falcon said. "Ray, Cletus, and Billy. I assume these are the ones you are talking about."

"Yes," Garrison said.

"From my brief time on the train with them, I would say that Billy is actually quite a nice young man. It is unfortunate that he is saddled with two worthless brothers."

"And an even more worthless father," Garrison said. "To make matters worse, the Clintons have Sheriff Belmond on their side."

"Yes, I heard Belmond was elected sheriff of Bent County. I must confess that surprised me a bit. The only way I would have ever thought Mark Belmond would wind up in a sheriff's office is if he were behind bars. That is, if I'm thinking of the right man."

Garrison nodded. "You are thinking of the right man, all right," he said. "Mark Belmond is as crooked as they come. When the three freight wagons were attacked, Belmond did nothing, even though it happened in the county, in his jurisdiction. The truth is, I wouldn't be surprised if he knew who did it."

"Why is Belmond in cahoots with Clinton?"

"Clinton financed Belmond's campaign for sheriff. Financed him, campaigned for him, coerced people to vote for him. You might say he practically appointed Belmond sheriff."

"What about the town marshal?"

"Titus Calhoun is a good man. In fact, he ran against Belmond for sheriff, and would have been elected if the election had been honest. But as it is, Calhoun is very limited in what he can do. First of all, the town doesn't have a big enough budget to pay for a deputy, so Titus's brothers, Travis and Troy, volunteer when deputies are needed. Also, our biggest problems come from the cowboys who don't live in town, so Titus is helpless to do anything once they leave the city limits."

"I know Titus Calhoun, and he is a good man," Falcon said. "I'm beginning to get the picture," Falcon said.

"I hoped that you would. Falcon, I'm going to make a lot of money from this railroad, that's true enough. But I also think it would be very good for this part of the state. I'm determined to see this thing through, but I'll be honest with you—I don't think I can see it through by myself."

"I'll do what I can to help," Falcon said.

A broad smile spread across Wade Garrison's face. "I knew you would," he said. "Say, where are you staying? You could stay with us. Kathleen wouldn't mind moving to a cot in the kitchen."

"No, no, that's not necessary," Falcon replied quickly. "I would not want to put Kathleen out. I've already taken a room at the hotel."

"All right, if you're sure."

"I'm sure," Falcon said.

"I have another wagonload of building material coming in a few days," Garrison said. "I've hired Thompson Wagon Freight to meet the train and bring the material back. If you don't mind, I would like you to ride with the wagons to meet the train, and then come back with them to see that the supplies get here safely."

"I'll be glad to do it," Falcon said. "But now, if you don't need me for anything else, I think I'll take a look around town and maybe meet a few folks."

"Yes, yes, good idea," Garrison said. "Oh, and maybe at the outset, you shouldn't tell anyone that you are here at my behest. You might learn more if people don't perceive an affiliation between us."

"My thought as well," Falcon replied. He tipped his hat toward Kathleen. "Miss Garrison," he said.

"Mr. MacCallister," Kathleen replied with a subtle dip of her head.

Even from the front of the CNM&T Railroad office, Falcon could see the sign displayed on the false front of the building. Painted in large red letters, outlined in black, was the name of the saloon, Golden Nugget, as well as the names of the two owners; Corey and Prentiss Hampton. It was a short walk from the railroad office to the saloon, and in less than a minute, Falcon was stepping up onto the porch to go inside.

Falcon had come to the saloon, not only to enjoy a cool beer, but also to visit with the Hampton brothers. Though it was not generally known around town, Falcon was the one who had loaned the Hampton brothers the money they'd needed to open their saloon. He'd done that because he had known the Hampton brothers for many years. They had been childhood friends, growing up near MacCallister, and like Falcon and some of his brothers, Prentiss and Corey had fought on opposite sides in the war. Also, as with Falcon and his brothers, that had been put behind them so that the familial bonds were as strong as they ever were.

"I only ask two things of you," Falcon said when he backed their operation. "Keep all the card games honest, and don't water your whiskey. Because if you treat your customers fairly, I have no doubt but that you will do a good business."

The Hamptons had kept their promise to him and the Golden Nugget had prospered.

From the moment Falcon stepped inside, he felt some relief from the heat. Borrowing a trick developed by the Indians, the Hampton brothers kept gourds of water hanging throughout their establishment. The evaporation of the water resulted in a saloon that was noticeably cooler than the outside temperature.

It was dark enough inside that Falcon had to stand for a moment to allow his eyes to adjust to the lack of light. The Hampton brothers were particularly proud of the bar, which had been shipped by rail and freight wagon all the way from New York.

Above the mirror was a large oil painting of a night train, its headlamp sending a beam ahead. Every window of every car was shining from interior light, and in every window there was a passenger, each passenger individually and painstakingly detailed. One of the passengers, by design, was Falcon MacCallister. The Hampton brothers were also depicted. That was because the painting had been commissioned specifically for the Golden Nugget Saloon.

Prentiss Hampton was standing at the far end of the bar, polishing glasses and laughing and joking with some of the customers, when he saw Falcon. With a big smile, he put down the glass and cloth, and walked quickly to Falcon's end of the bar to extend his hand in welcome.

"Falcon!" he said. "What a pleasant surprise! Checking up on us, are you?"

Falcon laughed and shook his head. "Why should I do that? You boys paid back every cent you borrowed from me a long time ago." He thought it best not to share the information that General Garrison had sent him a letter inviting him down.

"Wait until I tell Corey you are here," Prentiss said.

"You will have dinner with us tonight, won't you? We have a new restaurant in town that's really quite nice. It's called the Vermillion."

"Great, I'd love to eat with you," Falcon said.

Looking toward the back of the saloon, Falcon saw a young woman come through the back door, then stop for just a moment to survey the room. The woman was very pretty, with raven-dark hair, high cheekbones, hazel eyes, and full lips. She was thin, but generously rounded in the right places. Falcon's first thought was that she might be a bar girl, hired to tease the customers into buying more drinks. But as he looked at her more closely, he saw that she wasn't dressed in the provocative manner of such women. Also, she had a young, innocent look about her, with no hint of the dissipation bar girls quickly acquired.

"Who is that?" Falcon asked.

Prentiss smiled. "Ah. I see you are taken with our pianist."

"Piano player? You have a woman piano player?"

"She isn't a piano player, she is a pianist," Corey Hampton said, and hearing the voice of his friend, Falcon turned to greet him.

"Hello, Corey. What did you call her? A pianist?" Falcon asked.

"It's what she calls herself. In fact, she absolutely insists upon the term," Corey said.

"How did you get a—pianist—especially one as pretty at this young woman, to play piano in a saloon?"

"Her name is Rachael," Corey explained. "She came to La Junta with a group of players, but the manager of the troupe absconded with all the money, leaving the players stranded. Most left, but I happened to be in La Junta at the time. I had heard her play, so I prevailed upon her to come to Higbee to play for us."

"Rachael?"

"Rachael Kirby," Corey said. He smiled as he saw Falcon's lingering appraisal of the young woman. "She is pretty, isn't she?"

Falcon nodded. "Yes, very," he said.

Rachael smiled at a few of the customers, then sat at the piano.

"Wait until you hear her play," Prentiss said.

Rachael began to play then. The piece, though Falcon didn't actually recognize it, was Beethoven's Piano Concerto Number One. The music spilled out from the piano in grand, crashing chords, but with a continuing and melodic theme, weaving in and out like a golden thread through a rich tapestry.

Falcon looked around at the customers and saw that all were so entranced by the music that none of them were drinking. He chuckled.

"It's beautiful music," he said. "But it can't be doing much for your business." He took in the nondrinking customers with a wave of his hand. "Nobody is buying drinks."

"On the contrary, she is great for business. She draws people to the saloon just to hear her play," Corey said. "Every night we let her play one or two pieces like that. Then she has to play 'drinking' music."

Finishing the piece with a grand crescendo, Rachael got up from the bench to smile and curtsy in response to the applause.

"Saloon customers applauding a piano player," Falcon said. "I don't believe I have ever seen that. Most of the time, they don't even know the piano player is there.

The piano player is like an extra chair or a potted plant or something."

"It's impossible not to notice Rachael," Corey said. He laughed. "You certainly noticed her fast enough."

Falcon nodded. "Yeah, well, she's definitely not a chair or a potted plant," he said with a chuckle.

Sitting back down, Rachael began playing "Buffalo Gals," and with the change in musical fare, the customers once again began drinking and visiting with each other.

"You've been standing here with your mouth open, listening to Rachael," Prentiss said. "Would you like a beer?"

"Listening, hell, he's been looking at her," Corey said with a little laugh.

"I've been doing both," Falcon admitted. "And, yes, I'd very much like a beer."

When that song was over, someone requested that she play "I'll Take You Home Again, Kathleen." Rachael complied, and the music elicited more than a few tears as the patrons stood at the bar or sat at the tables, drinking. Now, business was brisk as bar girls moved quickly about the room, carrying drinks to those who ordered them.

"See what I mean about her being good for business?" Corey asked, pointing to the sudden activity.

"Yes, I see," Falcon replied. "About this dinner we're going to tonight. Do you think if we invited Rachael, she might come along with us?"

Corey laughed. "I think she might," he said.

"Falcon MacCallister," a friendly voice said. "I heard you were in town."

Turning toward the sound of the voice, Falcon saw a tall, bearded man.

"Titus Calhoun, how are you?" Falcon said warmly. "Still wearing a star, I see."

"Yes, I'm the city marshal here," Calhoun replied.

"Let's see, the last time I saw you, you were sheriffing down in Arizona," Falcon said.

"That's right," Calhoun said. "And if you hadn't stopped by for a drink that day, I'd still be in Arizona, lying under six feet of dirt."

Falcon nodded as he recalled that meeting.

Picacho, Arizona Territory, two years earlier*

As he stood at the bar, a tall, broad-shouldered, bearded man stepped in through the back door. At first, Falcon wondered why he had come through the back door. Then he saw that a star was barely showing from beneath the vest he was wearing. The sheriff pointed a gun toward one of the tables.

"I just got a telegram about you, Kofax," the lawman said. "You should'a had better sense than to come back to a town where ever'one knows you."

"Let it be, Calhoun," Kofax replied. "I ain't staying here long. I'm just waitin' around for the train to take me out of here."

The sheriff shook his head. "I don't think so. You won't be catchin' the train today," he said. "You're goin' to jail."

Kofax stood up slowly, and stepped away from the table.

"Well, now, you're plannin' on takin' me there all by yourself, are you, Calhoun?" Kofax asked.

The quiet calm of the barroom grew tense, and most of the other patrons in the bar stood up and

*Pride of Eagles

moved to both sides of the room, giving the sheriff and Kofax a lot of room.

Only Falcon didn't move. He stayed by the bar, sipping his beer and watching the drama play out before him.

"You can make this a lot easier by dropping your gunbelt," the sheriff said.

Kofax chuckled, but there was no humor in his laugh. "Well, now, you see, there you go. I don't plan to make it easy for you," he said.

"Shuck out of that gunbelt like I told you, slow and easy," the sheriff ordered.

Falcon saw something then that the sheriff either didn't see, or didn't notice. Kofax's eyes flicked upward for an instant, then back down toward the sheriff. Kofax smiled almost confidently at the sheriff.

"Sorry, Calhoun, but like I said, I don't plan to make this easy for you."

Curious as to why Kofax wasn't more nervous, Falcon glanced up and saw a man standing at the top of the stairs. The man was aiming a pistol at the sheriff's back. That was what Kofax had seen when he cut his eyes upward, and that was what was giving him such supreme confidence.

"Sheriff, look out!" Falcon shouted.

"Stay out of this, you son of a bitch!" the man at the top of the stairs shouted. He turned his pistol toward Falcon.

Falcon dropped his beer and pulled his own pistol, firing just as the man at the top of the stairs fired. The shooter's bullet missed Falcon and hit a whiskey bottle that was sitting on the bar. The impact sent a shower of whiskey and splinters of glass.

Falcon's shot caught the shooter in the chest, and he dropped his pistol and clasped his hand over the entry wound, then looked down at himself as blood began to spill between his fingers. The shooter's eyes rolled up in his head and he tumbled forward, sliding down the stairs, following his clattering pistol all the way down. He lay motionless at the bottom, his head and shoulders on the floor, his legs still on the steps.

Although the sound of the two gunshots had riveted everyone's attention, the situation between Kofax and the sheriff had continued to play out, and almost before the sound of the first two gunshots had faded, two more shots rang out. The sheriff's bullet struck Kofax in the neck forcing him back against the cold, wood-burning stove, causing him to hit it with such impact that he knocked it over, pulling down half the flue pipe.

As the smoke from four gunshots drifted through the saloon, only the sheriff and Falcon of the four original participants were still standing. Both were holding smoking pistols in their hands, and they looked at each other warily.

"I thank you for taking a hand in this, mister," the sheriff said. "Most folks would have stayed on the sidelines."

"How'd you wind up in Higbee?" Falcon asked.

"My brothers brought me here," Calhoun said. "We bought a restaurant together. With the railroad and all, seems to us like the only thing this town can do is grow."

"They own the Vermillion," Corey said. "The one we were telling you about."

"Good for you," Falcon said. "I hope it goes very well for you."

"We're working at it," Calhoun said. "Right now, my brothers are wearing two hats. They run the restaurant, and they are acting as my deputies when I need them."

"That must keep them busy."

"Only when the Clintons are in town," Calhoun said. "Ray and Cletus are bad enough by themselves. But somehow, they seem to attract the very dregs of society to ride for them."

"We're coming to your restaurant for dinner tonight," Corey said.

"Are you now? Well, in that case, I'll tell Travis to give you the best treatment. And the meal will be on me."

"Marshal, you don't have to do that," Corey said. "Prentiss and I will be happy to pay."

Calhoun shook his head. "You don't understand, Corey," he said. "Falcon saved my life once. I figure that's worth a meal."

Chapter Ten

All through dinner, Rachael wore an enigmatic smile. Finally, Falcon could take it no longer and picking up the bottle of wine, he refilled Rachael's glass and looked pointedly at her.

"Miss Kirby, would I be out of line to ask you what amuses you so?" Falcon asked.

"I would have known who you are, Mr. MacCallister," Rachael said, "Even if we had not been introduced. You are just as Rosanna and Andrew described you."

"You know my brother and sister?" Falcon asked in surprise. Falcon's siblings, Rosanna and Andrew, were twins and quite famous show personalities in New York.

"Oh, yes, I know them quite well. We did a show together last year," Rachael said. "I was very honored to appear with them. They are exceptionally talented."

"They are," Falcon said. Smiling, he shook his head. "But I have no idea where that talent came from. None of the rest of us has any talent."

"Alas, I should have listened to them," Rachael said. "When I told them I was going to tour the West with the J. Garon Troupe, they cautioned me about him. It turns out that they were right, Mr. Garon ran away with all the funds."

"Then I say we toast Mr. J. Garon," Falcon said, lifting his glass.

"What?" Rachael asked, surprised by his response.

Falcon smiled. "Had Garon not abandoned you here, we would not have met."

"Rosanna said you were a silver-tongued devil," Rachael observed as she lifted her glass to Falcon's.

"Don't you two mind us," Corey said. "Prentiss and I will just sit here quietly."

"Why, Corey," Rachael said flirtatiously. "If I didn't know better, I'd think you were feeling left out."

"Left out? No, not at all. I think it is great sitting here watching the two of you ignore us. Don't you, Prentiss?"

"Absolutely," Prentiss said. "Never let it be said that a Hampton stood in the way of Cupid."

Falcon laughed and Rachael blushed.

Five miles east of Higbee at the ranch, La Soga Larga, Ike Clinton bit the end off his cigar and licked it along each side. Firing a match, he held a flame to it, puffing until the tip began to glow. He squinted his eyes as he stared through the billowing cigar smoke at the three boys, recently returned from a business trip, who were in the den with their father.

"What kind of price did you get for the cattle?" Ike asked.

"We didn't get no offer a'tall," Ray replied.

Ike looked surprised. "What do you mean, you didn't get no offer? Didn't you go see Mr. Westpheling?"

"Yeah, Pa, we went to see him," Ray said.

"So? What did he say?"

"He didn't say nothin'."

"He didn't say anything?" Ike asked, the inflection of his voice showing his disbelief. "How could he not say anything?"

"He didn't say nothin' 'cause we didn't see him," Ray said.

"I thought you said you did go to see him."

"Yes, sir, well, what I meant to say is, we went to where he was supposed to be, but he wasn't there. And when we checked up on him, we found out he was already gone."

Ike shook his head. "I don't understand. I got a letter from him that said he would be at the Cattlemen's Exchange Bank at two o'clock Monday afternoon."

"Yeah, well, he might'a said that, only he wasn't there."

"How long did you wait for him?"

"We waited at least half a hour, till the bank closed," Cletus said.

Ike took another puff of his cigar and stared at Cletus. He continued to stare until his oldest son became discomfited by it.

"Let me get this straight," he said. "You stayed for half an hour, and then the bank closed?"

"Yes, sir."

"The Cattlemen's Exchange Bank closes at four P.M. What time did you get there?"

"Oh, uh . . ." Ray said, realizing now that he had been tripped up. "We got hung up, Pa. We didn't get to the bank till three-thirty."

"And where did you get hung up? In a saloon somewhere?"

"Well, yeah, we was in a saloon. But we was talkin' business, Pa. We really was," Ray said. He looked over to Cletus for support. "Wasn't we, Cletus?"

"Yeah, we was, Pa," Cletus said. "It's just like Ray said, we was talkin' business. You know, cattle market and such."

"I see," Ike said disgustedly. After a long, hard stare at his two oldest, he looked over at Billy. "What about you, boy? Was you in the saloon, too?"

"Ha!" Cletus said. "You think Goody Two-shoes here would hang out in a saloon with us? Like as not, he was up in his room suckin' on a sugar tit or somethin'."

Ray laughed.

"Was you in your room, boy?"

"No, sir," Billy answered.

"Where was you?"

"I was meeting with Mr. Westpheling."

"What?" Ray and Cletus both shouted at the same time.

"Don't you remember, Ray? You told me to go ahead and go to the meeting. So I did exactly what you told me to do."

Ray realized then that Billy was covering for him, and he recovered quickly. "Yes, yes, that's right. That's exactly what I said," Ray said. "Ain't that right, Cletus? I told Billy to go ahead and go to the meetin', do you remember?"

"I don't remember you tellin' him nothin' like that," Cletus said.

It took a long moment and an intense glare from Ray before Cletus caught on to what they were doing. Then, suddenly realizing what was expected of him, he nodded enthusiastically. "Oh, wait, yeah, now that I do think about it, Pa, that's right. Me'n Ray was talkin' business, so we told Billy to go meet with Mr. Westpheling."

"What kind of business could possibly be more important than getting a good price for our cows?"

"Well, I thought that—uh—Billy could use the experience," Cletus said. "Go ahead, Billy. Tell Pa what you found out."

"And did he make us an offer?" Ike said.

"Yes, sir, he did."

"What was the offer?"

"Mr. Westpheling will take twenty-five hundred head, Pa, at thirty dollars a head," Billy said.

"Twenty-five hundred head? That's more than twice what he indicated in the letter," Ike said.

"What do you think, Pa?" Ray asked. "See there? You send us off to do business for you, and we bring back a deal worth . . ." He paused, trying to figure out the worth of the deal.

"Seventy-five thousand dollars," Billy said.

"Yeah, seventy-five thousand dollars," Ray said.

Ike stared at the three boys for a moment, then nodded his head and left the room.

Ray waited until he was gone before he turned to Billy. "Why didn't you tell us that you met with Westpheling?" he asked angrily.

"I did tell you," Billy said. "But you and Cletus were both so drunk that you don't remember."

Ray raised his finger and pointed it at Billy. "Yeah, well, don't you be tryin' to turn Pa against me, boy, do you hear me?" he said. "Brother or no brother, I won't put up with it."

"I have no intention of turning him against you," Billy said. He looked at Cletus. "Against either one of you. You are my brothers. All I want to do is look out for you."

"Yeah? Well, you don't need to look out for me. I can look out for myself," Cletus said.

* * *

It was three days later when Cletus asked Ray and Billy if they would like to go into town.

"I mean, when you think about it, we ought to celebrate the good deal Billy got us on the cows," he said.

"Good idea," Billy agreed. "We could all have a nice dinner at the Vermillion."

"The Vermillion?" Cletus replied with a scoffing laugh. "Are you serious? In case you have forgotten, the Vermillion is owned by the Calhouns."

"I know it's owned by the Calhouns. But they serve the best food in town."

"Little brother, you eat to stay alive, not to have a good time," Cletus said. "What about you, Ray? You comin'?"

"What the hell good is it to go into town?" Ray asked. "We can't go to Maggie's whorehouse no more. And the whores at the Hog Waller are so ugly, they'd make a train take five miles of dirt road. I don't see no need to go into town a'tall."

"Ahh, you're both useless," Cletus said with a dismissive wave of his hand. "I'll get a couple of boys from the bunkhouse to go in with me."

At the Golden Nugget, Falcon was sitting at a table with Corey and Prentiss viewing the architectural drawings of a theater they planned to build.

"We've bought the lot next door, so we can expand in that direction," Corey said. "That way, you can enter the theater from the street or from the saloon."

"How many seats in the theater?"

"Three hundred and fifty," Prentiss replied.

Falcon whistled. "That's more people than there are in town."

"Well, it is now," Corey agreed. "But I think it's like Marshal Calhoun said. Once General Garrison gets his railroad built, people will be coming here from all around. I figure we'll have more'n a thousand people here the first year after the railroad is built. And when that happens, I believe they will welcome a theater."

"And I think people would come just to hear Rachael play," Prentiss added. "Not drinking music, her kind of music."

Even as they were looking at the drawings, Rachael was playing the Moscheles Piano Concerto Number Two and Falcon turned to look at her. Sensing his look, Rachael glanced back toward him, then smiled and bobbed her head as she continued to play.

"I agree with Prentiss," Falcon said. "I think that many would come just to hear her play."

Across town, Billy Clinton stepped into the Vermillion Restaurant. He stood there for a moment, looking around at the customers, then saw what he was looking for, a pretty young woman sitting alone at a table in the back. There was an empty table next to her, and Billy walked back to take it.

He said nothing to her, nor did he make eye contact. Sitting down, he picked up the menu and began to study it.

"Hello, Kathleen," he said as he studied the menu. He spoke quietly enough that only Kathleen could hear him, and because he appeared to be looking at the menu, it would not be apparent to the casual onlooker that the two were even aware of each other.

"Hello, Billy," Kathleen replied.

"I hear there is a dance next Saturday night. Will you be going?" Billy asked.

"Yes."

"Maybe I could stop by your house and walk to the dance with you," Billy suggested.

"Oh, Billy, no," Kathleen said. "Please don't do that. My father would—well—let's just say my father would not approve."

"I've done nothing to your father," Billy said.

"Not you personally, but your family has. You know how adamantly your father opposes the railroad. And right now, the railroad is my father's entire life."

"Maybe so, but that's my family, not me," Billy said. "Anyway, why should our families have anything to do with something that is just between you and me?"

"Billy, you know there is no way for that to be," Kathleen said. "I will see you at the dance. For now, we must be satisfied with that."

"Trade menus with me," Billy said.

"I beg your pardon?"

"Trade menus with me," Billy repeated.

"All right," Kathleen replied, puzzled by the request. She handed her menu to Billy and took his. When she opened it, she saw a piece of paper. "What is this?" she asked.

"It's something I wrote for you while I was in Pueblo," Billy said.

To Kathleen

Like a blooming flower to behold,
Your beauty shines through.
If only I were so bold
To declare my love for you.

But cruel is the fate
That keeps us apart.
Divided by families that hate,
I cannot speak what is in my heart.

Were I free to share with you
The words that I hold so dear,
There is nothing I would rather do
Than to whisper them in your ear.
But a Clinton am I, and Garrison you are,
Enemies, or so it seems.
I can but love you from afar
And hold you only in my dreams.

"Oh, Billy, it's beautiful," Kathleen said. "Nobody has ever written a poem for me before."

"Please don't tell anyone I wrote it for you."

"Why not? It is beautiful, you should be very proud of it. I know that I am."

"You don't understand," Billy said. "If my brothers found out that I wrote poetry, I would never hear the end of it."

"Oh, pooh on your brothers," Kathleen said. She sighed. "But under the circumstances, I will keep it quiet."

"Thanks," Billy said.

"Billy, I will keep it always," Kathleen promised.

"Here comes your father," Billy said. "It might be better if I leave now."

"I will see you Saturday?"

"Yes," Billy said.

"Mr. Clinton, are you not going to order dinner?" the waiter asked as he saw Billy leaving.

"Later perhaps," Billy said. "I just realized there was something I needed to do."

Billy passed Wade Garrison just as he was coming into the restaurant.

"Good evening, General," he said.

Garrison nodded, but said nothing in reply. Walking to the rear of the restaurant, he pulled a chair out from his daughter's table.

"I see young Billy Clinton was in here," he said as he sat down.

"Yes, he was."

"Did you talk to him?"

"Briefly."

"I've told you, I don't want you to have anything to do with him," Garrison said.

"Papa, he is not like the others," Kathleen insisted.

"He is a Clinton and you are a Garrison. That should say it all," Wade said, ending the conversation.

Kathleen did not respond. She was glad the conversation had ended.

Chapter Eleven

When Cletus and two of his cowboys came into the saloon, Cletus gave a loud whoop.

"Yippee, boys, Cletus Clinton is here, hang on to your beer!"

One of the cowboys laughed. "That rhymes," he said. "Here and beer."

At their table at the back of the room, Prentiss looked up when the three men came into the saloon. "Well, well," he said quietly. "It looks like we are going to have the pleasure of Cletus Clinton's company tonight."

"Yeah, some pleasure," Corey replied. He looked over at Falcon. "I believe you said you met him on the train?"

"Yes, I met him," Falcon said. "But he was so drunk you could hardly call it a meeting. Who are the two with him?"

"Those two boys with him ride for his pa," Prentiss said. "The ugly one, with the mustache, is Deke Mathers. The even uglier one, without the mustache, is Lou Reeder."

Falcon watched Cletus as he went from table to table, greeting everyone.

"Hey, missy, a round of drinks for this table!" he called to one of the bar girls.

"Thank you, Cletus, that's real nice of you," one of the men at the table said.

"Well, sir, don't let it ever be said that I ain't generous to my friends," Cletus replied. "What about you boys?" he asked the next table. "Would you like another round of drinks on me?"

"Why, yes, sir, that would be great!"

"Honey, when you finish with that table, take care of this one, too."

"What about us, Cletus?" someone at one of the other tables called out.

"You, too. Drinks for everyone," he said.

The saloon patrons let out a cheer.

"He certainly seems to be popular," Falcon said.

"Yeah," Prentiss replied. "Cletus's funny that way. One minute he is everyone's friend, the next he's ready to fight."

"I know what you are talking about," Falcon said. "In the short time I've seen him, I've seen him both ways. Well, if you gentlemen will excuse me, I think I'll find a friendly card game."

Taking his beer with him, Falcon saw an open chair at one of the tables where cards were being played, and walking over, asked permission to join.

"Yes, sir, Mr. MacCallister, we'd be honored to have you play with us," one of the men said. He stuck his hand across the table. "The name is Denham, Harold Denham. I'm publisher of the *Higbee Journal*."

Falcon met the other players, then began playing cards. When the game finally broke up about an hour later, he was neither the biggest winner nor the biggest loser. The other players left, and Falcon, who remained at the table, had started to deal himself a hand of solitaire when Cletus came over.

"Do you want to play by yourself? Or would you like someone to play against?"

From the expression on Cletus's face, and the tone of his voice, Falcon realized that Cletus didn't even remember him from the train. Billy had told him that Cletus wouldn't remember, and he was right.

"Sure, have a seat," Falcon offered. "We'll play. What will it be?"

"I don't particularly like two-handed poker. You choose the game," Cletus suggested.

"All right," Falcon replied. "How about this one?"

Falcon took three cards from the deck, a jack, a king, and an ace. He put the three cards facedown. "Find the ace," he said.

"What do you mean, find the ace?"

"It's a simple game, like finding a pea under the shell," Falcon explained. "Only in this case, you'll have to find the ace."

Falcon moved the three cards around for a few seconds, then took his hand away. "See if you can find it."

Cletus turned up the ace.

"Ha, that's not very hard."

"I let you win that one," Falcon said. "But if we do it for real, I don't intend to let you win."

"All I have to do is find the ace?"

"Yes."

"Ha! You can't stop me from winning. This is going to be the easiest dollar I ever made!" Cletus said. He put a dollar on the table; Falcon matched it, then moved the cards around, doing it much more quickly than he had the time previous.

"It's right there," Cletus said, reaching for a card. The card he turned over was a king.

"Damn."

"Again?" Falcon asked.

"Yeah."

Cletus lost another dollar, then another one.

"Wait, I'm going to get another beer," Cletus said.

Falcon watched Cletus walk over to the bar and order a beer. While Cletus was at the bar, he spoke to one of the men who had come into the saloon with him. Then, carrying the beer, he returned to the table.

"I hear tell you are Falcon MacCallister," Cletus said.

"Yes."

"I've heard of you."

"Have you?"

"My name is Cletus Clinton. I reckon you've heard of me as well."

"I have," Falcon said.

"Damn!" Cletus replied with a broad grin. "I figured you'd heard of me. I reckon all us famous people have heard of each other."

Falcon suppressed a smile. At that moment, the man Prentiss had identified as Deke Mathers came over to the table. This was the same man Cletus had spoken to when he went to the bar to buy his beer.

"Mr. MacCallister, is it true they's a whole town named just after you?" Deke asked.

"It's not named after me," Falcon replied. "It was named after my father."

Cletus watched Deke engage Falcon in conversation. This was by design, for Cletus wanted Falcon's attention diverted away from the three cards just for a moment.

With Falcon's head turned, Cletus reached across the

table and put a small, barely noticeable crease on one corner of the ace. Let Falcon switch the cards around all he wanted, Cletus would make no attempt whatever to follow them. He would simply select the card with the creased corner.

"You going to play cards, or are you going to talk all day?" Cletus asked.

Falcon turned back to the table. "Why, I'm going to play cards, Mr. Clinton," Falcon said, smiling easily.

"Good," Cletus said. "Only, this time, let's bet enough for me to get even." He put a ten dollar bill on the table.

"That's a pretty steep bet for a little friendly game like this, isn't it?" Falcon asked.

"If it's too rich for you, just say so," Cletus said.

Falcon drummed his fingers on the card table for a moment. By now, several other patrons of the saloon had wandered over to the table, and what had started out as a quiet, two-man game was quickly turning into a spectator sport.

"So, what are you going to do, Mr. MacCallister?" Cletus asked. "Are you going to play or not?"

"I'll play," Falcon said, reaching into his own pocket to bring out a ten dollar bill to match the bet.

Cletus took one last look at the creased card. So far, Falcon hadn't noticed it.

"Hey, I'm bettin' Cletus gets it this time," Deke said, putting a dollar down on the table.

"You're on," someone said.

"I'll bet on Cletus."

"I'm bettin' on MacCallister."

Within a few moments, there were several dollars in side bets on the table, and by now, nearly everyone in the house was aware of the game.

Falcon picked up the three cards, shuffled them around a few times, then put the cards down on the table. He started moving them around, in and out, over and under with such lightning speed that the cards were nearly a blur. Then he stopped and the three cards lay in front of him, waiting for Cletus to pick the ace.

With a smug smile, Cletus reached across the table to make his selection. Then suddenly, he froze in mid-motion and the smile left his face. He hand hung suspended over the table.

"Go on, Cletus, pick out the ace. You can do it," Deke said.

Cletus stared at the three cards with a sickly expression on his face. All three cards now bore that same creased corner. Falcon had not only seen it, he had, somehow, managed to duplicate it on the other cards with such exactness that Cletus had no idea which card he had marked.

Falcon reached across the table and put his hand on Cletus's shoulder, using his thumb to lift the vest away, ever so slightly.

"Is there something wrong?" Falcon asked. "You look a little piquèd."

Cletus glared at Falcon. Irritated, he pushed Falcon's hand away from his shoulder, then reached down to turn up one of the cards.

The card he turned up was a jack.

"Damn!" he said.

There was a collection of cheers and groans from the others around the table, many of whom had their own bets riding on the outcome.

"I guess I'm just lucky," Falcon said as he reached for the money.

"No, wait a minute!" Cletus said. "I don't believe the ace is even on the table."

"Sure it is, I'll show you," Falcon offered. He started to reach for one of the cards.

"Wait a minute, I'll turn it over," Cletus said. "For all I know you have an ace palmed. You can make it appear anywhere you want."

"All right, you turn it over." Cletus reached for the card Falcon had started for and flipped it over. It was the ace.

"He got you there, Cletus," one of the men in the crowd said.

"Oh, and Mr. Clanton, as far as my being able to make an ace appear anywhere, why don't you check your shirt pocket?" Falcon said.

"I beg your pardon?"

"Check your shirt pocket," Falcon repeated. "Under your vest."

Cletus opened his vest and stuck his hand down into his shirt pocket.

"What the hell is this?" he asked, coming out with a card. There, in his hand, was the ace of hearts. "How did that get there?"

The others in the saloon laughed uproariously as Falcon picked up the money.

It was a sullen and subdued Cletus who returned to the table where Deke and Lou were sitting.

"How'd he do that, Boss?" Lou asked.

"How'd he do what?"

"Get that ace in your pocket like that?"

"How the hell do I know?" Cletus replied angrily.

"He's a card cheat, that's how. That's how he got that card in my pocket, and that's how he won."

"I'll say this for him. He sure is good at it," Deke said.

"He's a cheat," Cletus insisted. "There ain't nothin' good about bein' a cheat."

"No, sir, you're right about that," Lou said. "There ain't nothin' good about bein' a cheat."

"Drink up, boys. Like I told you, tonight it's all on me," Cletus said.

"Damn, that's real good of you, Boss," Deke said.

"Yeah, I've worked for other men who've bought me a drink," Lou said. "But I ain't never worked for no one who was willin' to buy drinks all night long."

"Ladies and gentlemen, may I have your attention please?" Corey Hampton shouted. He held up his hands in a call for quiet. "May I have your attention, please?"

There were dozens of conversations ongoing at that moment, most of them dealing with the mystery as to how Falcon MacCallister was able to get the ace into Cletus's shirt pocket. Those conversations fell quiet at Corey's call for attention.

"Ladies and gentlemen," Corey repeated.

"What ladies?" Cletus called out. "They ain't nothin' but whores in here. There ain't no ladies."

There were a few nervous chuckles at Cletus's comment, but no general laughter.

"Ladies and gentlemen," Corey said again, this time putting a lot of emphasis on the word "ladies."

"The Golden Nugget is pleased to present for your listening pleasure this evening, Miss Rachael Kirby!"

There was a round of applause as Rachael took her

place at the piano, then began playing Chopin's Sonata Opus 58.

Cletus pointed to the piano player. "You know what I think? I think that girl would make a good whore. Fact is, she'd make a better whore than she would a piano player. What kind of music do you call that shit she's playin' right now? Hell, you can't even sing along with it."

"Some folks like that kind of music," Deke said.

"Yeah, well, I don't."

"Shhh!" someone at the adjacent table said. "Why don't you folks be quiet so the rest of us can hear?"

Cletus glared at the man who had shushed him, but he said nothing. Instead, he just took a drink of his whiskey.

As Rachael played, she was aware that Falcon MacCallister was in the saloon as well, and she was unable to shake his presence. She had heard about him from Rosanna and Andrew, but they had left out how handsome he was. Maybe because he was their brother, they had lost all perspective. She knew that he had been married, and she knew also that his wife was dead. What she didn't know was whether or not he would be interested in ever being married again.

Rachael, stop thinking such nonsense, she told herself. You just met him.

Rachael forced thoughts of Falcon out of her mind by concentrating more intently on her playing. Then, with a grand crescendo, she finished her piece. Standing up, she turned and curtsied graciously to accept the applause.

"Thank you very much for your applause," she said.

"And now, the rest of the evening belongs to you. What would you like me to play?"

"Hey, piano player!" Cletus shouted in a loud voice. "I'm tired of listening to all this shit you call music. Play 'Tying a Knot in the Devil's Tail'!"

"Oh, I'm afraid I don't know that one," Rachael said, smiling politely despite the rude customer's outbreak. "Perhaps you could suggest another one."

"I want to hear 'Tying a Knot in the Devil's Tail'," Cletus said again.

"I'm very sorry, sir," Rachael replied without losing her composure. "But I really don't know that one and I don't have the music for it. I would be glad to play something else for you."

"I don't want anything else," Cletus said.

"I'm sorry, sir," Rachael said again. "Does anyone else have a request?"

"How about 'Streets of Laredo'?" another customer suggested.

Rachael smiled. "That one I can do," she said, turning back to the piano.

The customer who had requested "Streets of Laredo" sat back down, but Cletus Clinton did not. Instead, he stood there, glaring angrily at the pianist's back as she sat at the piano.

Rachael began to play the requested song, but was interrupted by a loud crash when Cletus suddenly picked up his chair and brought it crashing down on the table beside him.

Rachael let out a little cry of fear and shock, and there were several shouts of anger and surprise from the others in the saloon.

Cletus stood in the middle of the saloon floor holding the remnants of the chair in his hand.

"Don't you turn away from me, you bitch!" Cletus said, pointing at Rachael. "Nobody turns away from Cletus Clinton!"

Rachael turned to face him. Falcon was surprised to see that though she was facing a very angry man, the expression on her face wasn't one of fear, but rather one of resolute anger.

"Mr.—Clinton is it? You are rude and distruptive. I told you that I don't know that song and even if I did know it, I would not play it for you. Now please sit down."

Several in the saloon laughed and cheered.

"That little lady sure put you in your place, Cletus," someone called from across the room.

Cletus raised one leg of the chair over his head and took a step toward her. "Oh, you'll play it all right or I'll smash up the piano so that you never play anything else on it."

The deadly sound of a pistol being cocked stopped Cletus in his tracks.

"Clinton, if you don't drop that club now, I'm going to put a ball between your eyes."

Cletus lowered the club but he didn't drop it. He smiled, though it was a smile without mirth. "Now here, Mr. MacCallister, is that right? I mean after me'n you just had us a real friendly game of cards, you go and pull a gun on me behind my back. Is that nice? What kind of way is that for friends to act?"

"I don't consider us friends, Mr. Clinton," Falcon said. "And I don't take kindly to anyone who would threaten a lady."

"I was just trying to get her attention."

"Really. And you got my attention instead. Funny how

it works out like that sometime. Now, drop your pistol belt on the floor and get out of here."

"What? Why the hell should I drop my pistol belt on the floor?" Cletus asked angrily. "I ain't the one holdin' a gun in my hand. You are."

"You just answered your own question, Clinton. You should drop your pistol belt because I am the one holding the gun. And I'll kill you if you don't do it. Come back tomorrow when you are sober and you can pick it up."

Cletus's eyes narrowed as he continued to glare at Falcon. "Mister, I reckon you must be new in these parts. Otherwise, you would know that I ain't the kind of man you want to have as an enemy," he said menacingly.

"You don't say," Falcon replied calmly.

"Please go, Cletus," Prentiss said quietly. "Do what the man says and get out of here. Otherwise, he will have to kill you, and I don't want you bleeding all over my floor."

There was a scattering of nervous laughter.

Cletus hesitated a few seconds longer. Then he dropped the chair leg, unbuckled his gunbelt, and let it drop to the floor. He pointed at Falcon.

"Mister, you made a mistake tonight. A big mistake. This ain't over between us."

"Clinton, you had better hope that it's over," Falcon said quietly.

"Are you threatening me?" Clinton asked.

"Call it more of a promise," Falcon said.

Cletus curled his hands into fists, then walked to the door and stepped outside.

"Miss Kirby, are you all right?" Prentiss called over to the piano player.

"Yes, thank you, I'm fine," Rachael replied in a tight voice.

While everyone else was reliving the scene in excited conversation and minute detail, very few paid any attention to Falcon when he walked over to pick up the club Cletus had dropped. With the club in his hand, Falcon stepped up to the batwing doors, then moved to one side and backed up against the wall. He waited.

He didn't have to wait long, because seconds later the doors were pushed open with a bang.

"You son of a bitch! Nobody braces Cletus Clinton and gets away with it! *Nobody!*" Cletus shouted in a loud voice, totally oblivious of the fact that Falcon was standing no more than a few feet from him,

Cletus's eyes were flashing, and his face was twisted into a mask of rage, but nobody was looking at his face. What everyone was looking at was the double-barrel 12-gauge Greener shotgun he had thrust out in front of him.

"Look out!" Corey shouted.

There were other shouts of alarm as everyone in the saloon hurried to get out of the way.

Those who had kept their eyes glued on Clinton were surprised when they suddenly saw Falcon smash the cowboy in the forehead with the club he was holding.

For a long moment, everyone remained quiet and still, shocked into silence by what they had just witnessed.

"Son of a bitch," someone finally said, the words almost reverent.

Then all began talking at the same time, the voices rising louder and louder in their nervous excitement.

Deke and Lou looked at the prostrate form of their boss as he lay on his back on the saloon floor.

"Is he dead?" Deke asked.

"No," Falcon said. "Now, get him out of here."

"Mister, I hope you know what you done. Cletus has a bad temper. He ain't likely to forget this."

"I don't intend for him to forget it," Falcon said. "Now, get his sorry carcass out of here."

At that moment, Marshal Calhoun pushed his way through the batwing doors and, seeing Cletus on the floor, looked around the smoke-filled room.

"Son of bitch, is that Cletus Clinton?" he asked.

"Hello, Marshal Calhoun. Yes, that's him, all right," Prentiss said.

Deke and Lou started to pick up Cletus. "Leave him be for the moment," Calhoun said. "Is he dead?"

"No such luck," Corey said. "Falcon just laid him out, is all."

Calhoun saw the shotgun lying on the floor, then looked up at Falcon. "You the one he was coming after, Falcon?"

"I was," Falcon replied.

"Why didn't you save us all a peck of trouble and kill the son of a bitch? If he came after you with a shotgun, you certainly had cause."

"I guess I was just feeling generous," Falcon said.

Marshal Calhoun chuckled. "Falcon MacCallister feeling generous," he said. "I like that."

"Marshal, what are you going to do about this fella hittin' Cletus right between the eyes, like he done?" Lou asked. "He could'a kilt him."

"He should've killed him," Calhoun replied.

"Can we take Cletus home now?" Deke asked.

"No, but you can take him down to the jail," Calhoun replied.

"What? The hell you say. You ain't goin' to put 'im in jail," Deke said angrily.

"That's where you are wrong, because that is exactly what I am going to do," Marshal Calhoun said.

"It ain't in no way right for you to put him in jail," Deke insisted. "Cletus is the one that got hit. Right between the eyes, it was, and with a club as big around as your wrist. Ike ain't goin' to like this. He ain't goin' to like this none a'all."

"Take him down there and put him in jail now," Calhoun ordered, pointing toward the jailhouse, "or I'll throw the two of you in there with him."

Struggling with the deadweight of the unconscious form, Deke and Lou left the saloon carrying Cletus.

"All right, folks, all the excitement is over," Prentiss said to the saloon patrons, who were still gathered around watching the proceedings with intense curiosity. "Go on back to your tables now and enjoy your time with us. The next beer is on the house."

"Good!"

"Thanks!"

"Good man."

As the patrons crowded the bar for their free beers, Rachael, after a nod from Corey, returned to the piano and began playing.

"I've been here at least a half-dozen times," Falcon said. "I've heard of Ike Clinton, but I don't think I've ever met him."

"That's because until there was talk of a railroad, Clinton pretty much stayed to himself," Calhoun said.

"Where did he come from?"

"Some say he rode with Doc Jennison and the Kansas Jayhawkers; others say he rode with Bloody Bill Anderson and the Bushwhackers of Missouri," Calhoun explained. "If you want to know the truth, I think they are both right. I think our friend Clinton played both sides for whatever he could get. I know he came out here not too long after the war with more than ten thousand dollars in cash."

"Folks say he's never seen an acre he didn't claim, or a cow he didn't brand," Corey said.

"Yes, and if he has his way now, he'll put his brand on General Garrison's railroad," Prentiss added.

"Knowing the general, I think that may be a bit bigger project than Clinton can handle," Calhoun said.

"It just might be," Falcon said.

Calhoun studied Falcon for a long moment, then he laughed. "I'll be damned, Falcon, I just figured out why you are here. You were with the general durin' the war, weren't you?"

"Yes, I was with him for a while," Falcon agreed.

"I thought as much. The general brought you out here, didn't he?"

Falcon paused for a moment, recalling Garrison's suggestion that he not tell anyone. But he knew it would be impossible to maintain that façade, so he just took a deep breath and answered truthfully.

"Yes, I got a letter from the general asking me if I would come."

Calhoun nodded. "Good, good. The general is a good man, he needs somebody like you on his side."

"You're on his side," Falcon replied.

"Yeah, I'm on his side. But only to the edge of town," Calhoun said. He sighed. "Unfortunately, that's as far as my jurisdiction goes."

"Wait until the next election, Titus," Corey said. "You'll be the sheriff then."

Calhoun chuckled. "I don't know, I didn't do all that well in the last election."

"We've learned a few things since then," Prentiss said.

"I appreciate your support," Calhoun said. "But now, I guess I'd better get on down to the jail before my prisoner wakes up."

"Good night, Marshal, thanks for responding so fast," Corey said.

Calhoun nodded without answering, then pushed outside into the darkness.

"There goes a good man," Prentiss said. "I don't know where this town would be without him."

"We would be run over roughshod by Sheriff Belmond more'n likely," Corey replied.

Chapter Twelve

The next morning, Billy Clinton came into town driving a buckboard. He stopped in front of the general store where Carl Moore, the proprietor, was sweeping off the store's front porch.

"Mr. Moore, have you seen my brother Cletus?" Billy asked.

"Not since yesterday, Billy," Moore answered.

"Do you mind if I leave the buckboard parked here until I find him?"

"No, sir, I don't mind a bit," Moore said.

"Thanks."

Climbing down from the buckboard, Billy started up the walk toward Little Man Lambert's Café. If Cletus was still in town, like as not he would be having breakfast, and given that the Calhoun brothers owned the Vermillion, it wasn't very likely he would be there. And even if Cletus wasn't in town, Billy was hungry, so Little Man's was as good a place as any to start looking for him.

"Mornin', Billy," someone said as he passed Billy on the board sidewalk.

"Good mornin', Mr. Clark," Billy replied. "Say, have you seen my brother this morning?"

Clark shook his head. "Haven't seen him this morning, but I saw him at the Golden Nugget last night. He was feeling pretty good, if you know what I mean."

"Drunk?"

"Yes."

"Did he get into any trouble?"

"Well, now, that I can't tell you," Clark said. "Seein' as I didn't stay too much longer after he got there. He wasn't in no trouble last time I seen him, though."

"Thanks, Mr. Clark."

Billy left the sidewalk and crossed the dirt street, picking his way gingerly through the horse droppings. He pushed the door open at Little Man's, and saw Cletus sitting at a table in the back.

Billy gasped. Both Cletus's eyes were black and his nose was purple and swollen. He was also so drunk that it was all he could do to hold his head up.

Billy walked back to the table and sat down.

"What happened to you?" he asked.

"What do you mean, what happened to me?" Cletus asked.

"Your eyes are all black."

"They are?" Cletus touched himself between his eyes and winced in pain. "Damn," he said. "That hurts."

"Well, I should say it hurts," Billy said. "It's a wonder you can even see out of them. What happened?"

"I don't know."

"Did you get into a fight?"

"I don't know," Cletus repeated. "I must have. But I don't remember anything about it."

"Where did you spend the night? Do you at least know that?" Billy asked.

"Yeah, I know that."

"Where?"

"In the jail," Cletus said. "I spent the night in jail. What about Deke and Lou? Where are they?"

Billy shook his head. "I don't know, I haven't seen them this morning. Did they get into a fight, too?"

"I don't know."

Billy sighed. "Look at you. You are so damn drunk, you don't know anything."

The waitress brought a plate of eggs, potatoes, and fried ham to set before Cletus. Cletus looked at his breakfast stupidly for a moment, as if having difficulty making his eyes focus. Then he smiled.

"Oh, yeah," he said, grinning. "I was sittin' here waitin' on another drink, but I must've ordered breakfast." His face paled as he looked at the food, then he pushed it away. "Why'd I order breakfast? I can't eat this shit," he said.

"Give it to me, I haven't eaten yet," Billy said.

"You can eat it?"

"Yes, I can eat."

"How can you eat it?"

"I can eat it because I'm not hungover from a night of drinking, fighting, and who knows what else you were doing."

"Oh yeah, I forget," Cletus said. "You are the good boy of the family. Pa thinks me and Ray should be more like you. Tell me, little brother, do you think I should be more like you?"

"Would it do any good if I said I thought you should?"

Billy asked. He cut a piece of ham and stuck it in his mouth.

"No, it wouldn't do no good a'tall," Cletus said. "Besides which, I got me a score to settle with Marshal Calhoun."

"What score do you have to settle with him?" Billy raked his biscuit through some egg yellow, then took a bite.

"I don't know."

"That doesn't make sense, Cletus," Billy said. "You say you have a score to settle with Marshal Calhoun, but you don't even know the reason?"

"I've got these here two black eyes!" Cletus shouted. "Ain't that reason enough?" Cletus's voice was so loud that a few of the others who were eating their own breakfast looked around nervously.

"You're making a scene, Cletus," Billy cautioned.

"I don't care. This here thing with Marshal Calhoun and his two brothers has gone far enough. I'm goin' to stand up to them today. Are you goin' to stand up with me? Or are you goin' to turn tail and run?"

"What do you plan to do?" Billy asked.

"It don't matter what I plan to do. What I want to know is, whatever I do, will you be there with me?"

"I'm your brother," Billy said.

"I know you're my brother," Cletus said. "That ain't the question. The question I'm askin' you is will you be there with me?"

"I hope it never actually comes to that, but it if does, yes, I'll be with you."

"What if it actually comes to gunplay? Would you be there to back me up?"

Billy sighed. "Yes," he said. "Like I told you, you're my brother. If it comes to gunplay, I'll back you."

Suddenly, the anger left Cletus's face and he grinned

broadly. "I was hopin' you would say that," he said. "Just knowin' I can count on you makes me happy. Come on."

"Where are we going?"

"We're goin' home," Cletus said. He laughed. "If Calhoun and his brothers want to have a shootout, why, they can just have it amongst themselves."

Billy laughed happily. "Now you're making sense," he said. "Come on, I have a buckboard parked just down the street."

"A buckboard? Where's my horse?"

"It came back to the ranch last night," Billy said.

Kathleen Garrison stood at the front window of the CNM&T office and watched as Billy drove by in the buckboard. Billy's brother, Cletus, was sitting in the seat beside him, his head hanging forward as if he were asleep.

She wondered if Billy would glance toward the window, and when he did, she felt a little thrill pass through her. She waved at him, and she saw the small smile play across his face as he nodded in response.

Leaving the front window, she returned to the desk, then pulled out the poem he had written for her. She read the poem again, allowing each word to go to her heart.

Then, the joy she was feeling was suddenly replaced with a jolt of reality.

He had said it in the poem.

She was a Garrison.

He was a Clinton.

Kathleen heard her father's footsteps on the front porch, and quickly, she folded the poem and stuck it between the pages of a copy of Charles Dickens's *Great Expectations.*

"Hello, Papa," she said to him as he came in.

"I was just down to the telegraph office," Garrison said. "All the material I need for building the depot has arrived in La Junta. Mr. Thompson is sending wagons after it tomorrow."

"That's wonderful, Papa," Kathleen said. "Let's just pray that it arrives without anyone being killed or hurt."

"Prayer is good," Garrison agreed. "But you've heard the old expression 'God helps him who helps himself'?"

"Yes, of course."

Garrison nodded. "I'm helping myself," he said. "I'm sending Falcon MacCallister along with the wagons. I pity anyone who tries to stop them this time."

Mounted on a horse supplied by Wade Garrison, Falcon was on the way to La Junta with the wagons. They had left Higbee at first light, and were now halfway between Higbee and La Junta.

Garrison wasn't the only one to take steps to ensure the safety of the shipment. For this trip to La Junta and back, Thompson had hired guards to ride with the drivers, arming each of them with double-barrel shotguns.

As the wagons rolled slowly toward La Junta, the three guards shouted directions at each other.

"Tom, you check the tree line over there. Do you see anything?" one of the guards called.

"No, what about you?" Tom replied. "Anything in those rocks?"

"Nothing I can see."

"Uh, Tom, Larry, and, Frank, is it?" Falcon asked.

"Yes."

"Do you mind if I make a suggestion?"

"No, why should we mind? We're in this together," Larry replied.

"Good," Falcon said. "Take a look at the wagons."

"I beg your pardon?"

"The wagons," Falcon said. "Take a look at them. What do you see?"

The three guards looked at the wagons, then at each other, than at Falcon. It was obvious they had no idea what they were supposed to be looking for.

"I don't see anything," Tom said.

"Neither do I," Larry added."

"How about you, Frank? Do you see anything?"

"No," Frank replied, confused as to where all this was going.

"Good, good, you've just made my point," Falcon said. "Nobody is going to hit us with empty wagons," he explained. "If they are going to hit us, it will be on the way back, when they can do the most damage."

"Ha!" Smitty, the lead driver, laughed. "Shouldn't of been all that hard for you boys to figure that out."

"Yeah," Tom said sheepishly. "Yeah, I guess we should have thought about that."

When Falcon and the wagons reached La Junta, they stopped alongside a low, long, wooden building. A white sign on the either end of the building, bore the name of the station, in black letters.

LA JUNTA

"Whoa, hold it up here, boys," Smitty said. "Barnes, you and Morrell stay with the wagons. I'll go see Mr. Rudd and find out where our load is."

"I'll come with you," Falcon said.

"Here, Tom, hold the reins," Smitty said, handing the reins to the guard as he climbed down from the wagon. "I got the brake set, so they ain't goin' nowhere."

"I got 'em," Tom said.

Dismounting, Falcon followed Smitty into the little depot. There were a few passengers waiting for the next train: a drummer sitting alone with his case of samples, a couple of cowboys who were engaged in conversation, and a man, his wife, and two children. The smallest of the two, a little girl, was sleeping on the bench beside her mother. A little boy was sitting next to his father, playing with a wooden horse.

At one end of the depot, there was a ticket counter and telegraph station, and as Falcon and Smitty came inside, they could hear the telegraph clacking away. Evidently, La Junta was not the destination of the message because there was nobody at the instrument. Instead, the one man behind the ticket counter was busy with some printed documents. He looked up as Falcon and Smitty entered.

"Good morning, Smitty," he called.

"'Mornin', Poke. Is Mr. Rudd around?"

"Yes, he's back in his office."

Smitty nodded, then started toward the opposite end of the depot. Here, there was a closed door with a frosted glass windowpane. On the frosted pane were painted the words STATIONMASTER.

Smitty knocked lightly on the door, then pushed it open. "Mr. Rudd?" he called.

"Yes, come in," a voice answered from inside.

Rudd was a man in his sixties, with white hair and white muttonchop whiskers. He was sitting at his desk, writing in a ledger, but looked up, then nodded as he recognized Smitty.

"Mr. Smith," he said. "You would be here for the Garrison shipment, I take it?"

"Yes, sir. Did everything get here that was supposed to?"

"It did," Rudd replied. "It's the rearmost car at the back of the marshaling area. Let's see, the number of the car is"—he paused to consult a book—"yes, here it is. The number is 10031. Here, I'll write it down for you."

"Thanks," Smitty said, taking the number from Rudd. "Is all of it in the same car?"

"Yes, everything in that one car. Will you be signing for it?"

"No, I will sign for it," Falcon said.

"And you are?"

"Falcon MacCallister."

"Falcon MacCallister?" Rudd said, reacting to the name. "Are you the famous Falcon MacCallister?"

"I don't know about the famous part," Falcon replied.

"Yes, sir, this is the same Falcon MacCallister you've prob'ly heard about," Smitty said. "After what happened to our last shipment, General Garrison hired Mr. MacCallister to ride along with us."

"Yes, yes, I heard about what happened to the last shipment. What a shame. Mr. True was a fine man, a true gentleman. I will miss him. Uh, Mr. MacCallister, no offense, but do you have some authorization to sign for General Garrison's shipment? It's railroad regulations, you understand."

"No offense taken," Falcon said, showing the station-master the letter Garrison had given him before he left town this morning.

Rudd put on a pair of wire-rimmed glasses, hooking them carefully over one ear at a time. Then he read the letter slowly, as if going over each word. Then, he cleared his throat and put the paper aside.

"Sign here, please," he said, sliding a bill of lading toward Falcon.

Falcon signed the document, then he and Smitty returned to the wagons.

"Back there in the corner, boys!" Smitty called to the other drivers. He pointed to the car in the most remote part of the yard.

Lee Davis and Gene Willoughby had been cutting weeds around the depot when Falcon went in to talk to the stationmaster.

"Son of a bitch!" Davis said. "Son of a bitch, it's him!"

"It's who?" Willoughby said.

"Wait, I'll be right back."

"I ain't cuttin' all these damn weeds by myself, you know," Willoughby called out after Davis dropped his weed hook and started toward the depot.

Davis moved up close to the window that opened onto Rudd's office, then looked in. Seeing what he wanted to see, he hurried back to Willoughby, whose right earlobe sported a ragged, encrusted wound.

"It's him," Davis said.

"Yeah, that's what you said a while ago," Willoughby replied as he continued to swing the weed hook. "Only you ain't said who." The expression in his voice showed that he had little interest in whoever it was Davis was talking about.

"Who? Him, that's who," Davis said. "Falcon MacCallister, the fella that shot off your earlobe when we tried to hold up that stage."

That got Willoughby's attention and he looked up sharply. "What? Are you sure?"

"Damn right I'm sure. I not only recognized him, I heard him tell Rudd that was his name. You might remember, that's the son of a bitch that took our guns."

"Yeah, and our boots, too," Willoughby said. "Where is he?"

"He's with them wagons," Davis said, pointing to the three wagons that were now working their way across the tracks toward a freight car that was sitting alone.

"Well, what do you know?" Willoughby said. "I've been waitin' for a chance to get even with that bastard, and here it is."

Davis smiled. "Yeah, I thought you might be happy about this."

"Damn!"

"What?"

"We ain't got no guns," Willoughby said. "Like you said, MacCallister took 'em. So, how are we going to do this?"

"I know where there's a couple pistols," Davis said.

"Where?"

"In a cabinet in the back of Rudd's office."

"They loaded?"

"Yes, they keep 'em loaded all the time. But if you can get Mr. Rudd to come out here, I can get hold of 'em."

"How'm I goin' to get him out here?"

"Here," Davis said. "Put your hook under these

railroad spikes. I'll do it, too. We'll see if we can pull a few of them up."

Working together, they pulled up a couple of spikes, then were able to move the rail slightly out of line. "That'll get his interest," Davis said as he threw the spikes out into the adjacent woods.

Davis wandered off so that he wouldn't be noticed. Then he waited as Willoughby went in to summon Rudd. A moment later, he saw Rudd come out of the depot, then stand over the track looking down at it and shaking his head.

"I'm glad it's not the high iron," Davis heard Rudd say, referring to the main line. "But even though this is a spur, it has to be fixed. We can't be having cars run off the track here."

With Rudd engaged, Davis went into the station-master's office, opened the cabinet, and took out two pistols. Checking them quickly, he saw that both were loaded. He was back outside by the time Rudd returned from his inspection of the track.

"Did you get them?" Willoughby asked.

By way of answering him, Davis handed him one of the pistols.

"Let's do it," Willoughby said.

Falcon was standing by the front of the one wagon that had already been loaded, watching as the men loaded the second of the three. It wasn't that he was too lazy, or too good to help with the loading; it was that he appreciated professionalism, and the three freight wagon drivers were professionals. They knew exactly how to load the wagons to get the maximum efficiency from the available space, and also where to place the weight in order to make the wagon ride better and to enable the team of horses to work more efficiently.

Falcon scratched a match on the weathered wood of the wagon, and was just holding it up to light the cigarette he had just rolled when a bullet slammed into the wagon just inches away.

Drawing his pistol and spinning in the same moment, he saw two men standing about twenty-five yards behind him. There was something familiar about them, though for the moment, he didn't have time to consider what it was.

"Damnit, Davis, you missed!" one of the two men yelled. He fired his own gun even as he was yelling.

Falcon fired twice, and both men went down. With his gun held ready, he hurried toward them. When he got there, one was already dead, the other was dying. That was when he saw that they were the same two men who had tried to hold up the stagecoach between La Junta and Higbee.

"Damnit!" Falcon said angrily. "Are you crazy? I wasn't after you. Why did you do this? You got yourselves killed for no reason!"

"It was supposed to be the other way around," the one remaining outlaw said. This was the one with the mangled ear. "We was supposed to kill you."

"What's happening? What's going on?" the wagon drivers called, and seeing Falcon standing over a couple of bodies, they hurried down to see, drawn by a morbid curiosity. By the time they got there, both outlaws were dead.

"I didn't figure we would be hit until we were on the road on the way back," Smitty said.

"They weren't after the loads."

"They weren't?"

"No," Falcon answered. "This had nothing to do with the loads. This was personal. These men were after me."

"Damn, Mr. MacCallister, I hope you don't take this wrong, but if you have crazy sons of bitches like these two tryin' to kill you for no reason, just how safe are we with you?"

Chapter Thirteen

Seth Parker relieved himself.

"Damn, ain't you got no more manners than to piss where we live?" Cletus Clinton asked.

"It ain't like we're livin' here, we're just campin' here," Parker replied as he aimed toward a grasshopper. He laughed as the grasshopper, caught in the sudden stream, hopped away.

"Yeah, well, I don't like anyone pissin' this close to where I'm sittin', so next time you have to shake the lily, go some'ers else to do it."

"I reckon I got a right to piss about anywhere I want to," Parker replied with a growl.

Cletus pulled his pistol. "How's this for a right? If you do it again, I'll shoot your pecker off," he said easily.

"We ain't goin' to get nowhere fightin' amongst ourselves," Bailey said. "Parker, you keep your mouth shut. We're ridin' for the La Soga Larga. That makes Cletus the boss."

"I thought Ray was the boss."

"We're both the boss," Ray said.

"Hey, Ray, how long you think it'll be before them wagons show up?" Deke asked.

"I figure no more'n forty-five minutes—maybe an hour," Ray answered. "I reckon it all depends on how long it took 'em to get loaded this mornin'."

"How many men will there be?"

"There's three wagons. Prob'ly after what happened last time, there'll be at least two on each wagon."

"That makes six of 'em," Bailey said. "I thought you said this would be easy."

"There's six of them and eight of you," Ray said. "Also, they won't be expectin' you. It'll be as easy as it was the last time."

"I notice you keep sayin' 'you' and not us," Parker said. "You ain't goin' with us?"

"No farther'n this," Ray said.

"Why not? You're the ones wantin' this job done, ain't you?"

"Folks would recognize Cletus and me," Ray said. "That wouldn't be good."

"What are these here wagons a'carryin' anyways?" Bailey asked.

"Lumber, nails, tools, and the like," Ray explained. "Things that Garrison needs for buildin' his railroad."

"Nothin' we can take and sell?" Parker asked.

"You're gettin' paid for the job," Ray said. "There ain't no need to be worryin' about sellin' anything."

"Here they come," Lou Reeder said, calling down to the others from his position atop a large rock outcropping.

"All right, boys," Ray said. "Hit 'em hard and hit 'em fast. If you do this right, they'll all be dead before they even know they're in danger."

* * *

As the iron-rimmed wheels rolled across the sunbaked earth, they picked up dirt, causing a rooster tail of dust to stream out behind them. Because the trail was wide enough, the wagons were moving three abreast. That was preferable to traveling in-line because it kept anyone from having to eat the dust of the wagon in front of them.

Falcon, who was riding in front, stopped, then held up his hand, signaling for everyone else to stop. From behind him, he heard the squeak of brakes being set and the commands of "Whoa" from the drivers as they called to their teams.

"What is it, Mr. MacCallister?" Smitty yelled up to him.

Falcon reached back into his saddlebag and drew out a telescope. Opening it, he looked at something far ahead.

"Do you see something?" Smitty asked.

"I saw a couple of men on horseback."

"What's wrong with that? This is one of the main trails, isn't it?" Barnes asked.

"Yes," Falcon replied. "And ordinarily, seeing someone wouldn't arouse any suspicion. But for some reason, these men don't seem to want to be seen. They were bent low over their horses, and they rode quickly across the open gap. Now, they are behind that ridge." He pointed.

"So, what do you think?" Tom asked. Tom was the guard riding with Smitty.

"I think we should have a little meeting."

Falcon turned and rode back toward the wagons. The drivers and armed guards looked toward him to see what he had to say.

"Did you say you only seen two riders?" Larry asked.

"There's seven of us." Larry patted the side of his Winchester. "What's the problem?"

"Have you ever seen just two cockroaches?" the driver asked the guard. "You heard Mr. MacCallister say they didn't want to be seen. You can count on there bein' more of 'em."

"What do you think they want?" Morrell asked.

"Hell, Morrell, you know what they want," Smitty said. "They want to kill us and burn our wagons, just like they done with True."

"Mr. MacCallister, what do you have in mind?" Barnes asked. "You think we should go in-line?"

"No," Falcon answered. "We'll stay abreast but we'll alter it a little. Smitty, you pull your wagon somewhat ahead. Morrell, you and Barnes drop back a little on each side so you form a V. When they hit, we'll get out of the wagons and get inside the V. That should give us a little protection. Tom, Larry, Frank, now is the time to keep your eyes open. All of you, get your guns ready."

The three guards, all of whom were carrying Winchesters, jacked shells into the chamber, then held the rifles, butts down and barrels up, by their sides. The drivers checked the loads in their revolvers.

"All right, let's go," Falcon said, resuming his position in front of the wagons.

They drove on for another fifty yards or so, silent except for the clop of the horses' hooves and the creak and rattle of the rolling wagons.

"Do you see that opening in the ridge, about a hundred yards ahead?" Falcon called back to them. He didn't point.

"I see it," Smitty replied quietly.

"That's where they'll hit us."

They rode on in silence for less than another minute. Then, suddenly, eight mounted men burst out through the opening in the ridge, exactly where Falcon had said they would be. With screams of challenge in their throats, they rode at a gallop toward the wagon party.

"Take cover behind the wagons!" Falcon shouted, jerking his horse around as he yelled. Stopping the wagons, the drivers and guards jumped down into the barricade formed by the V of the three wagons. All had their weapons ready.

The outlaws, with their pistols extended in front them, began firing. The flat popping sound floated across the open ground, reaching Falcon's ears at about the same time the bullets began whistling by.

"Take aim, but hold your fire!" Falcon shouted. Falcon aimed at one of the men and held it as the riders came closer. The outlaws continued pouring in a steady barrage of fire, and as they got closer the bullets came closer. Some of them were hitting the wagons now, sending out splinters as they made a solid, thocking sound.

"Now!" Falcon shouted.

Falcon pulled the trigger. His target tumbled from his saddle. A second later, one of the other outlaws went down and the six remaining outlaws, suddenly realizing the precariousness of their position, jerked their horses to a halt. Then, turning them around, they started off at a full gallop.

"What just happened back there? I thought it was going to be easy!" one of the riders demanded. "Hell, we had two men down almost before you could take a breath!"

"You should've kept on going," Ray said. "A little shooting and you all turned tail and ran."

"A little shooting? Deke and Seth was killed right off. There wasn't none of us countin' on gettin' killed."

"You took your fifty dollars, didn't you?"

"Yeah, but I wouldn't of took it if I'd knew they was folks goin' to get killed."

"Quit your bellyachin', Cooper. You should'a known it wasn't goin' to be a walk in the park," Lou Reeder said. "You took your money like the rest of us, and you ought to have enough sense to know that you don't get paid fifty dollars just for a walk in the park. Besides, you was with us the last time."

"That big bastard they had with 'em today wasn't with 'em the last time," Cooper said.

"What big bastard?" Cletus asked.

"Ha. Someone you would be interested in," Lou said. "It was that same man you tangled with in town the other night."

"I didn't tangle with him exactly," Cletus said. "He hit me when I wasn't lookin'."

"But that was the same one. It was Falcon MacCallister is who it was," Lou said.

"You're sure?"

"Damn right I'm sure. He ain't the kind you can just forget about. He's also not the kind of fella you want against you," Lou continued.

Cletus turned in his saddle and pointed his pistol at Lou. "If you say one more word about Falcon MacCallister, I'll shoot you. Do you understand that?"

"What?" Lou gasped, throwing his hands up in alarm. "Cletus, come on, I don't mean nothin' by it. I'm on your side, remember?"

"Then shut up about Falcon MacCallister," Cletus ordered.

"Sure, Cletus, you want me to shut up about 'im, I'll shut up about 'im," Lou said. "I ain't goin' to say another word about him, no, sir. I ain't even goin' to mention Falcon MacCallister's name again."

Cletus glared at Lou, then he put his pistol away. The eight men rode on, though they were no longer riding at a gallop.

"What do we do about Deke and Seth?" Cletus asked Ray.

"What do you mean, what do we do about them?" Ray asked.

"I mean, what are we goin' to do about them? We just left them lyin' back there."

"They won't mind," Ray answered.

"But they're dead," Cletus said.

"Like I said. They won't mind."

When the three wagons rolled into Higbee an hour later, they were met by Wade Garrison, who came toward them with a big smile on his face.

"Well, you got through, I see," he said. "I'm glad you didn't have any trouble, but I thought . . ." He stopped in mid-sentence because he saw two canvas-covered lumps lying in the back of one of the wagons. "What's that?" he asked.

Dismounting, Falcon walked to the rear of the wagon and jerked the covers off, disclosing two bodies.

"I'll be damn!" Garrison said. "That's Deke Mathers and Seth Parker. They ride for Ike Clinton," Garrison said. "Or rather, they did," he added, correcting himself.

"Yes, I recognized Mathers," Falcon said. "Lou Reeder was with them, too."

"Are you sure?"

"I'm sure. I recognized them because I saw both of them with Cletus Clinton the other night."

"Did you see any of the Clintons?" Garrison asked.

Falcon shook his head. "No, I didn't see any of them."

"It doesn't matter," Garrison said. "If these two, who were known to ride with Clinton, were part of it, and you say you saw Lou Reeder as well, there shouldn't be any doubt in anyone's mind who's behind all this."

By now, news that the three wagons had arrived had caused several of the townspeople to gather round. When they learned that there were two bodies in the back of one of the wagons, the news spread quickly so that several others gathered around as well.

"What happened?" Denham asked. The editor of the *Higbee Journal* had his pencil poised over his notebook.

"We were attacked on the road," Morrell said.

"But they didn't get far," Barnes said quickly. "We fought 'em off."

"And as you can see, we killed two of them," Morrell concluded.

By now, Marshal Calhoun had arrived as well, and he looked at the two bodies, then at Garrison.

"These are a couple of Clinton's riders," Calhoun said.

"Marshal, I told you that I believed Clinton was behind the last attack on my wagons," Garrison said. "I took my complaint to Sheriff Belmond, but he said he couldn't find anything to back me up. Seems to me like this ought to be all the evidence we need."

"I'll ride up to Las Animas and see the sheriff," Calhoun said. "Maybe this time we can get something done."

When Marshal Calhoun arrived in Las Animas, he rode straight to the sheriff's office, which was located on Powers Street. Sheriff Belmond was sitting in a chair with the two front legs raised and the chair leaning back against the front wall of the jail. He was paring an apple, trying to do it in one long peel. The peel was now hanging from the apple all the way to the floor of the porch.

Calhoun dismounted, then looped the reins around the hitching rail.

"Now, why do I believe you are bringing me a problem to deal with?" Belmond asked, without looking up from his task at hand.

"I'm bringing you the problem and the solution," Calhoun said as he stepped up onto the porch.

"Wait, don't get off the stoop," Belmond said. "I don't want you to jinx my operation here."

Calhoun stood on the step for a moment until, finally, the peel collapsed to the floor.

"Ha!" look at that!" Belmond said. "I'll bet if you measured that, it would be one of longest peels ever to come off in one piece."

"It's long, all right," Calhoun agreed.

Belmond cut the apple in half, then offered one half of it to Calhoun.

"No, thanks," Calhoun replied.

"All right, Calhoun, what is this problem and what is the solution?" Belmond asked. He took a bite of the apple.

"You remember when Mr. Thompson's freight wagons

were attacked? The drivers were killed, and the wagons burned."

"Yeah, I remember it. I looked into it, but couldn't find enough evidence to pin it on anyone."

"It was Ike Clinton. He was behind it."

"So you said, Calhoun, so you said. But the truth is there was not one shred of evidence that pointed to Clinton."

"What about the fact that he is going around preaching to other ranchers, telling them to resist the railroad?" Calhoun asked.

"Calhoun, Calhoun, Calhoun, you are, what is it they say—grasping at straws? Ike Clinton has every right to say he doesn't want a railroad to come through Higbee. The fact that he says that openly does not mean he was behind that attack on the wagons."

Calhoun smiled. "Maybe not, but the wagons were attacked again, and this time we do have evidence."

"What sort of evidence do you have?"

"I have the bodies of two of the men who attacked the wagons," Calhoun said. "Deke Mathers and Seth Parker. They are back in Higbee now."

"Deke Mathers and Seth Parker, you say?"

"Yes. You may recall, they ride for—that is, they did ride for Ike Clinton."

"I'll look into it," Belmond promised.

"Belmond, I'm going to need you to do more than just look into it," Calhoun said.

"What do you mean?"

"They're guilty as hell, and we have the proof lying in the undertaker's. I want you to bring in the Clintons for murder."

"Murder? That's a serious charge," Belmond said.

"Yeah, I mean it to be serious," Calhoun replied.

Belmond carved off the last piece of apple and put it in his mouth.

"Well, I'll tell you what, Titus," he said. "Since this all allegedly happened in my county, suppose you just let me decide whether or not there should be a charge of murder."

"I'm not trying to tell you how to do your job," Calhoun said. "I'm just giving you the benefit of the evidence I have."

"Yes, well, remember, you did run for sheriff against me in the last election, didn't you?" Belmond said. "And how did that turn out now? Oh, right, I won, didn't I?"

"Let me put it this way, Belmond. If I learn that you are purposely covering up for the Clintons, I will go to the governor."

"I'll do my job," Belmond said. "You just stay the hell out of my way."

When Billy Clinton rode off, he told his father that he was going to look for strays. Once he got out of sight of the main house, though, he cut across Vachille Creek toward the McKenzie Ranch. Emma McKenzie was a widow, and though she still lived there, she made her living by leasing her grazing and water rights to other ranchers.

Emma had been very good friends with Billy's mother when she was alive, and had often taken care of him when he was younger. Billy called her Aunt Emma, even though she was not related to him.

It was not unusual for Billy to call on Emma from time to time, but today was a little unusual because he and Kathleen had made arrangements to meet there. Emma knew and liked them both, and was the only person in the county who could understand the attraction these two star-crossed people had for each other.

Billy was a little nervous as he rode toward Aunt Emma's place because this was the first meeting that he and Kathleen had ever arranged. He didn't know if she would actually show up or not. As he approached, he looked around the place for any sign of Kathleen, but saw nothing. Did she not come?

Emma stepped out on the front porch to greet him as he arrived.

"Hello, Billy." she said.

"Aunt Emma," Billy replied. He continued to look around for any sign of Kathleen.

Emma laughed. "Don't get yourself all worried. She's inside," Emma said. "She's making lemonade."

"Oh," Billy replied. "I, uh, didn't see her horse or anything, I was wondering."

"We put her surrey in the barn," Emma said. "If someone rode by and saw your horse here, why, they wouldn't think anything of it. You are here often. But this is the first time Kathleen has ever been here, and if someone happened to see her surrey and your horse, well, you can see what problems that might cause."

"Yes, ma'am, I truly can," Billy said. "Aunt Emma, I appreciate this, I hope you don't get into any trouble over it."

"Don't be silly," Emma said. "I'm an old widow woman who lives alone. I have every right to have anyone I want as friends."

Emma brushed her hands against her apron. There was about her the smell of flour and cinnamon, as she had been baking in the kitchen, and for a sudden, brief moment, he remembered the days he had spent with her when he was a little boy.

"Heavens, I didn't even bother to take off my apron," Emma said self-consciously. "I thought I would make some cookies for you and your friend. I must look a mess."

"You look beautiful to me, Aunt Emma," Billy said. "But you always have."

Kathleen came outside then, and she smiled at Billy.

"Hello," she said.

"Hi," Billy replied.

"Oh," Emma said just before she went back inside the house. "I made a picnic lunch for you. Billy, I thought your friend might like to see the overlook."

"The overlook?" Kathleen asked.

"It's our secret place," Emma said. "Billy's and mine."

"Oh, my, should I be jealous?" Kathleen teased.

"No. Aunt Emma, I mean, Mrs. McKenzie, she . . ." Billy said, attempting to explain.

Kathleen laughed. "You don't have to explain," she said. "I know Mrs. McKenzie raised you. She told me all about it this morning. I was just teasing. And I would love to see the overlook."

With the picnic lunch loaded in Kathleen's surrey, Billy drove along a trail until he reached a high escarpment. The trail climbed a large rock outcropping, then went beyond a group of aspen trees until Billy finally stopped near an overhang. He helped Kathleen down from the surrey.

"I call this my secret place," Billy said, "but there are markings and signs here from who knows who or how long ago. See?"

"Pictographs," Kathleen said.

"What?"

"They are called pictographs," Kathleen explained. "Some think drawings and carvings on rocks like this may be over a thousand years old."

Billy laughed.

"What is it?"

"I guess that means I wasn't the first to discover this place then, huh?"

Kathleen laughed with him.

"I wish you could be up here at twilight sometime," Billy said. "It's very pretty when the clouds are lit from below by the setting sun so that they glow pink and gold against the purple sky. It's especially beautiful in the spring, with the flower carpeting the valley floor in every hue. It's even beautiful at night when the stars sparkle above like diamonds on velvet, and the owls talk quietly among themselves."

Kathleen took Billy's arm and held it. "Oh, Billy, it's no wonder you are a poet," she said. "I don't have to be here in the spring, or at twilight, or at night. Your words have brought all that to me."

Kathleen looked into Billy's eyes, and he knew then that she wanted to be kissed. He moved her lips to hers, and she leaned against him. They kissed.

"Oh," Kathleen said, pulling breathlessly away from him. "I think we had better not do that again."

"Why not?"

"Because I don't trust myself as to where it might lead," Kathleen said.

"Let it go where it goes."

Kathleen shook her head. "No, Billy, not yet. Not while our families are—"

"You don't have to go on," Billy said. "I know what you mean."

"Billy, do you think we will ever be able to be like everyone else? To love who we want to love?"

"I don't know," Billy said. "God help me, I don't know."

"We could run away," she suggested.

"Run away where. And do what?"

"We could run away and get married," Kathleen said. "That is—if you actually do want to marry me."

"Kathleen, I want to marry you more than anything in the world," Billy replied. "But I also want to be able to make a living for you. What would I do if we ran away?"

"We'd find something to do," Kathleen said. "I know we would."

"I need to think about that," Billy said.

"I'm sorry, I shouldn't have pushed."

"No, no," Billy said. "Kathleen, I can't think of anything that would be more wonderful than to marry you. But let's wait and see if we can't do it on our own terms, without having to run away like thieves in the night. Besides, what would that do to your father?"

"You're right," Kathleen said, nodding her head. "I got carried away a bit there, but you're right. I could never leave my father like that."

"Are you hungry?"

"A little," Kathleen admitted.

"One thing I know about Aunt Emma, she is one hell of a cook," Billy said. "Let's see what we have here."

"We have cookies, of course," she said, taking one out and biting into it.

"Hey, you aren't supposed to eat the cookies until after we have our lunch," Billy said, taking the cookie from her. As soon as he took it, he popped the whole cookie into his mouth.

"Oh, you!" Kathleen scolded, laughing as she did so. "You just did that so you could have the cookie."

"It worked, didn't it?" Billy teased. "What else do we have?"

"We have sliced ham and freshly baked bread," Kathleen said. "And potato salad, and some canned peaches. And, of course, a bottle of wine."

"Sounds good," Billy said, reaching for the loaf of bread.

"Just be patient. I'll set it out for you," Kathleen said. She spread a blanket, then put out the food. Billy made himself a big sandwich and took a healthy bite.

"Fantastic," he said, smacking his lips in appreciation. "Absolutely fantastic."

"Wine?" Kathleen asked, pouring some into a glass.

After they had eaten, they sat on the blanket enjoying their wine. They talked of inconsequential things for a while, then Kathleen laughed.

"What's so funny?"

"Tomorrow night, at the dance," Kathleen said, "you and I will have to pretend that we are practically strangers. Yet all the time, we will know about this wonderful day we have shared today."

Chapter Fourteen

When Kathleen awakened the next morning, she lay in bed for a long moment, enjoying the gentle breeze that lifted the muslin curtains and brought on its breath the fragrance of roses that grew just outside her window.

She thought of the picnic yesterday and of the time she and Billy had been able to spend together, without having to look over their shoulders, without having to explain their relationship to anyone else.

What a bittersweet time that had been; sweet because she and Billy were together, bitter because they both knew that it was stolen time—it could not, and it would not, last.

Billy kissed her yesterday, and smiling, Kathleen touched her fingers to her lips. Because the kiss was so recent, and because Kathleen was blessed with a strong imagination, she was able to recreate that kiss, almost as if it were happening now.

Thinking about it, Kathleen reached under her mattress where she was hiding the poem Billy had written for her, and took it out. She reread it for what had to be the tenth time.

Billy had not wanted anyone to know about the poem because he was afraid of the ribbing he would take from his brothers.

His brothers, Kathleen thought. What evil and despicable men they were. How was it possible that Billy had been born into that family? So many people who didn't know Billy the way she did thought of him in the same way they thought of Ray and Cletus. Even her own father thought of Billy in that way.

It wasn't fair. It just wasn't fair.

Out at La Soga Larga Ranch, the object of Kathleen's mental meanderings was at the pump on the back porch washing up when he saw Sheriff Belmond riding into the front yard. Curious as to what might have brought the sheriff there, he walked around front, even as he was running the towel through his hair. Billy's father and two brothers were standing on the front porch.

"Hello, Sheriff," Ike said warmly. "What brings you out here? Get down, come on in."

"Thanks," Belmond said, swinging down from his saddle. He tied the horse off, then followed Ike and the others into the parlor of the large house. Billy went inside as well and stood, leaning against the wall next to the window.

"Would you like something to drink, Sheriff? Whiskey? Lemonade?"

Belmond laughed. "Whiskey in the morning is a bit much, even for me. But a glass of lemonade might taste just real good after a long, hot ride."

"Rosita, bring a glass of lemonade for the sheriff," Ike called to his maid.

"*Sí, señor,*" the large Mexican woman replied.

"Hello, Ray, Cletus, Billy," he said. Then, taking a second look at Cletus, he took in a short breath. "Damn, Cletus, what the hell happened to you?"

Both of Cletus's eyes were black and his nose was swollen and purple.

"Nothin'," Cletus muttered.

"It sure don't look like nothin'."

"What brings you out here, Sheriff?" Ike asked.

"Deke Mathers and Seth Parker," Belmond replied.

"What about 'em?" Ike said. "I fired those two no-accounts a couple of days ago. What trouble have they got themselves into now?"

"Wait a minute," Belmond said. "Are you telling me them two don't work for you?"

"Not after I fired 'em, they don't work for me. So, tell me, Sheriff, what have they done?"

Rosita returned with a glass of lemonade. "Your *limonada,* señor," she said.

"*Gracias,*" the sheriff said. He drank the entire glass, then wiped his mouth before he responded to Ike's question. "They've got themselves kilt, is what they've done," Belmond replied.

"I'll be damn," Ike said. He stroked his chin, then sighed. "Well, I don't know as I can say it surprises me all that much. Get into a barroom fight, did they?"

"No, sir. They was killed while they was attacking some freight wagons out of La Junta, headed toward Higbee."

"That was damn stupid of them, trying to rob some freight wagons," Ike said. "But neither one of them boys was ever what you would call particular smart."

"I don't think they intended to rob them," Belmond said.

"Well, then, what the hell was they after?"

"The wagons belonged to Thompson Freight, but they was carrying goods bound for General Garrison. Lumber and the like, for building his railroad depot."

"The hell you say? Well, that might explain it then," Ike said.

"Explain what?"

"Deke and Seth knew the way I felt about this railroad," Ike said. "Once Garrison gets it built, he's plannin' on holdin' up all the cattlemen in the county. Being the only railroad, he'll charge us an arm and a leg to ship anything, and that'll just make all the other railroad people raise their prices, too. I figure that Deke and Seth were probably thinking that if they could stop those wagons, then they could keep the railroad from being built. The way I see it, them boys was just trying to get back on my good side."

"So you're sayin' you didn't have nothin' to do with it?" Belmond asked.

"I never left my ranch," Ike replied. "After they stopped the wagons, I don't have no doubt but that they was goin' to come ask me for their old jobs back."

Belmond stroked his chin and nodded. "Yeah," he said. "Yeah, I guess I can see that."

"Were any of Thompson's men hurt?" Ike asked.

"No. None of them were hurt."

"Well look here, Sheriff, if nothin' was done to the wagons, and none of the drivers or guards was hurt, then why are you even involved? The only ones hurt was Deke and Seth, and they got themselves kilt."

"How did you know there were guards?" Belmond asked.

"Didn't somebody burn three wagons and kill the

drivers the last time Garrison tried to get a shipment delivered?" Ike asked.

"Yes."

"Then, don't it stand to reason that they would have guards with them this time?"

"I reckon that's right. Turns out also that they had Falcon MacCallister riding with them."

"Falcon MacCallister? Funny you should mention him, Sheriff. I've been thinking about swearing out a complaint against him."

"A complaint? What kind of complaint?"

"Why, an assault-and-battery complaint," Ike said. "You see the way Cletus looks here. That's 'cause MacCallister hit him with a club the other night."

"He would'a never got away with it if I had'a seen him," Cletus said. "He hit me when I wasn't lookin'."

"Why would he have done that?"

"No reason, Sheriff. No reason a'tall. What happened was, me'n Deke Mathers and Lou Reeder was in the Golden Nugget the other night, when Deke started gettin' a little rowdy, yellin' at that woman piano player they got. Well, I was tryin' to calm Deke down when this here fella MacCallister pulled a gun on me. So, me bein' unarmed, I went out to my horse to get a gun, and when I come back in to the saloon, MacCallister was waitin' just inside and he hit me with a club. I never seen it comin'."

"That's why I'm sayin' I want you to arrest Falcon Mac-Callister," Ike said.

Belmond shook his head. "I'm afraid you'll have to take that up with Marshal Calhoun," he said.

"Ha, a fat lot of good that'll do," Ike said. "Those town dogs have Calhoun in their hip pocket. He ain't goin' to take no cattleman's word over anyone from town. Anyway,

I thought you had jurisdiction over the whole county. You're the sheriff. You tellin' me you can't arrest anyone in Higbee?"

"I can, yes, but as a matter of professional courtesy, I tend to let the city marshals control their own towns."

"I see. So, what you are saying is, you're just goin' to let this MacCallister fella get away with it."

"I'll keep an eye on him," Belmond promised.

"Yeah, you do that," Ike insisted. "Only, it's too late for Deke and Seth now, ain't it? They're already dead."

"You didn't really fire Deke and Seth, did you, Pa?" Billy asked after the sheriff left.

"Doesn't make any difference whether I fired them or not," Ike replied. "They're both dead."

"They were worthless as tits on a boar hog anyway," Ray said. "If they had listened to me instead of ridin' out ahead like that, they would both be alive now, and those wagons would be nothn' but burnt-out cinders."

"Wait a minute," Billy said. "Ray, you and Cletus were with them, weren't you. You set out purposely to destroy those wagons. Deke and Lou were with you—they weren't doing it on their own."

"So what if we were with them?" Ray challenged.

"So that means you got them killed," Billy said.

"Son, you might say we're in a war with the railroad right now," Ike said. "And in times of war, folks get killed. That's what wars are all about."

"But I don't understand," Billy said. "Pa, can't you see the advantages of a railroad?"

"Of course I can see the advantage of a railroad if we own it," Ike said.

"What? What are you talking about?"

Cletus chuckled. "I told you that boy wasn't none too bright, Pa," he said.

"Think about it, Billy," Ike said. "Whoever owns that railroad will control everything hereabout for five hundred miles."

"You—you want General Garrison to fail so you can take it over," Billy said.

"Well, now, you were wrong about our little brother, Cletus," Ray said. "It looks like he does understand."

"That isn't right, Pa," Billy said. "That's no way right."

"I tell you what, Billy. You let me worry about what is right and what is wrong," Ike said. "All you have to do is remember that you are a Clinton."

"You're wastin' your time talkin' to him, Pa," Cletus said. "He ain't got no more gumption than a milk-fed puppy."

"Get on out of here, let me talk to Billy," Ike said.

"Why do you want to do that?" Cletus asked. "I'm tellin' you, you're just wastin' your time."

"Get out," Ike ordered.

"I reckon it's your time to waste, Pa," Cletus said. Turning, he and Ray left. Billy started to go, too.

"No, you stay," Ike said to Billy.

"Cletus's right, Pa," Billy said. "I don't have the stomach for this."

"You stay and listen to me," Ike said.

With a sigh, Billy came back inside.

"Have a seat," Ike said, pointing to the sofa.

Billy sat, and Ike sat on a chair across from him. Ike stared at Billy for a long time.

"Billy, why do you think I'm doing all this?" Ike finally asked.

"Why do I think you are attacking General Garrison's wagons?"

"No, not that. Well, yes, that, but more. Much more. What I mean is, why do you think I'm working so hard to make the ranch bigger and more successful? I mean, when you think about it, I'm already the richest man in the county. I wouldn't have to do another thing for the rest of my life if I didn't want to, and I could live out the rest of my life like a king."

"I don't know, Pa. I'll be honest with you, I have wondered about that very thing."

"Well, it ain't all that hard to figure out, son," Ike said. "I'm doin' it for you."

"You're doing it for me?" Billy asked in disbelief.

"Yes, for you, Ray, and Cletus."

"I don't understand."

"No, I don't reckon you do understand," Ike said. "Look, there are three of you. Right now, I do have a lot of money, but there is only one of me. After I'm gone, everything I have is goin' to have to be divided up three ways. And if there's not enough to go around, well, you know how Ray and Cletus are. It wouldn't surprise me none if they didn't start fightin' among themselves. Only—and this here is where you come in, Billy—you bein' the youngest, and you bein' the, well, let's say the meekest of the three, you're the first one that would get hurt."

"No, I wouldn't get hurt," Billy said. "I'd walk away and let them have it."

"You would, huh? And where would that leave you and that little girl you've been sniffin' around?"

"Do you mean Kathleen?"

"Yes, I mean Kathleen. You ain't exactly keepin' it a

secret how you feel about her. And I wouldn't be surprised if she didn't feel the same way about you."

"Well, she does, I think," Billy said. "Only—"

"Only right now things ain't goin' too well between her pa and me," Ike said, finishing Billy's sentence. "I can see how that might be a problem. But after one of us is gone, either Garrison or me, it won't be a problem no more. And then you'll need money to make her happy."

"I don't think Kathleen is the kind of girl that needs money to make her happy."

Ike chuckled. "All women is that kind," he said. "Whether you're talkin' 'bout the whores that work for Maggie, or girls like Kathleen. It takes a heap of money to keep 'em happy. And if I can take over the railroad from Garrison, you won't never have no money problems. And look at it this way," he added. "If you wind up marryin' his daughter, why, all the money goes back to him anyway."

Chapter Fifteen

Saturday morning, a large banner was stretched across Higbee Avenue.

DANCE TONIGHT!

MORNING STAR HOTEL

Come one, come all

The musicians had come to La Junta by train from Denver; then arrangements were made for them to have a special stagecoach that would take them to Higbee. They arrived in Higbee just after noon, with their instruments securely lashed to the top of the stage.

The arrival created a great deal of excitement as children and dogs met the stage at the edge of town, then ran alongside it as the coach came the rest of the way. Occasionally, one of the children would run up very close to the stage and poke a stick into the whirling wheels, laughing as the stick was jerked from his hands and thrown back onto the road.

By the time the coach reached the Morning Star Hotel, several of the townspeople had gathered as well to watch the musicians disembark.

"Careful with that violin, my good man!" one of the musicians called up to the top of the stage when an eager onlooker took it upon himself to help.

"With the what?" the would-be helper replied.

"With the . . . fiddle," the musician said.

"Oh, hell, don't worry 'bout that. I ain't goin' to drop it or nothin'."

The musician cringed as the fiddle was handed down to him. Soon, all the instruments were off-loaded and the band was met by Mayor Charles Coburn.

"Welcome, welcome, gentlemen, to Higbee," Mayor Coburn said, extending his hands to all of them. "We have a nice lunch prepared for you, and have rooms for you here in the hotel. Which one of you is Edwin Mathias?"

"I am Edwin Mathias."

The man who answered was a tall, very dignified-looking man, with a neatly trimmed beard and a touch of gray at the temples.

"Ah, good, good, you are the one I have been corresponding with, I believe. Do you have any questions?"

"If you don't mind, I would like to see where we are to perform tonight," Edwin said.

For a moment, the mayor looked confused. "Perform? Uh, Mr. Mathias, you do understand that you aren't actually going to perform, don't you? You have been hired to provide music for a dance."

"Mayor, I am a professional musician," Edwin said. "Indeed, we are all professional musicians." He took in the others with a wave of his hand. "Do you think for one minute that providing music for a dance isn't performing?"

"I—I suppose if you put it that way," Mayor Coburn said.

"Good, then we are in agreement."

"Yes, yes, I suppose we are," he said. "Well, come with me then, and I'll show you the ballroom."

Edwin and the other musicians followed the mayor into the hotel, where they were greeted by the concierge and the desk clerk as well as several others.

"I must tell you, Mr. Mathias, this annual dance is the highlight of our social life."

"Social life," Edwin repeated, and though he didn't slur the words, there was an implied degree of condescension in the tone of his voice.

"Yes, sir, social life," the mayor repeated. "Oh, I'll admit, Higbee doesn't look like much now, but we'll be havin' our own railroad through here soon. And once that happens, we'll grow like weeds. I've seen it happen time and time again."

"Yes, of course," Edwin said. "Please forgive me, Mayor, I didn't mean to be patronizing."

"That's all right. I know people who see Higbee for the first time, and who don't know 'bout the railroad, don't really understand. But you might be interested in knowing that we already have a famous musician living right here among us. I'll admit, she hasn't been here very long, but she's here now, and that's all that counts."

"Oh? And who would that be?"

"Rachael Kirby," Mayor Coburn said.

Edwin had turned away from the mayor to walk over and examine more closely the platform upon which they would be performing that night. He had asked the question without any real curiosity, because he was certain that the "famous" musician the mayor was about to name would be of no interest to him.

But when he heard the name Rachael Kirby, he stopped and turned back toward the mayor.

"Who did you say?" he asked.

"Rachael Kirby. She plays piano in the Golden Nugget Saloon."

"Are you sure it is *the* Rachael Kirby?"

"Aha!" the mayor said with a broad smile spreading across his face. "So you have heard of her?"

"If she is the person I'm thinking of, yes, I have heard of her," Edwin said. "But I don't understand. What is Rachael Kirby doing in a place like this?"

"I told you, she's playin' the piano."

"What I mean, my good man, is, how did the likes of Rachael Kirby wind up in a—a—" He searched for a word, then shook his head. "Place as small as this," he concluded.

"The way I heard it, she was with a group of players, some acting company called J. Garon or something like that. Well, sir, this fella Garon took all the money and ran away, leaving all his actors stranded."

"But, Rachael isn't an actor," Edwin said. "She is a pianist."

The mayor laughed and pointed at Edwin. "You know, that's a funny thing," he said. "That's exactly what she calls herself. She says she's a pianist, not a piano player. Can you believe that?"

"Yes, Mayor," Edwin said. "I can believe it."

Edwin's knees felt weak and his stomach turned. He'd had no idea he would ever run into Rachael Kirby again. Especially not in a tiny town like Higbee, Colorado.

* * *

Rachael was playing the Fantasie in C Minor by Mozart. Falcon was seated at one of the tables, enjoying the music while eating a ham sandwich and drinking a beer. There was a spattering of applause when she was finished. Then, after acknowledging the applause, Rachael walked over to Falcon's table.

"Do you mind if I join you?" she asked.

Falcon stood quickly and pulled out a chair for her. "It would be my pleasure," he said.

"When did you last hear from Andrew and Rosana?" Rachael asked.

"It hasn't been that long," Falcon said. "In fact, they came out to Colorado to give a performance at the Broadmoor for Count James Pourtales."

"Well, I'll bet they enjoyed that," Rachael said. "Seeing you again, and returning to the West they both love so."

Falcon chuckled.

"What is it? What is so funny?"

"I'm not sure they 'love' the West all that much. They have spent their entire adult life in New York. Plus, there was another little factor involved."

"Another factor?"

"They were taken hostage and held for ransom," Falcon said.

"Oh, heavens! How awful that must have been for them!"

"You would think so, wouldn't you?" Falcon said. "But apparently, they took it as one grand adventure. I wouldn't be surprised if by now they were reenacting the entire experience in daily matinees."

Rachael laughed out loud. "You know, I think you may be right."

"Are you going to the dance tonight?"

Rachael smiled. "I thought you would never ask," she said.

For a second, Falcon was confused. Then he realized she thought he was asking her to the dance. He recovered quickly.

"If you would allow me, I would be happy to call for you and escort you to the dance," he said.

"I would like that very much," Rachael said.

"All right. Seven o'clock?"

"Yes, seven would be fine." Looking around the saloon, Rachael saw that a few more patrons had arrived. "We always get a crowd early on Saturday. I guess I had better get back to the piano. I'll see you tonight at seven."

"Rachael Kirby?" a man's voice said.

Rachael was halfway back to the piano when she heard her name. Turning, she looked at the person who addressed her, then let out a little gasp.

"Edwin Mathias!" she replied. "What on earth are you doing here?"

"My group is providing music for the dance tonight," the tall, dignified man replied. "I heard over at hotel that you were here, playing in a"—he looked around with obvious distaste—"saloon? I was certain it would not be you, yet here you are."

"Yes," Rachael said. "Here I am."

"May I ask why you are here?"

"Everyone has to be somewhere," Rachael answered. "I came west with the J. Garon troupe, and when he absconded with all the money, I found myself stranded and in need of a job. This opportunity came up, so I took it."

"So, the story the mayor told me is correct," Edwin said. He made a clucking sound, and shook his head. "Rachael, Rachael, Rachael. I could have warned you about Garon. Everyone in the business knows what a crook he is."

"Apparently, not everyone," Rachael replied. "I had no idea that the man's reputation was anything but sterling."

Seeing that Falcon was following the conversation between the two of them, Rachael stepped back toward the table. "Edwin, I would like you to meet a friend of mine, Falcon MacCallister. Falcon, this is Edwin Mathias."

Falcon stood and extended his hand.

"MacCallister," Edwin said. "Would he be any—"

"He is their brother," Rachael said, answering Edwin's question before he finished asking it.

Edwin smiled and dipped his head slightly. "If you are the brother of Andrew and Rosanna MacCallister, then it is certainly my honor and privilege to meet you, sir."

"The honor is mine," Falcon said.

"Falcon, Edwin and I are old . . . friends," Rachael said, setting the word "friends" apart from the rest of the sentence. "We have performed together many times."

"Well, by all means, have a seat, Mr. Mathias," Falcon invited. "I'll just get out of your way here. I'm sure you two have much to talk about."

"You needn't leave, Falcon," Rachael said.

"I was about to leave anyway," Falcon said. "I need to buy a new shirt for the dance tonight."

"Then I will be seeing you again, sir?" Edwin said.

"Yes," Falcon replied.

"Very good, I shall look forward to it."

As Falcon left, he glanced back to see that Rachael and Edwin were already engaged in serious conversation. From the tone of their voices, and the way they behaved toward each other, he got the idea that their past acquaintance was more than just casual.

"I was afraid I would never see you again," Edwin said after Falcon left.

"It might have been better if you hadn't," Rachael said.

"Rachael, please, don't be that way. You have no idea what I went through when you left."

"What *you* went through?" Rachael said. "Edwin, may I remind you that you did not come to my apartment and catch me with a man. It was I who caught you with a woman."

"But she meant nothing to me, Rachael. Can't you understand that? She—she came up to me after the performance that night—she was an outrageous flirt. At first I was just flattered by the attention. Then—"

"Please," Rachael said, interrupting him. "I don't want to hear all the details."

"All right," Edwin said. He sighed. "I wish you were as pleased to see me as I am to see you. I did read the reviews. Rachael, the critics loved us. We could have had it all, the season in New York, the European tour. It was there for us—and we just threw it away."

"*We* threw it away?"

"Well, all right, I threw it away," Edwin said. "But if you had just been a tiny bit more tolerant. I would have made it up to you, Rachael. I swear to you, I would have made it up to you."

"Your beer, sir," Corey said, bringing the mug over to the table at that moment.

"Thank you, my good man," Edwin said.

"Oh, for heaven's sake, Edwin, must you always be so pompous?" Rachael asked. "He isn't your 'good man.' He is the owner of this establishment, and he is my boss."

"I see," Edwin said. He looked around the saloon. "You call this an establishment, do you? If you call it an establishment rather than a saloon, does that make it seem a bit more palatable for you to be playing piano in such a place?"

"If I ever wondered what happened to us, I need only to spend a few minutes with you," Rachael said. "And who are you to criticize me? Here you are, playing for a square dance in a hotel, not performing in a concert theater."

Rachael started to get up from the table, but Edwin reached out for her.

"Wait, please," he said.

Rachael looked down at him.

"Please," he said again. "Another moment?"

Rachael sat down again.

"I'm sorry," Edwin said. "You are right, I am playing music for a square dance and I am a little pompous."

"A little pompous?"

"A lot pompous," Edwin corrected with a smile, and Rachael smiled with him.

"What a joy to see a smile on your beautiful face," Edwin said.

"Don't think that it means anything," Rachael said. "Because it doesn't."

Edwin sighed. "Is it MacCallister?"

"What?"

"MacCallister, the man I just met. The brother to Andrew and Rosanna."

"I don't know what you are talking about."

"Of course you know what I'm talking about. Are you in love with this man MacCallister?"

Rachael hesitated.

"My God, you are, aren't you?" Edwin ran his hand through his hair, then sighed. "Well, I should have known better than to think you would just still be out there some-where unattached."

"I'm not in love with him," Rachael said. "I confess that I find him fascinating. Do you know that they actually write adventure novels about him?"

"Adventure novels?"

"He is quite a daring figure," Rachael said. "They say he has faced death many, many times."

"But you aren't in love with him?"

Rachael shook her head. "No, I'm not in love with him. And it is for sure that he feels nothing more than friendship for me."

"Good, good, then there is a chance," Edwin said.

"No, Edwin. There is no chance."

Edwin smiled. "I won't take that as an answer."

"Edwin, what are you doing out here anyway?" she asked. "The last I heard, you were going to Europe on a grand tour of the continent."

Edwin shook his head. "I didn't go," he said.

"It's obvious you didn't go, because you are here. My question is, why didn't you go?"

"The maestro thought it better that I not go."

"But why would he think that? Edwin, you are gener-ally acknowledged to be one of the best violinists in the business."

"At the risk of being 'pompous' again, I agree with you," Edwin said.

"Then what happened? I mean, what really happened?"

Edwin took a sip of his beer, then set the mug down. "The maestro's wife," he said.

"Lucinda?" Rachael gasped. "My God, Edwin, please tell me you were not being indiscreet with Lucinda."

"It was more her doing than mine," Edwin said quickly.

"Well, now, that I can believe. Lucinda is the biggest flirt in the business. Everyone knows that she has an eye for men. For any man," Rachael said. "I just can't believe that you were foolish enough to fall into her trap. No, wait, as I recall, you seem to have a problem in that department as well."

"Rachael, you aren't being fair," Edwin said. "You had just left and I was feeling—"

"Oh, no, you aren't going to blame that on me," Rachael said, interrupting him.

Edwin shook his head. "No, I'm sorry, I didn't mean for it to sound that way. It's just that I was depressed, and I wasn't as smart, or diligent, as I should have been." He sighed. "So now, instead of playing the violin in a concert orchestra, I'm playing . . . the fiddle for barn dances." For the last five words he abandoned his normal cultured enunciation for a Western twang. He laughed. "Could you ever imagine me—a'playin' the fiddle?"

Rachael laughed with him, then reached across the table to put her hand on his. "I don't mean to laugh, Edwin. But I am glad that you can laugh at yourself. And I must confess that I think I could like the fiddle player more than I like the concert violinist."

"If we couldn't laugh, we would surely cry," Edwin said. "I do not believe that it is mere coincidence that the

symbol for thespians is two masks, one with a laughing face
and the other with a crying face. When you think about
it, we could be in the grandest theaters in Europe, performing before kings and queens, but circumstances"—
he paused, then nodded—"of my own making, to be sure,
have put us here in Higbee playing in a saloon and a hotel
lobby—casting pearls before the swine, so to speak."

"Or bringing culture to a grateful audience," Rachael
suggested.

"Oh, my, I was getting pompous again, wasn't I?"

Rachael nodded.

"I must work on that," Edwin said. He stood. "If you
will excuse me, I have to meet with my—orchestra."

"I will see you tonight," Rachael said.

Chapter Sixteen

By dusk, the excitement that had been growing for the entire day was full blown. The sound of the practicing musicians could be heard all up and down Higbee Avenue. Children gathered around the glowing, yellow windows on the ground floor of the hotel and peered inside. The ballroom floor was cleared of all tables and chairs, and the musicians had been installed on the platform at the front of the room.

Horses and buckboards began arriving, and soon all the hitching rails on Higbee Avenue, as far up as Front Street and as far down as Bent Road, were full. Men and women streamed along the boardwalks toward the hotel, the women in colorful ginghams, the men in clean, blue denims and brightly decorated vests.

Once they were inside, the excitement was all it promised to be. Several young women were gathered on one side of the room, giggling and turning their heads in embarrassment as young men, just as embarrassed, made awkward attempts to flirt with them. At the back of the dance floor, there was a large punch bowl on a table, and Billy saw one of the cowboys look around to make certain he wasn't being seen, then pour whiskey into the punch bowl from a bottle he had concealed beneath his vest. A moment later, another cowboy did the same thing.

Billy had been there when the doors opened because he wanted to be there before Kathleen arrived. Now his wait was rewarded when he saw Kathleen step through the front door, pause, and look around the room. When her eyes caught his, she smiled. Billy nodded toward the table that held punch and cookies, then started toward it.

"Good evening Miss Garrison," he said when Kathleen joined him at the table.

"Good evening, Mr. Clinton," she replied. She reached for a cup, but he put his hand on hers to restrain her.

"I wouldn't drink any of that punch if I were you," he said.

"Oh? Why not?"

"There may be a little more in it than you think."

"I don't—" she began, then she paused in mid-sentence and smiled. "Oh, I think I see what you mean."

"The coffee is all right," he suggested.

"Well, I don't really need anything right now," Kathleen said.

"We have a few minutes before the dance actually starts," Billy said. "Could we take a walk?"

"No, I—" Kathleen began, then she paused in mid-sentence again. "All right, why not? There can be no harm in a walk."

Stepping outside, Billy and Kathleen walked the entire length of the board sidewalk until they reached the edge of town. They continued on for another hundred yards or so until the sounds and the lights of the town were behind them. The Golden Nugget was closed for the dance, but the Hog Waller was still open and its patrons seemed to be trying extra hard to prove that they didn't have to be at the dance to have a good time. Billy and Kathleen heard a woman's scream, not in fear obviously, because it was followed by her laugh, which carried clearly above everything else.

Ahead of them lay the mountains, great slabs of black and silver in the soft wash of moonlight.

A sudden blaze of gold zipped across the sky, and Kathleen squealed with delight.

"Oh, look!" she said. "A falling star!" She shivered. "Oh!"

"What is it?" Billy asked.

"Someone has just died."

"Why do you say that?"

"That's what a falling star means. There is a star in heaven for every person on earth. And when someone dies, their star falls."

Billy chuckled. "You're serious, aren't you?"

"Yes. At least, that's what I've always heard."

"That's not true. Besides, stars don't fall."

"What? Of course they do. We just saw one."

"What we saw was a meteor," Billy said. "Aunt Emma has a book about meteors, and I've read all about them. They are actually small chunks of rock which are traveling through space. From time to time, one of them falls to earth. I saw one once."

"What do you mean, you saw one once? We just did see one."

"No, I mean I saw one after it hit. I held it in my hand."

"Oh, I bet it was beautiful," Kathleen said. "They must look like a large diamond, they glow so when you see them at night."

"They glow because they are heated up as they are

falling. Actually, they just look like any other rock. There isn't anything spectacular about them."

"That's a shame," Kathleen said. "I rather like thinking of them as beautiful things."

"Well, they are beautiful when you see them the way most people see them," Billy said. "So they will always be beautiful in your eyes."

You are a strange one, Billy Clinton."

"Why do you say that?"

"You aren't like any other man I know. You are different."

"I hope that is a good different," Billy said.

"It's a very good different."

They heard music from the hotel, not disjointed bits and pieces as if the band was warming up, but a complete number, indicating the dance had begun.

"I think we should get back now," Billy said.

"Yes," Kathleen said.

Turning, they walked quickly back to the hotel, stepping in through the door as the caller shouted, "Choose your partners for the Virginia reel!"

Billy offered Kathleen his arm. "May I have this dance, Miss Garrison?"

"I would be honored," Kathleen replied.

The music began then, with the fiddle loud and clear, the bass fiddle carrying the rhythm, the guitars providing the counterpoint.

Although the band supplied the music, Prentiss Hampton had stepped in as the caller.

"All go forward and all go back,
  Once more time forward and back.
  Make a turn with your right elbow.

A big wide swing and around you go.
Those in front sashay down
And sashay back.
Now let's have the elbow reel.
A right to the middle and a left to the side,
A right to the middle, then reel on down.
Touch in the middle and a'work your way back.
Sashay around and down you go."

Around the dance floor, those who were without partners watched the dancers, including those who were too old and those who were too young. A few danced along the sidelines as if they had partners, but most participated in the dance by clapping their hands and stomping their feet.

"Oh, my," Kathleen said when the dance was finished. She fanned her hand back and forth in front of her face. "That was most invigorating."

"Would you like to step outside for a breath of fresh air?" Billy suggested.

"Yes," Kathleen said enthusiastically. "Yes, I think I would enjoy that."

Kathleen and Billy were standing out front when Falcon and Rachael Kirby came walking up.

"Good evening, Miss Kirby, Mr. MacCallister," Kathleen said.

"Good evening," Billy added.

"Good evening," Falcon replied.

"Now, there's a sight I never thought I would see," Rachael said as she and Falcon stepped inside.

"What is that?"

"General Garrison's daughter with one of Ike Clinton's sons. Those two men are bitter enemies."

"Surely, being in the business you are in, you know that such a thing isn't without precedence," Falcon said.

"What are you talking about?"

"Romeo and Juliet?"

Rachael laughed. "Why, Falcon MacCallister," she said. "Who would have ever thought you were such a romantic?"

When Ray and Cletus stepped into the hotel ballroom, the dance was already in progress and out on the floor couples moved and skipped, swayed and bowed as the music played and the caller called.

"What we comin' to the dance for?" Cletus asked. "We ain't got us no women to dance with."

"Looks like there's some women over there that ain't dancin'," Ray said.

Cletus looked toward the women. "Damn," he said. "No wonder they ain't dancin'. They're uglier than cow plop." He looked around the room. "I'm thirsty. Ain't there no bar in this place?"

"There's a punch bowl over there," Ray said.

"Hell, I don't want punch. I want somethin' to drink," Cletus said.

Ray chuckled. "Believe me, at things like this, punch ain't what you think it is. Come on."

The two men walked over to the table to get a cup of punch. Cletus got his, then smiled after he took the first swallow. "You're right. This here ain't half bad," he said.

The set ended and the couples left the floor. Cletus finished his drink, then wiped his hand across his mouth. "I'll be damn," he said. "Lookie over there."

"Where?" Ray asked.

"Over there, just comin' in through the door," Cletus said. "That's our little brother with the Garrison girl."

"What the hell is he doin' with her?" Ray asked.

"Why don't we just go find out?" Cletus replied. Putting the empty cup down, he started across the room toward Billy and Kathleen.

"Oh, no," Billy said under his breath.

"What is it? What's wrong?"

"My brothers are what's wrong," Billy said. "They're coming over here to make trouble."

"Maybe they won't. I mean, not in a public place like this."

"You don't know my brothers."

"Well, now, Billy boy, what do we have here?" Ray asked, coming up to them then. "You mixing with the enemy, are you?"

"Enemy?" Kathleen asked.

"Yeah, Miss Garrison, the enemy," Ray said. "Maybe you don't know that not all the cattlemen want you pa puttin' in a railroad here."

"Ray, whatever is goin' on between pa and General Garrison has nothing to do with Kathleen and me."

"Boy, you ain't got the sense of a day-old goose," Ray said.

"Oh, I don't know, Ray," Cletus said. "She is a good-lookin' heifer, you gotta give him that. What do you say, little brother? Can I dance with your girl?"

Billy felt Kathleen cringe beside him, and he reached out to take her arm reassuringly.

"If you so much as even look at her, I'll—"

"You'll what, little brother?"

Billy sighed. "Go away, Cletus. Go away and leave us alone."

Cletus laughed wickedly, then held up his hands. "All right, all right, don't get yourself in a piss soup over it."

As Cletus and Ray turned away from Billy and Kathleen, they saw Falcon MacCallister standing close by and looking at them.

"What the hell do you want?" Cletus asked.

"Are these men giving you any trouble, Miss Garrison?" Falcon asked.

"Please, Mr. MacCallister, it's nothing I can't handle," Billy said.

Falcon stared for a moment longer, then he nodded. "You know, I believe you can at that, Billy," he said. He started to turn away.

"Hold it, mister, don't you be turnin' away from me now," Cletus called in a loud, angry voice.

Falcon stopped and turned back to Cletus and Ray. "You have something to say to me?" he asked.

"Yeah, I have something to say to you," Cletus replied. "Ray, this here is Falcon MacCallister, the fella I was tellin' you about."

"The one who gave you two black eyes?" Ray asked.

"Yeah," Cletus said. Cletus forced another smile. "Only this time, he ain't holdin' a gun, he ain't holdin' a club, and he ain't behind my back."

"That's right," Falcon said. "I'm standing right here in front of you."

"Well, you ain't goin' to be standing long," Cletus shouted and, stepping forward, he threw a wide, arcing roundhouse right fist toward Falcon.

Falcon dodged the blow easily, then counterpunched

with a straight left jab that landed at the point of Cletus's nose that was right between his eyes.

"Oww!" Cletus shouted in pain, and he threw both his hands up to protect his nose.

"Heavens!" one woman said aloud.

"Oh, my!" another added as several were in position to witness the disturbance.

Falcon threw a second punch to the gut, and when Cletus bent over with an audible expulsion of breath, Falcon followed up with a right cross to the chin.

Cletus went down and out.

"Ray, get Cletus out of here," Billy said.

"Yeah, I will," Ray said.

Seeing Ray move toward Cletus, Falcon turned away.

"Falcon, look out!" Rachael shouted.

Almost on top of the warning, Falcon felt a blow to the side of his head. He saw stars, but even as he was being hit he was reacting to the warning, so though it didn't prevent the attack, it did prevent him from being knocked down.

Instead of picking up his brother as he had said he would, Ray Clinton had swung at Falcon, trying to take him down with one, huge blow.

He'd almost succeeded, but when Ray swung at him a second time, Falcon was able to avoid him. With his fists up, Falcon danced quickly away from Ray in order to have room to maneuver.

"MacCallister," Ray said with a low growl. "I think it's about time you got your due."

"Fight!" someone shouted. "They's a fight!"

Almost instantly, the music stopped as the dancers and observers all crowded around Falcon and Ray.

"Ray, why don't we take this outside?" Falcon suggested. "There's no need to break up the dance."

Ray smiled, an evil smile. "Hell, what do I care if we break up the dance?" he asked. "I ain't got me no woman like my little brother here."

"You don't have a woman?" Falcon said.

"No."

"Well, now, do you think it might just have something to do with your personality?"

Some in the crowd laughed nervously.

"Enough talk, you son of a bitch!" Ray said. "I'm going to whip your ass good."

Ray swung wildly at Falcon, but Falcon slipped the punch easily, then counterpunched with a quick, slashing left to Ray's face. It was a good, well-hit blow, but Ray just flinched once, then laughed a low, evil laugh.

"Five dollars says Ray whups him," someone said.

"I don't know. Falcon ain't quite as big as Ray, but I hear tell he's tough as rawhide. I'm going with Falcon."

With an angry roar, Ray rushed Falcon again, and Falcon stepped aside, avoiding him like a matador sidestepping a charging bull. And like a charging bull, Ray slammed into a support post, smashing through it as if it were kindling. He turned and faced Falcon again.

"Damn, these two fellas could bring the building crashing down on us if they keep this up," someone said.

A hush fell over the crowd now as they watched the two men. They were watching the fight with a great deal of interest. They knew it would be a test of quickness and ability against brute strength, and they wanted to see if Falcon could handle Ray. Falcon and Ray circled around for a moment, holding their fists in front of them, each trying to test the mettle of the other.

Ray swung, a clublike swing that Falcon leaned away from. Falcon counterpunched and again he scored well, but again, Ray laughed it off. As the fight went on, it developed that Falcon could hit Ray at will, and though Ray laughed off his early blows, it was soon obvious that there was a cumulative effect to Falcon's punches. Both of Ray's eyes began to puff up, and there was a nasty cut on his lip. Then Falcon caught Ray in the nose with a long left, and when he felt the nose go under his hand, he knew that he had broken it. The bridge of Ray's nose exploded like a smashed tomato and started bleeding profusely. The blood ran across his teeth and chin.

Falcon looked for another chance at the nose, but Ray started protecting it. Falcon was unable to get at it again, though the fact that Ray was favoring it told Falcon that the nose was hurting him.

Except for the opening blow, Ray hadn't connected. The big man was throwing great swinging blows toward Falcon, barely missing him on a couple of occasions, but as yet, none of them had connected.

After four or five such swinging blows, Falcon noticed that Ray was leaving a slight opening for a good right punch, if he could just slip it across his shoulder. He timed it, and on Ray's next swing, Falcon threw a solid right, straight at the place where he thought Ray's nose would be. He timed it perfectly and had the satisfaction of hearing a bellow of pain from Ray for the first time.

Ray was obviously growing more tired now, and he began charging more and swinging less. Falcon got set for one of his charges; then as Ray rushed by with his head down, Falcon stepped to one side. Like a matador thrusting his sword into the bull in a killing lunge, Falcon sent a powerful right jab to Ray's jaw. Ray went down and out.

By now, Cletus had gotten back onto his feet, and he was glaring at Falcon.

"Get him out of here," Falcon said, and Cletus and Billy grabbed hold of Ray's unconscious form and dragged him away. As Ray was pulled away, the crowd began to disperse.

"Did you ever think anyone could handle Ray like that?" someone asked.

"Hell, look at Falcon. His hair ain't even none messed up," another said.

Falcon followed them outside, and saw Cletus and Billy put Ray belly-down across the saddle.

"Billy, you can come on back in," Falcon told him.

Billy shook his head. "No, sir, I can't," he said. "These are my brothers. I'd better stay with them." Then, leading Ray's horse, Billy and Cletus rode away.

Inside, the music had yet to start up again.

"I'm sorry about that," Falcon said, returning to Rachael Kirby.

Rachael was standing in front of the orchestra, talking to Edwin Mathias.

"Is that how all disputes are settled out here?" Edwin asked. "With an approach like that, it is no wonder this is called the 'wild' West."

"I didn't have much of a choice," Falcon replied. "It was either stand there and fight, or get hit. I chose to fight."

"And you like it out here, do you, my dear?" Edwin said to Rachael.

"Yes," Rachael replied, "I do like it."

"Maestro, more music!" someone called.

Edwin sighed. "If you will excuse me, I must jump through some hoops now."

"Mr. Mathias seems to be a bitter man," Falcon said.

"Edwin Mathias had a taste of glory once," Rachael replied. "It is always difficult when one falls from glory."

When the music started, Rachael smiled and offered Falcon her arm. Falcon joined her on the dance floor.

After the dance, Falcon escorted Rachael away from the dance floor. He had just said something funny and they were both laughing when they looked up to see the stern, staring, angry eyes of Wade Garrison confronting his daughter.

"Is it true that you took a walk with Billy Clinton?"

"Pa, it isn't what you think," Kathleen said.

"Oh? And tell me, daughter, just what am I thinking?" Garrison replied.

"That we did something wrong," she answered.

"You went for an evening walk with him, did you not? Without a chaperone?"

"Yes."

"Then don't tell me you weren't doing anything wrong. I wouldn't approve of that kind of behavior no matter who you were with. But this is much worse. Kathleen, this man is the son of Ike Clinton. Ike Clinton is our sworn enemy, you know that."

"Billy isn't like the others."

"Darlin', Billy is a Clinton," Garrison said. "When it gets right down to it, it always comes out the same. He is a Clinton."

"I love him, Papa."

"What? What did you say?"

"I said I love him."

"No, that can't be."

"Papa, I can't help it. This isn't something I can just turn on and off."

"Let him go, child, let him go," General Garrison said gently, putting her hand on her shoulder.

"It's not fair, Papa," Kathleen said. "It's just not fair."

"Life isn't fair, darlin'," Garrison replied. "It never was, and it never will be fair."

Chapter Seventeen

From the *Higbee Journal*

DISRUPTION AT DANCE !

*But One More Example of
Clinton Mischief.*

Saturday night last, nearly everyone in town repaired to the Morning Star Hotel for the fifth annual Higbee dance. The music was provided by a group of musicians headed by Edwin Mathias, who is regarded by many as the finest fiddle player in America. Beautifully decorated, the reception hall of the Morning Star Hotel was an ideal place for the festivities, and the dance was proceeding with high spirits and merriment.

But such was not to be for very long, for the Clinton brothers, Ray and Cletus, in keeping with their nature of troublemakers, did institute a fight.

Alas, the brothers Clinton did not consider the consequences of their plan, for the man with whom they picked the fight was none other than Falcon MacCallister. Having attended the dance, this reporter was there to witness the action, and it was a joy to behold the two thugs get their comeuppance. Falcon dispatched both Clinton brothers with little effort on his part.

If picking a fight and disturbing the peaceful pursuit of a pleasurable evening be the only offense of Ray and Cletus Clinton, this paper would have little to say of the issue. But there is strong evidence that the Clintons have been involved in dealings of a much more serious, and nefarious nature.

It is no secret that Ike Clinton wishes to prevent General Garrison from constructing a railroad that would benefit all. Would that he express his dissatisfaction with the railroad by peaceful petition, one might espouse some sympathy for his position. But his protest has already erupted into violence and bloodshed, costing, at last count, some five lives.

It is the strong opinion of this newspaper that the Clinton family in whole, and Ray and Cletus in particular, were directly involved in all five deaths. For that reason, this paper will institute a vigorous campaign to urge the sheriff to begin an investigation of the Clintons and all their activities.

It was noon on Wednesday, and Falcon was in the Golden Nugget, having a beer with Marshal Calhoun;

Harold Denham, the newspaper editor; and Corey Hampton. The marshal was reading Denham's article and, after finishing it, laid it down, nodded, then picked up his mug of beer.

"That's it?" Denham asked. "All you are going to do is just nod? Aren't you going to say anything about the article?"

"Well, what is there to say, Harold?" Calhoun replied. He shook his head. "I'll give you this, that's one hell of an article. It might be a bit overstated, but it is one hell of an article."

"What do you mean it's overstated? It's true," Denham insisted. "Every word of it is true."

Calhoun sighed. "As far as the fight at the dance is concerned, there were more than one hundred witnesses, so I don't think anyone is going to disagree with you. But as to the other, we have no direct proof that the Clintons were involved."

"Come on, Titus, you know damn well they were. Hell, everyone in town knows that they were."

"Knowing and proving are two different things," Calhoun said. "You can't prove something in a court of law simply by saying that you know it to be so. You have to have solid evidence and concrete proof, or it won't make it past the judge and jury."

Denham chuckled. "Well now, that's where I've got you, Titus," he said.

"What do you mean?"

"In my profession, I don't need to prove anything in a court of law. All I have to do is prove it in the court of public opinion, and that, my friend, I can do."

"He's got you there, Titus," Falcon said. "There is

nobody who is going to read this article without a sure and certain belief that the Clintons are as guilty as sin."

"Let's say that's true. What good will it do to prove this in the court of public opinion? That has no bearing on the legal status."

"The Clintons are a school of sharks," Denham said. "And sharks need a friendly ocean in which to swim. In the case of the Clintons, the people of Higbee and the county of Bent make up their ocean. If the people aren't friendly to them, they won't last long."

Calhoun chuckled. "You do believe in the power of the written word, don't you?"

"It's why I chose this profession, Marshal," Denham replied.

"Marshal! Marshal Calhoun!" someone was shouting from outside. Falcon could hear the rapid approach of boots on the boardwalk; then the batwing doors slapped open and the grocer, Moore, ran inside, while the batwing doors swung back and forth behind him.

"Marshal Calhoun!" Moore called. "Is the marshal in here?"

"I'm back here, Mr. Moore," Calhoun called out. "What's wrong?"

"It's the newspaper office, Marshal," Moore said. "There are some fellas down there now, tearing the place up something fierce."

"There are people in my office?" Denham shouted, standing up quickly. "What is it? What are they doing?"

"I don't know what all they are doing," Moore said. "But I can tell you for sure that it isn't anything good. It's probably best that you get down there and look for yourself."

Denham started toward the door, but Calhoun called out to him.

"Hold on, Harold! Don't you go gettin' down there before the rest of us! If there are a bunch of people down there tearing up your office, it wouldn't be too smart for you to confront them all by yourself."

"All right, I'll wait, but hurry, Titus. Please hurry," Denham said.

As they got closer, Denham called out in anger and alarm. "My type!" he said. "That's my type in the street!"

Two other trays of type came hurtling through the broken window and Calhoun, with his gun drawn, ran toward the newspaper office. He stepped in through the front door just as four men were trying to pick up the Washington Hand Press that Denham used to print his paper.

"Hold it!" Calhoun shouted. "Get your hands up!"

The four cowboys who had been trashing the newspaper office stopped and lifted their hands.

"Oh, now, Marshal," one of them said, laughing. "You had to come along and spoil our fun."

"Fun? You call this fun?" Denham yelled, barely able to control his anger. He looked around at the trashed office. "Why would you do such a thing?"

"We work for the Clintons, and we don't like what you said about 'em."

Denham waved his hand over the mess. "It'll take me all day to put this together again."

"No, it won't," Falcon said.

Denham shook his head. "I'm afraid it will."

"No, these boys are going to pick it all up for you."

"Ha! In a pig's ass we will," one of them said.

Suddenly Falcon drew his pistol. Then he brought it around hard alongside the head of the cowboy who had just spoken. The cowboy went down.

"Hey, what the hell did you do that for?" one of the three remaining cowboys shouted. "Marshal, did you see that? He hit Bart right up alongside the head."

"I didn't see anything," Calhoun replied.

"What do you mean, you didn't see anything? What the hell, you was standin' right here."

"Start picking up the type and everything else you threw out of here," Falcon said.

"Why should we do that? Marshal, if you're goin' to take us to jail, go ahead and take us now. Mr. Clinton will more'n likely bail us out first thing in the mornin'. I'll go to jail, but I'll be damn if I'm goin' to pick up one damn thing."

"That's too bad," Falcon said. Again, his gun was out, and again he slammed it against the head of the cowboy who had just stated he wasn't going to pick up anything.

"Shit! He did it again!" one of the two remaining men said in alarm.

"It would have been an easier job if all four of you had done it," Falcon said. "Now there are only two of you, unless one of you wants to refuse."

"Mister, about the only way you're goin' to make me pick up anything is to shoot me."

"Your terms are acceptable," Falcon said, speaking in a very quiet, cold, and calm voice. He pointed his pistol at the head of the cowboy who had just spoken, and cocked it.

"Mister, do you think I actually believe you are going to shoot me?"

"Shut up, Clyde," the other cowboy said sharply. He continued to stare at Falcon. "I believe this son of a bitch would shoot us. Marshal, you heard him. This fella just threatened to kill us, and he ain't no lawman. I demand that you arrest him."

"Mr. Falcon, I hereby appoint you a temporary deputy," Calhoun said.

"That ain't legal for you to do that," Clyde said.

"You see any judges around here?" Calhoun asked.

"What? No, I don't see no judges."

"Then for the time being, it's legal, simply because I say it is legal. Now, pick all this up, or I'll shoot you myself."

The two cowboys looked at each other, then, under the guidance of Harold Denham, they began picking up, and reassembling, the scattered type and other components of the newspaper office. A few minutes later, the other two cowboys, still groggy, began helping as well.

All the while the four men were working, citizens of the town were gathered around, laughing and calling out instructions to them.

"Bart! You missed the piece over here!"

"Virgil, it don't look to me like you're holdin' up your end."

Finally, the newspaper office was put back together except for the broken window. And even though it couldn't be repaired at the moment, all the shattered glass was swept up.

"Damn," Denham said after Marshal Calhoun marched the four down to jail. "It'll take me two weeks to get a replacement for that window."

"No, it won't," Corey Hampton said.

"What do you mean it won't?"

"One of the windows back at the Golden Nugget is cracked. It's about the size of this window, and I've ordered a replacement. It should be here in a few more days. I'll let you have that one, and I'll order another one."

"Would you? That's damn decent of you, Corey."

"Well, like you, I believe in the power of the press," he said.

"Really? Well, if you believe in the newspaper that much, why not increase your advertising?"

Corey laughed. "That's what I like about you, Harold. You are always doing business."

Totally unaware of the fact that four of his father's employees were currently locked up in the jail, Billy Clinton rode into town that night. He'd told his brothers and his father that he planned to have dinner at the Vermillion, then stop by the Golden Nugget to hear Miss Kirby play the piano.

"Ha!" Cletus teased. "It's too bad we don't have an opera house. 'Cause more'n likely Billy would go there ever' night for tea and trumpets."

"That's crumpets," Billy said.

"Crumpets? What are crumpets?"

"Never mind, it doesn't matter what they are," Billy said with a sigh. "You just go your way and I'll go mine."

It was dark by the time Billy got into town and tied his horse at a hitching rail in front of the Golden Nugget, which would suggest to anyone who recognized his horse that Billy was in town enjoying a drink at the saloon. But in fact, Billy slipped through the darkness alongside the saloon to the alley behind. Then, with his movements masked by the night, he hurried up the alley to the Garrison house, where he climbed a picket fence, then stood in the dark shadows of a cottonwood tree. The shadows were necessary because the moon was exceptionally large and exceptionally bright tonight, and if he wandered out from under the tree, he could easily be seen.

Looking up to the second floor, to the window on the extreme right side of the house, he saw that the room was well lit. He knew also that this was the window of the room that belonged to Kathleen.

Billy had come down the alley a few times, thinking about calling up to Kathleen, but always before he had lost his nerve before climbing the fence. Kathleen did not know, nor did he ever want her to know. He would come, look up toward her room whether it was lighted or not, and feel closer to her.

Tonight, just standing in the alley wasn't enough, so he climbed the fence and moved into her garden. It was not his intention to let her know he was here tonight, but as he started to leave, she stepped out onto the balcony and, because the moon was so bright, he was forced to remain, very quietly, in the shadow cast by the tree.

"Señorita Garrison, you should have a coat," a maid's voice called from inside the room. "You will catch your death out there in the cold."

"It is not so cold, Maria," Kathleen replied. She wrapped her arms about herself. "Oh, the moon is glorious tonight. Have you ever seen anything so beautiful?"

"Yes, I have," Billy answered, though speaking too quietly to be heard. "You are more beautiful than the moon, the sun, or all the stars."

"Maria, have you ever been in love?" Kathleen asked.

"Si, señorita. Everyone has been in love," Maria answered, still from inside Kathleen's room.

"Yes," Kathleen said. "Everyone has been in love, haven't they? Why, then, did it become my fate to love someone who's very name is an abhorrence to my father? If only I could be a Smith, or a Jones, or even a Gonzales."

"Señorita, no, you cannot say such a thing," Maria said. "That would be denying your father."

"I would gladly deny my father if Billy would deny his," Kathleen said.

"You cannot ask someone to deny who he is, señorita."

"You don't understand, Maria," Kathleen said. "I'm not asking him to deny who he is, only to deny his name. If he were a Miller or a Kelly, he would still be Billy. What is the old saying? A rose by any other name would smell as sweet?"

"I have never heard that saying, señorita."

"Trust me, it is a famous saying," Kathleen said. She giggled. "I just don't know who said it."

"Your bed is turned down, señorita," Maria said. "I am going now. Good night."

"Good night, Maria," Kathleen said.

Billy waited until he was sure that the maid was gone. Then he called up to the balcony.

"For your love, Kathleen, I will call myself by any name you choose."

"What?" Kathleen gasped. "My God, Billy, what are you doing out here hiding in the dark?"

"I'm sorry, I didn't mean to frighten you."

"I'm not frightened of you, don't you understand? I'm frightened *for* you. If my father finds you here—or your brothers, I don't know what would happen."

"I'm not afraid of your father or my brothers," Billy said. "The only thing I fear is losing you."

"Billy, go now, please," Kathleen said. "I think I hear my father coming up the stairs."

"I'm not going until you tell me you love me."

"I do, I do love you. Now, please, go. Go quickly."

"Kathleen?" Billy heard Garrison call from within the house. "Kathleen, are you up here?"

"Good night, Kathleen," Billy called. Moving quickly, he darted through the moon-splashed garden, then climbed over the fence.

Kathleen watched him until he reached the fence, then breathed a sigh of relief that he was gone before her father appeared.

"I thought I heard voices. Were you talking to someone out here?" Garrison asked, as he came onto the balcony.

"I was talking to the moon, Papa," Kathleen said, pointing to it. "Have you ever seen it more beautiful? It is huge, and golden."

"Yes, it's what they call a harvest moon," Garrison said. He chuckled. "You know, I proposed to your mother under such a moon."

Her father suspected nothing, and Kathleen was relieved.

"Why, Papa," Kathleen said, laughing. "I had no idea you were such a romantic."

"I said I proposed to your mother under such a moon," Garrison said. "I didn't say I stood out on the balcony talking to it."

"Is it true you met Mama while you were a cadet at West Point?"

"Yes, that's true," Garrison said. "Her father owned a livery stable near there."

"Mama was a Northern girl, but you were a Southerner, from Virginia."

"That's true."

"Grandpa could not have been too happy with you when you resigned your commission in the Union Army so you could fight for the South."

"Whew," Garrison said, shaking his head and chuckling. "That's putting it lightly. From the day I resigned my commission, your grandfather never had another thing to do with me."

"And yet, you and Mama loved each other and your marriage was strong."

"Yes, it was very strong, until the day she died," Garrison said. Then, suddenly, he realized where Kathleen was going with this conversation. "No, it's nothing like that," he said. "It's nothing at all like the situation between you and the Clinton boy."

"Yes it is, Papa. It's exactly like that," Kathleen insisted.

"No. Your mother and I were already married when the war split up our family. And it was the war, Kathleen—the war, something that was far bigger than any of us."

"Papa, didn't you tell me that you and the Clintons were at war?"

Garrison shook his head. "It's not the same thing," he said again. He shivered. "It's getting cool. I think I'm going to bed. I would recommend that you do the same thing."

"Yes, Papa." Kathleen kissed her father on the cheek. "I love you, Papa," she said. She thought, but did not verbalize, *no matter what happens.*

Chapter Eighteen

The next day, Falcon was visiting Titus Calhoun's office, playing a game of checkers with the marshal, when Sheriff Belmond and Ike Clinton came in.

"Calhoun, I hear a few of my boys may have gotten drunk and a little out of hand yesterday," Clinton said.

"They were a lot out of hand," Calhoun replied.

"And you've got them in jail, do you?"

"I do."

"Well, no harm done," Clinton said. "I'm willing to pay for any damage they may have done to the newspaper office."

Falcon looked up at him. "How did you know it was a newspaper office?"

"I guess word just got around," Clinton replied.

"Or you sent them in town to tear up the newspaper office," Falcon suggested.

"Are you saying I'm behind this?" Clinton demanded.

"That's exactly what I'm saying," Falcon replied. "I think you put them up to it because you didn't like Mr. Denham's article."

"That ain't true," Ike said. "More'n likely, the boys read it and was pissed off by what they read."

"Really?" Calhoun said. "They read it and were pissed off because they didn't like what they read? Is that what you're saying?"

"Yes, that's exactly what I'm saying," Clinton said.

"That's interesting," the marshal replied. He pulled open one of the desk drawers and took out a paper. "This is their arrest form," he said. "Here is where they signed." He pointed to the bottom of the page.

"What is all this about? What do I care about the arrest form, or where they signed?"

"Look at their signatures," Calhoun said.

Clinton looked at the form.

"If you notice, all four men made their mark where they were supposed to sign," Calhoun said. "Not one of them can read or write, Mr. Clinton. Yet you insist they tore up the newspaper office because they didn't like what they read."

"I don't know," Clinton said, clearly agitated. "Maybe somebody told them about the article."

"You sent them, didn't you, Clinton?"

"Did they tell you I sent them?"

"No."

Clinton smiled broadly. "Then you got no case, do you? All right, I'm here for them now. Turn them loose. I'm paying the bail."

"That's not possible," Calhoun said. "Bail hasn't been set yet."

Now it was Clinton's time to smile, and he turned to Sheriff Belmond.

"Tell 'em, Belmond," he said.

"I spoke with the judge this morning," Belmond said. "Bail has been set at twenty dollars each for the four men."

"Twenty dollars?" Calhoun said. "Bail is set for twenty dollars?"

"For each of them."

"That's preposterous!" Calhoun said. "It should be at least five hundred dollars apiece."

Belmond shook his head. "It's not your place to set bail. Pay the man, Mr. Clinton."

Clinton counted out four twenty-dollar gold pieces, then put them on the desk in front of the checkerboard. "Whoever is red has a jump here," he said, pointing to the board.

"Sheriff Belmond, you know damn well that twenty dollars is not an equitable bail for these men," Calhoun complained.

"Like I said, it's not for you to decide. Now, let the men out."

After a long, angry glare at Belmond, then a surrendering sigh, Calhoun walked to the back of the jail cells. A moment later, he returned with the four men. Two of the men had their left eyes blackened, and swollen shut.

"What happened to you two?" Clinton asked.

"Ask that big son of a bitch," Clyde said, pointing to Falcon. "He laid his pistol upside my head for no reason, and without warnin'. I wouldn't be surprised if this wasn't about the same thing he done to Cletus, if you think about Cletus's black eyes."

"Clyde is correct," Clinton said. "You seen my boy's eyes, Belmond, you know what they look like. Looks to me like this fella enjoys bullyin'."

"They were resisting arrest," Calhoun said.

"Resisting arrest? What does resisting arrest have to do with MacCallister?"

"I made him my deputy," Calhoun said.

"That's sort of convenient, isn't it?" Belmond asked.

"About as convenient as having bail set at twenty dollars, I'd say. Anyway, as I said, they were resisting arrest."

"We wasn't doin' nothin' of the sort," one of the other prisoners said.

"You're the one they call Jesse, aren't you?" Calhoun asked.

"Yeah, that's me."

"Well, Jesse, I say you were resisting arrest, and I have got half the town as witnesses who will swear that you were. So, if you want to take this all the way to court, I'm willing to do so."

"Shut up, Jesse," Belmond said. "That goes for the rest of you, too. Don't say another damn word, or I'll throw you into jail myself."

"I was just—" Jesse began.

"You was just nothin'," Belmond said. Then to Calhoun: "They have now been bailed out of the city jail. That ends your responsibility toward them."

"Then get them out of here," Calhoun growled. He looked at the four men and at the smug expressions on their faces.

"I reckon you don't have as much power as you thought you did, huh?" Bart said to the marshal.

Calhoun held up his index finger. "Here's how much power I have, sonny," he said. "If ever I see any of you in my town again, I will throw you in jail again."

"For what?" Bart asked defiantly.

"For breathing without permission," Calhoun said pointedly.

"What about our guns and such?" Virgil asked. "You plannin' on givin' 'em back to us?"

"They're hangin' over there," Calhoun said, pointing to four pistol belts, handing from nails protruding from the wall.

The four cowboys recovered their guns, then looked over at Ike with huge smiles. "Hey, Mr. Clinton, can we stop by the Hog Waller for a bit before we get back home?"

"No."

"Why not?"

"Just get on your horses and get back to the ranch, or leave your horses—they're mine, remember—and go off on your own. But we ain't stoppin' by the Hog Waller."

Falcon had been quiet during the entire episode, but after Clinton, Belmond, and the four men left, Falcon spoke up.

"You're going to have trouble with those men," he said.

Calhoun chuckled. "Hell, I've already got trouble with them."

Falcon shook his head. "No, I mean real trouble."

"You goin' to talk or play checkers?" Calhoun asked.

The two men returned to their checker game. Calhoun won that one, Falcon won the second one, and they were on the third set to determine a winner for best two out of three.

"Damn, I'm getting so sleepy I'm havin' a hard time keepin' my eyes open here," Calhoun said. He stretched, then stood up. "I've got some coffee over there. Would you like a cup?"

"That would be good, thanks," Falcon said.

Calhoun walked over to take two cups down from their hooks; then he picked up the coffeepot.

"Don't you be movin' none of them pieces now, you hear me?" he teased.

"Hell, Titus, you've got me in such a pinch now, I

wouldn't even know what pieces to move to help me," Falcon replied.

"Ha! What are you tryin' to do, lull me into a trap? You've got more pieces on the board than I do. I'm not even sure—unhh!"

Concurrent with Calhoun's grunt, came the sound of breaking glass. That was followed almost immediately by an entire barrage of shots, smashing through the front window and zinging around the room.

Falcon dived to the floor behind the desk, just as one bullet penetrated the chair where he had been but an instant before.

Even as the bullets were flying through the room, Falcon was on his stomach, working his way across the floor to Calhoun's prostrate form. But, by the way Calhoun way lying, and by the open eyes and slack jaw, Falcon knew, even before he put his hand on the marshal's neck to feel for a pulse, that the marshal was dead.

Suddenly, the shooting stopped, and Falcon heard the sound of receding hoofbeats as the assailants galloped away from the marshal's office. Standing up, Falcon grabbed a Winchester from the gun rack on the wall, then ran out into the street. By now, the two shooters were already more than one hundred yards away, scattering pedestrians as they fled the scene of the assassination.

Both sides of the street were lined with citizens of the town who, when they heard the barrage of gunshots, had poured out of the houses and businesses onto the boardwalks to see what was going on. There were two people crossing the street between Falcon and the fleeing men.

"Get off the street!" Falcon shouted, waving his hand. "Get out of the way!"

Seeing the galloping horses, as well as seeing Falcon

standing in front of the marshal's office with a rifle, the pedestrians were galvanized into movement, and they ran to clear a path between Falcon and the fleeing gunmen.

Falcon didn't bother to check to see who might be in the street beyond the fleeing men. He didn't have to. He knew that the bullets would not be going any farther than his intended targets.

Jacking a round into the chamber, Falcon raised the rifle to his shoulder, brought the front sight down on the rider on the left, then squeezed the trigger.

The rifle roared, and kicked back against his shoulder. The rider on the left tumbled from his saddle, and even before the smoke of the discharge had drifted away, Falcon had levered another shell into the chamber and fired a second time, knocking the other rider down. The two horses, now with empty saddles, continued to gallop.

From the *Higbee Journal*

MURDER SO FOUL !

Marshal Titus Calhoun Murdered.

Assailants Killed While Fleeing !

On the afternoon of the 15th, instant, Virgil Tate, Bart Gray, Jesse Jimmerson, and Clyde Newbury were arrested by Marshal Titus Calhoun. These four miscreants had busied themselves with the vandalizing and destruction of private property, to wit: this newspaper. Their stated motive for the vandalism was dissatisfaction with an article that had appeared in the Journal two days prior.

After spending but one night in jail, the four were freed from jail when their employer, Ike Clinton, paid bail. Shortly after being released, Jesse Jimmerson and Virgil Tate returned to the marshal's office and, firing through the window, killed Marshal Calhoun.

Falcon MacCallister, who was visiting with the marshal at the time, armed himself with a Winchester .44-.40 and with exceedingly accurate rifle fire slew both assailants as they attempted to flee.

Funeral for Marshal Calhoun will be held Saturday next.

The body of Marshal Titus Redfern Calhoun lay in a highly polished black coffin, liberally decorated with shining silver accoutrements. The lining of the coffin was white satin and the marshal, wearing his finest suit, lay in the coffin with his hands folded across his body and his head resting upon a red felt pillow. The undertaker had used clay to cover the bullet hole in his temple, and though he had been quite skillful, a close examination could locate the fatal wound.

The marshal lay in state in the front of the sanctuary of the Higbee Church of the Redeemer. The top half of the casket was open as mourners filed by to pay their last respects. At the request of the marshal's two brothers, Travis and Troy, Rachael played the piano.

The music Rachael chose was from Joseph Haydn's Mass in G, and as she played, the music filled the church and caressed the collective soul of the congregation. If there was anyone in town who did not know of the talent of the beautiful young pianist who played at the Golden Nugget, they soon realized that they were listening to a concert pianist of great skill.

Not one person in the congregation had ever read the story in the *London Times*, written by a British music critic, about Rachael Kirby, but if they had read it, they would have agreed with everything he said:

> Although some may question whether or not a woman can play music of concert quality, no one could question the renderings of Miss Kirby on this night. Her music was something magical, and one could almost believe that the very composers whose music she recreated were looking down upon her with deep appreciation of her skills.

It rained on the day of the funeral, and the Reverend E. D. Owen stretched out the eulogy and the service in an attempt to wait out the rain. He reviewed every aspect of the marshal's life, from the time he was a boy back in Ohio, through his military service during the terrible war that had so recently torn asunder the very fabric of civilization as brother fought brother, till his time as a peacekeeper, both in Arizona and there in Colorado. The Reverend Owen told about the marshal's two brothers, Travis and Troy, who had come to Higbee to join him and to begin a restaurant.

Finally, when it began to grow apparent that the mourners would rather brave the rain than listen to the preacher talk any longer, he brought the service to a close and indicated by a nod of his head that the pallbearers could now close the coffin and carry the body to the waiting hearse.

It was a measure of the respect that the citizens of the town had for Titus Calhoun that all braved the rain, standing under umbrellas as the coffin was lowered into a grave that was quickly filling with muddy water. After the funeral, many of the mourners gathered in the home of Troy Calhoun, where Troy and his wife had prepared cake, pie, and coffee.

At the gathering, Mayor Coburn; Carl Moore, proprietor of the general store; Harold Denham; Prentiss and Corey Hampton; as well as Travis and Troy Calhoun, all approached Falcon.

"We've been talking it over," Mayor Coburn said. "Falcon, we would like for you to become our new marshal."

Falcon's first reaction was to refuse the offer so vehemently that it wouldn't be repeated, but he knew that they were serious about it, and he knew also that the offer was actually one of honor and respect. He did not want to accept the job, but neither did he want to refuse it in a way that would be discourteous.

"I appreciate the offer," Falcon said. "But the truth is, if I accept the position, I would be bound by law to acting only within the city limits of Higbee. As it is now, working for General Garrison, I have a much wider range of authority."

"I don't understand," Mayor Coburn said. "What authority could you possibly have working for Wade Garrison?"

"I can explain that," Garrison said, stepping into the conversation.

"Please do."

"Although not one mile of track has yet been laid, the

Colorado, New Mexico, and Texas Railroad has been granted a charter. And because we are a chartered railroad, I am authorized to hire a railroad detective. By the state laws of Colorado and Texas, as well as federal and territorial laws which cover New Mexico and cross state lines, Falcon MacCallister is granted police enforcement authority. Gentlemen, by accepting an appointment as city marshal, you are limiting his jurisdiction to an area of about two square miles. But as a railroad detective, he has jurisdiction over fifteen hundred square miles."

"You mean he has jurisdiction over Sheriff Belmond?" Troy asked.

Garrison shook his head. "No, not over Belmond, but he has concurrent authority with Belmond on anything that pertains to the railroad."

Mayor Coburn laughed. "Why, that's wonderful," he said. "Mr. MacCallister, no disrespect meant, but the offer to be marshal of Higbee is hereby withdrawn."

"What do we do now?" Moore asked.

"I have a suggestion," Falcon said. "That is, if you are open to it."

"Yes, we're open to anything," Mayor Coburn replied.

Falcon looked up at Travis and Troy. "Both Travis and Troy have been acting as deputies," he said. "I would suggest that you hire one of them as the new marshal."

"Oh, no," Lucy Calhoun said, stepping up beside her husband. "We have two children. I don't want to take a chance of what happened to Titus happening to Troy."

"Darlin', there's always been that chance," Troy replied. "Even when I was deputying for Titus."

"It's not the same," Lucy insisted.

Troy shrugged his shoulders and looked at the mayor. "Sorry," he said. "But I guess that lets me out."

"I'll do it," Travis offered. He looked at Troy. "But that will put more work at the restaurant onto you."

"I'll help at the restaurant," Lucy said.

"I think you'd make a fine marshal, Travis," Troy said.

"Gentlemen, we have a new marshal," Mayor Coburn announced.

Chapter Nineteen

Rose Simpson's breasts were large and sagging. The sagging wasn't so bad, but what disturbed the symmetry was the fact that her left breast had only half a nipple, the other half having been carved off by a drunken sailor when Rose lived and worked in San Francisco.

Sitting up, she reached for a bottle of whiskey and poured a generous amount into a glass. She handed the glass to Ray Clinton, who was lying in bed alongside her. Like Rose, Ray was naked, but from the waist down Ray was covered with a sheet.

"Thanks."

"You're welcome," Rose said as she poured a second glass for herself.

"You ain't as pretty as any of them whores Maggie has, but you're a heap more friendly."

"I'll take that as a compliment," Rose said as she took a drink.

"Yeah, I mean, Maggie won't even let Cletus or me near any of her whores." Ray chuckled. "The only one she'll let be with her whores is Billy, which don't make no sense 'cause he don't want nothin' to do with any of 'em."

"I don't know Billy," Rose said. "He never comes into the Hog Waller."

"No, he wouldn't. He goes to the Golden Nugget from time to time, but he ain't much of a drinker."

"He don't whore, he don't drink, what does he do?" Rose asked.

"Ha! He sniffs around that Garrison girl is what he does."

"I thought the Clintons and the Garrisons didn't get along," Rose said.

"We don't, only Billy, he ain't quite learned that yet," Ray said. "I guess he sees that little ole gal and thinks she's so pretty that nothin' else matters. I reckon I'm goin' to have to learn him a thing or two."

"Folks say things is only goin' to get worse now," Rose said. "What with the marshal gettin' hisself killed and all."

"Did you go to the marshal's funeral?" Ray asked.

"The funeral was in the church."

"So?"

"I'm a whore, Ray, remember? I'm not the kind that would be welcome in a church," Rose replied.

Ray laughed. "No," he said. "No, I don't reckon you would be. I ain't welcome in no church neither, I don't think. Besides which, I wouldn't of gone to the marshal's funeral anyway."

"Did you go to Virgil and Jesse's funeral?" Rose asked.

"Hell, they didn't have no funeral," Ray said. "Not so's you could call it one anyway. We just buried both of 'em out on the ranch alongside Deke Mathers and Seth Parker is what we done."

"Looks to me like your hired hands are gettin' whittled down pretty good," Rose said. "That's four of 'em been killed in the last couple of weeks."

"Yeah," Ray said. "It's that murderin' son of a bitch MacCallister. What the hell is he doin' here anyway?"

"The way I heard it, General Garrison hired him as a railroad detective to protect the railroad."

"The railroad," Ray said, scoffing. "There ain't no railroad yet. And truth to tell, I don't think they's goin' to ever be one. You know what I think?"

"What do you think?" Rose asked.

"Well, Garrison, he's gettin' a lot of money from investors and such to build the railroad, ain't he?"

"That's right, you can't build a railroad if you don't have the money," Rose said.

"Yeah, that's what I know. So, what if you told a bunch of investors that you was goin' to build a railroad, and they all started givin' you money, but then it turns out you didn't build it? You'd have all that money and you wouldn't have to do nothin'."

"Oh, he's building it all right," Rose said.

"No, he ain't. Unless you call buildin' that depot buildin' the railroad."

"Yes, he is, he's building the actual railroad," Rose said. "In fact, there's a work party out right now leveling the right-of-way and getting ready to build a trestle."

"How do you know?"

"I know lots of things, honey," Rose said. "It turns out that when men are with whores, they do about as much talkin' as they do anything else."

"I'll be damn. So, what you're tellin' me is, they's actually some men out buildin' on the railroad now?"

"That's what I've heard."

"Where are they, do you know?"

"Right now, I think they're bridging the Thompson Arroyo."

"The Thompson Arroyo, huh?" Ray said. "I bet Pa don't know that. He's up in La Junta right now."

La Junta

At a table at the rear of the saloon, Jefferson Tyree sat with his back to the wall, playing a game of solitaire. When Sheriff Mullins came into the saloon, Tyree paid him no attention. Mullins had come in several times over the last few days and had not spoken to him. Tyree didn't know if Mullins had not spoken to him because he didn't know who he was, or because he was afraid of him. It seemed very unlikely that Mullins didn't know who he was. The state had been plastered with dodgers on Tyree ever since he escaped prison.

Tyree started to go back to his card game; then he noticed something that caught his attention, something different.

Sheriff Mullins was carrying a shotgun. That made Tyree suspicious enough, but when he saw who had come in with the sheriff, he knew that something was up. The man with Mullins was Darrel Crawford. Crawford had been chief of prison guards when Tyree was a convict at the State Prison in Cañon City.

Tyree knew this was no coincidence.

"Well, now, if it isn't Darrel Crawford," Tyree said. "What brings you to a jerkwater town like La Junta? Are you here on a little friendly visit?"

"Nothing about my visit is friendly," Crawford replied.

Tyree chuckled. "Let me guess. You are upset about the little fracas I had with Kyle Pollard back in the prison, aren't you?"

"It was more than a fracas. You killed him."

"Yes, well, that's just the way it worked out," Tyree said. "I wanted to leave, you see, and he didn't want me to. Killing him seemed the best way of settling our disagreement."

"Kyle Pollard left behind a child and a pregnant wife, did you know that? He was a good man," Crawford said.

"He couldn't have been that good of a man. I mean, what kind of man would take a dangerous job like prison guard when he has a family at home?" Tyree asked.

"You son of a bitch," Mullins said. "You don't have the slightest degree of contrition, do you?"

"Contrition?" Tyree replied. He laughed. "Ain't that somethin' you're supposed to get by goin' to church?"

"Enough talk, Tyree," Crawford said. "I'm taking you back to prison."

"Really? Well, now, how are you going to do that? I heard that you lost your job. The prison fired you for letting me escape. This is true, ain't it?"

"It's none of your concern whether that's true or not," Crawford said. "It has no bearing on what is right and what is wrong."

Tyree laughed. "I'll be damned," he said. "It is true, isn't it? But that leaves you with a little problem, Crawford. If you don't have a job, you don't have the authority to take me back. That's right, ain't it, Sheriff?"

"Normally, he would not have the authority," Mullins agreed. "But we have it worked out. I've appointed Mr. Crawford as my deputy."

Tyree clapped his hands gently. "Well, now, ain't that somethin'? I mean, our man Crawford here, goin' from bein' chief of guards in a state prison to being a deputy in some mud-hole place like this? My, how the mighty have fallen. Tell me, Crawford, does that make you real proud?"

"I told you, whatever my position is doesn't concern

you," Crawford said. "You're going back to prison with me. And this time, you'll hang."

"You think you'll get your job back if you take me in?"

"I don't care whether I get that job back or not," Crawford replied. "It's not about the job anymore. It's about honor."

"Honor?" Tyree laughed out loud.

"Yes, honor," Crawford said. "I know honor is a difficult concept for you to understand, but you will understand this." Suddenly, and inexplicably, Crawford smiled. "What I really want, even more than honor, is the privilege of watching you hang."

"Really? Well, don't get your hopes up, Crawford, because I can tell you right now that you ain't goin' to live long enough to see that," Tyree said.

Slowly, and without calling attention to themselves, the other patrons began moving away from the bar to be out of the line of fire should shooting break out. But they were faced with a dilemma. No one wanted to be close enough to be hurt, but everyone wanted to be close enough to witness whatever was about to happen.

"What about you, Mullins?" Tyree asked. "What part are you playin' in all this?"

"I am a law enforcement officer," Mullins said. "You are a wanted man. I intend to see that you are brought to justice."

"And just how are you going to do that?"

"Let's put it this way," Mullins said. He pulled the two hammers back on the double-barrel shotgun. "Before all this plays out, you are either going to leave here as Crawford's prisoner, or as a dead body."

Tyree shook his head slowly. "And here, I though me'n you had become good friends over the last few days. You knew all along who I was, but you never said or did anything about it," Tyree said. "I guess the reward got to you, huh? Just too much money for a greedy fella to pass up."

"Unbuckle your gunbelt and come along with us nice and easy," Mullins said.

"Sure, Sheriff, whatever you say," Tyree said, moving his hand down toward his pistol belt. Then, suddenly and unexpectedly, he drew his pistol, drawing and firing so fast that it appeared to be no more than a twitch of his shoulder. Seeing Tyree start his draw, Mullins pulled the trigger on both barrels of his shotgun, but it was too late. By the time he reacted to what he was seeing, it was over. The double-aught charges from his shotgun tore large, jagged holes in the floor of the saloon, even as the heavy bullet from Tyree's gun was slamming into his heart.

Nobody was more surprised that Crawford. He had not even bothered to draw his pistol, believing that, because Mullins had the drop on Tyree with a double-barreled shotgun, the situation was well in hand. He realized too late that he was wrong, because even as his pistol was clearing leather, Tyree's second shot crashed into his forehead. Crawford went down, dead before his body hit the floor.

"You all saw it!" Tyree shouted, still pumped up from the excitement of the incident. He pointed to the two bodies. "They drew on me first."

"That's 'cause they was lawmen," one of the patrons said. "They was here to arrest you."

"Are you saying it wasn't self-defense?" Tyree challenged. He looked directly at the man who had pointed out that Mullins and Crawford were lawmen.

"If you ask me, it was self-defense," one of the other men said. "Mullins was pointin' a double-barrel shotgun right at him."

"Of course he was. He was tryin' to arrest him," the first man said.

"Don't you understand, Bob? It was self-defense pure and simple," the second man said, staring pointedly at Bob.

Suddenly, Bob realized that he might be placing his own life in jeopardy. "Oh, uh, yes," he said. "Yes, now that I think about it, it *was* self-defense."

The others in the saloon, catching on quickly, began agreeing that it surely was self-defense.

"But here's the thing, Mr. Tyree," one of the men said. "I don't see no way folks ain't goin' to hear about what just happened here, and they're bound to come after you. Now, far as I'm concerned, and ever'one else for that matter, I mean, you've heard 'em." He took in the others with a wave of his hand. "They all say you didn't have no choice except to do what you done. But if more law was to come here, why, it's just goin' to wind up makin' trouble for you. So, if I was you, I'd leave now."

"Leave and go where?" Tyree asked.

"You might come to work for me," a new voice said.

Tyree looked over toward the man who had just spoken. He was an older man, but with a hard look about him.

"Who the hell are you?" Tyree asked.

"The name is Clinton. Ike Clinton. I own a ranch near Higbee."

Tyree laughed. "You wantin' to hire me to punch cows, do you?" He shook his head. "Sorry, Mr. Clinton, but I ain't no cowboy."

"I've got plenty of cowboys," Ike replied. "Cowboyin' ain't what I have in mind."

"Then I don't understand. If you own a ranch, and

you want me to work for you, but not as a cowboy, what do you want me for?"

"Oh, for about a hundred dollars a month," Ike said.

Everyone in the saloon gasped. One hundred dollars per month was four times as much money as a cowboy normally received.

"A hundred dollars a month?" Tyree replied.

"That's right," Ike replied. "Are you interested?"

"Who do you want me to kill for that much money?"

Ike chuckled, then took a swallow of his beer before he answered. "Funny you would ask me that, Mr. Tyree," he said. "Because the answer is, I want you to kill whoever I tell you to kill."

Tyree stared at Ike for a long moment. Then suddenly, he broke into a great belly laugh. "What did you say?" he asked.

"You asked who did I want you to kill, and I answered that I want you to kill anyone I tell you to kill."

Still laughing, Tyree slipped his pistol back into the holster. "Mister, I like the way you think," he said. "I'd say you just hired yourself a ranch hand," he said.

"How long will it take you to get ready to leave?" Ike asked.

"About as long as it takes me to walk out to my horse," Tyree replied.

"Let's go," Ike said.

Thompson Arroyo

"How long is your pa going to be gone?" Lou asked.

"I don't know, he didn't say," Ray replied.

"You sure he knows about this?"

"It don't make no difference whether he knows about this or not," Ray said.

"It's just that I don't like to do things without him knowin' about it."

"Reeder, as far as you are concerned, anything me or my brother tells you to do is the same as Pa tellin' you to do it," Cletus said.

"Yeah, I know that, but—"

"There ain't no buts," Cletus said.

"Stop talkin'. If my information is right, we'll be comin' up on them soon," Ray said.

"Your information is right, big brother," Cletus said. "There they are," He chuckled. "Look at them. Ha! It'll be like shooting ducks in the water."

Cletus pointed in the predawn darkness to the construction camp, consisting of a dozen or more sleeping rolls circling the still-burning campfire.

"Looks like they're making it easy for us," Cletus said. "They've even kept the fire lit to light the way for us."

"Yeah," Ray replied.

"How are we going to handle this, Ray?" Pete asked. Pete was one of the La Soga Larga riders.

"We're goin' to handle it real easy," Ray replied. "We're just goin' to ride down there and start shootin'."

Ray pulled his pistol, then cocked it. "Is everyone ready?"

"Ready," the others replied.

"Let's go!" he shouted, slapping his legs against the side of his horse.

The horses thundered down the gentle rise that led to the carefully arrayed bedrolls. Ray fired first, and had the satisfaction of seeing a little puff of dust fly up from the roll and the point of impact of his bullet.

The others began firing as well, and within a few

seconds they were right on the camp, shooting into the bedrolls.

Cletus noticed it first.

"Ray!" he said. "Ray, hold it! There ain't nobody in them bedrolls!"

"What?" Ray replied.

"Look at 'em! The bedrolls is all empty!"

"What the hell? What's goin' on here?"

"Now!" they heard a voice call from the darkness, and the riders suddenly discovered that the tables had been turned. Instead of shooting at targets, *they* were the targets, and muzzle flashes from the nearby rocks had bullets whizzing by in the night.

"Let's get out of here, boys!" Ray called, spurring his horse into retreat.

The sun was just coming up by the time Ray, Cletus, and the others returned to the ranch. They pulled to a halt in front of the porch.

"Does someone want to tell me what the hell happened back there?" Lou Reeder asked. "I thought this was supposed to be easy!"

"They was waitin' for us," Ray answered.

"Hell, yes, they was waitin' for us," Lou said. "But my question is, why? I thought they was not supposed to be nothin' but a bunch of dumb gandy dancers."

"Someone must have been with them. Someone must have organized them."

"It ain't no mystery who that someone is," Cletus said. "It was Falcon MacCallister."

"How do you know that? Did you see him?" Ray asked.

"I didn't have to see the son of a bitch," Cletus replied.

"I've got to where I can smell the son of a bitch anytime I get a mile away from him."

"Yeah?" Lou said. "Well, it might'a helped us tonight if you had smelled him before we ran into that hornet's nest."

Pete was weaving in his saddle, and his face was pasty white. It wasn't until then that the others noticed he was bleeding.

"Pete," Cletus said. "Pete, what's wrong with you?"

Pete was holding his hand over his stomach, and he pulled the hand away from his wound. The palm of his hand was filled with blood, and it spilled down onto his saddle and down his pants leg, though, as his saddle and trousers were already soaked with blood, it was hard to discern new from old.

"I got hit back there, when all the shootin' started," Pete said. He weaved back and forth a couple of times, then fell from his saddle.

"Pa!" Cletus shouted. "Pa, get out here!"

Ike Clinton came out onto the patio then, and saw Pete's blood-soaked body lying very still.

"What the hell happened?" Ike asked, kneeling beside Pete. He put his hand on Pete's neck, felt for a pulse, then looked up. "He's dead."

"Damn, they killed him," Cletus said.

"Funny, Pete never said a word the whole time we was comin' back," Ray said.

"Who killed him?" Ike asked. "Where were you? What were you doing?"

"Pa, while you was gone, I found out that Garrison was beginnin' to build his railroad," Ray said. "So what we done is, we rode out at the railroad construction site just to stir things up a bit."

"Yeah, we figured we could catch 'em all sleepin'," Cletus said.

"When we got there, the bedrolls was all spread out around the fire an' all, so we started shootin' at 'em. We rode all the way into the camp shootin' at them bedrolls. But it turns out, there wasn't nobody in any of them. They was all empty."

"And the next thing you know, all hell broke loose," Cletus said.

"Yeah," Ray said. "Yeah, the whole thing was an ambush. They was hidin' in the rocks just outside the camp, and they opened up on us."

"That's when they killed Pete," Cletus said.

"They didn't kill him, sonny. You two boys did," a sibilant voice said.

Both Ray and Cletus looked at the man who had spoken. Neither of them had ever seen him before.

"Who the hell are you?" Cletus asked.

"Boys, this is Jefferson Tyree," Ike said.

"Jefferson Tyree?" Cletus said. "Wait a minute. Do you mean the outlaw Jefferson Tyree?"

"I mean Jefferson Tyree," Ike said without commenting on the outlaw reference.

"What's he doin' here?"

"I hired him."

"You hired him? Pa, he's an outlaw!" Cletus said.

Ike chuckled. "Hell, son, if it weren't for the fact that we got Belmond in our hip pockets, we would be outlaws, too," he said.

"Well, what the hell do you need him for anyway?"

"I thought we might be able to use him in our little disagreement with General Wade Garrison," Ike explained.

"You don't need him, Pa. You got me'n Ray. What do you need someone else for?"

"Because, like you said, I have you and Ray," Ike said. "Two of the must useless sons a man has ever been cursed with."

"Yeah? Well, what is he goin' to do that we can't?" Cletus challenged, pointing to Tyree.

"If I had been with you tonight, I would've smelled the trap, and I wouldn't have gotten a man killed. Like I said, you're the ones who got him killed. You killed him by going out there without knowing what you were doing," Tyree said. He crossed his arms across his chest and leaned back against one of the columns that fronted the patio. "Don't be doing anything like that again, unless I give you permission."

"Now, wait just a damn minute here," Cletus said angrily. "If Pa hired you, then that means you work for me, I don't work for you. So you won't be giving me permission to do anything."

Tyree uncrossed his arms. "Sonny, I not only don't work for you," he said. "I no longer work for your pa." He started toward the barn.

"What do you mean, you don't work for me?" Ike called after him.

"Ought not to be that hard to figure out," Tyree replied without looking back. He continued walking toward the barn.

"No, wait!" Ike called after him. He glared at his son. "Ray, Cletus, Tyree is right. Neither one of you have any business messing in his business. And from now on, you won't do one damn thing unless he tells you to do it."

Ray stood there for a moment, seething, as he clenched and unclenched his fists.

"This ain't right, Pa!" Ray said. "This ain't in no way right, and you know it!"

"Boy, you know me well enough now to know that I don't give a tinker's damn what's right or wrong," Ike said. "I only care for results. And so far, neither you nor Cletus has given me any results. That's why I hired Tyree."

"We don't need him, Pa," Ray said. "Me'n Cletus can take care of—"

"So far you and Cletus haven't been able to take care of shit," Ike said, interrupting his son in mid-sentence. "I've hired Jefferson Tyree because I'm tired of getting my men killed. I think it's time we started killing a few of Garrison's men. Do you understand that?"

"Yeah," Ray said, biting off his words. "Yeah, I understand it."

"And you won't go off on your own anymore. You won't do anything like that unless Tyree tells you it's all right. Do you understand that?"

Ray sighed. "Yeah."

"Yeah, what?"

"Yeah, I won't do anything unless Tyree tells me it's all right," Ray said, nearly choking on the words.

"Cletus? What about you?"

"Hell, Pa, it weren't my idee to go over there in the first place," Cletus said. "It was all Ray's idee and I was just doin' what he said."

"Then I take it that you agree to do nothing without Tyree's permission?" Ike asked.

"Yeah, sure, whatever you say, Pa," Cletus said, looking away so as not to have to face the angry glare he was getting from Ray.

"Tyree?" Ike called. "You heard all this?"

"I heard it," Tyree replied from over by the barn.

"Will you stay?"

Tyree didn't make a verbal response, but he answered in the affirmative by making an almost imperceptible nod of his head.

"What about Billy?" Cletus asked.

"What about him?"

"Are you saying Billy is to take his orders from Tyree same as us?"

Ike shook his head. "Billy ain't a part of this," he said.

"What do you mean, he ain't a part of it?"

"You boys know what Billy is like. When it comes to something like this, he's as worthless as tits on a boar hog. Hell, I ain't even told him about Tyree yet."

When he heard the early morning commotion out on the front porch, Billy got out of bed and came down to see what was going on. He intended to step out on the front porch to be closer to what was happening, but when he heard them talking about Tyree, he stopped and stood just inside the door in the parlor, drinking a cup of coffee. When he heard his father's assessment of him, he turned and left the parlor, not wanting to be there when they came back inside.

Chapter Twenty

When Tyree, Cletus, and Ray rode into town, Harold Denham was standing on the front porch of his newspaper officer, supervising the replacement of the window that had been broken out.

"Son of a bitch," he said quietly as the three rode by him, then dismounted in front of the Hog Waller.

"What is it, Mr. Denham, what are we doin' wrong?" one of the workers asked.

"What?" Denham asked. Then, realizing that he had said the words "son of a bitch" aloud, he shook his head.

"No, nothing to do with what you boys are doing," he said. "You're doing a fine job."

"Thanks."

"Look, you seem to have everything in hand here. You just keep going the way you are. I need to walk down to the marshal's office and have a word with Travis. I'll be back in a few minutes."

"Yes, sir, Mr. Denham."

When Denham reached the marshal's office, he saw Travis sitting at the desk, the top of which was covered with a rather messy spread of papers. The new marshal looked up as Denham stepped inside.

"Would you look at all this?" Travis said. "How did Titus keep up with it all? I had no idea there was so much paperwork involved in being a marshal. It could be that I'm just not cut out for this job."

"You'll do fine," Denham said. "I think it was a smart decision to appoint you."

"We'll see, we'll see," Travis said. "What brings you by?"

"Do you have anything in there about Jefferson Tyree?" Denham asked.

"Jefferson Tyree? Hmm, seems to me like I've heard that name. Now, why is that name familiar?"

"He murdered an entire family a year or so ago. He was caught and put in prison for life, but last month he escaped from prison," Denham said.

Travis nodded. "Jefferson Tyree," he said again. "Yes, I do remember that now. Well, if he is a murderer and an escaped prisoner, I'm sure there must be something on him in here somewhere." Travis started shuffling through the papers on his desk until he turned up a poster. "Ah, yes. Here it is."

WANTED!

DEAD OR ALIVE

JEFFERSON TYREE

$5,000.00 REWARD !

The poster also had a woodcut picture of the outlaw. "Is this the man you're talking about?"

"Yes," Denham said. "He's here, Travis. Jefferson Tyree is here."

"Here?"

"In Higbee. I just saw him."

"Are you sure?" Travis asked. He pointed to the picture. "Because, to be honest, these woodcuts aren't always that good."

"It doesn't matter how good the woodcut is," Denham said. "I know it is Tyree. I just saw him ride in with Ray and Cletus Clinton."

"How can you be so sure that it's Tyree?"

"Because I covered his trial last year," Denham replied. "I sat in the courtroom and looked at that son of a bitch all through his entire trial."

"And you say he's with the Clintons?"

"Yes."

Travis sighed. "In that case then, there's not much doubt about why he's here, is there? It looks like the Clintons have just upped the ante by hiring themselves a gun."

"Where's Falcon MacCallister?"

"He's with the crew that's putting up the bridge," Travis said.

"Maybe we'd better send for him."

Travis stood up, then pulled his pistol, and turned the cylinder to check the loads.

"No, there's no need for that," he said. "I'm the marshal now. If I can't handle this, I've got no business wearing this badge."

"Travis, no," Denham said. "This man is a cold-blooded killer."

"So what am I supposed to do, Harold? Let the cold-blooded killers go and just handle people who spit on the boardwalks?"

"You could send somebody after Falcon."

Travis dropped the pistol back in his holster, put on his hat, and squared his shoulders.

"No," he said. "No, I can't do that."

Denham followed Travis down the street, then into the Hog Waller.

Recently, there had been some discussion before the city council as to whether or not the Hog Waller should be closed. Those who spoke against it talked about it as a health hazard, and if filth had anything to do with disease, as Denham believed, then there was some justification for it, because the Hog Waller literally reeked with filth.

In addition to being filthy, the Hog Waller appealed to the lowest common denominator of citizen, attracted by the cheap women and the cheaper whiskey.

The move to close the Hog Waller failed for two reasons. Prentiss Hampton was a member of the city council, and he felt that he could not support the proposal because it would appear as if he were trying to stifle the competition. Also, it was pointed out that most of the card cheating, fistfights, and other acts of disreputable behavior took place in the Hog Waller.

"It's as if we have a place marked off just for such behavior," Moore said in arguing against the proposal. "Maybe as long as we keep it contained there, it won't spread through the rest of the town."

In the end, Moore's argument prevailed, and the city council took no action in closing the Hog Waller.

The first thing Denham noticed when he stepped

inside was the smell. It was overpowering, but it didn't seem to be bothering any of the patrons.

"Is he here?" Travis asked quietly.

"Yes. That's him, standing next to Cletus. Tyree is the fella with the gray shirt."

"Thanks," Travis replied. Travis pulled his pistol from his holster. "Now, step back out of the way."

What Travis did not realize was that Tyree had seen him through the window before he came into the saloon. Tyree had also seen the badge on Travis's vest, so he knew why Travis was coming.

Unnoticed by anyone else at the bar, Travis had pulled his pistol and cocked it and was holding it in front of him, concealing it between his stomach and the bar, even as the marshal came in.

"Jefferson Tyree, turn around," Travis called authoritatively.

Tyree spun around and fired, catching Travis by surprise. Even so, Travis reacted quickly, pulling the trigger on his own pistol so soon behind Tyree that those who only heard the sounds of the gunshots thought the fight was much closer than it really was. In truth, Travis's bullet plunged into the floor right in front of him.

"Travis!" Denham shouted, running toward the collapsed form of his friend.

Tyree stood for a long moment, holding the still-smoking pistol as Denham attempted to administer to his friend.

"Is he dead?" Tyree asked calmly.

"Yes, he's dead," Denham replied. "You murdered him."

"You might've noticed he already had the gun in his hand when he braced me," Tyree said.

"He didn't brace you, Tyree. He was attempting to arrest you," Denham said.

"Arrest me, huh? Well, maybe he should've said somethin'. I thought he was just somebody trying to build a reputation by killing Jefferson Tyree."

"One doesn't build a reputation by killing polecats or rattlesnakes," Denham said. "And compared to you, the polecat and the rattlesnake are some of God's noblest creatures."

"You have a big mouth, don't you, friend?" Tyree said. He looked over at Cletus. "This fella always have a way with words like that?"

"Oh, yes," Cletus said. "This is Harold Denham, the publisher of our local newspaper."

"The local newspaper, huh?" Inexplicably, a broad smile spread across Tyree's face. "So, are you going to write about me, Mr. Newspaperman?"

"I am indeed," Denham said, still on his knees next to Travis Calhoun's body. "If you think you can frighten away the press, you have another think coming."

"Oh, I don't want to frighten you away. I want you to print the story, just as it happened. And I want you to say that when this fella braced me, he was already holding a pistol in his hand, but that I was so quick that I turned, drew, and shot him before he could shoot me."

"I will not make anything heroic out of this," Denham said.

"I ain't askin' you to make me a hero, mister," Tyree said. "I'm just askin' you to tell the truth, that's all."

* * *

When Falcon saw the buckboard with General Garrison and his daughter arrive at the site where the bridge was being built, he walked over to them.

"Hello," he said, greeting them with a smile. "Are you out here to check on the progress?"

"I wish that was the only reason," Garrison replied.

Falcon noticed the grim expressions on their faces.

"What is it?" he asked. "What has happened?"

"Marshal Calhoun has been killed."

Falcon frowned for a second, wondering why they would be telling him what he already knew. Then, suddenly, he realized they weren't talking about Titus, they were talking about Travis.

"Wait a minute! Travis?" he said. "Are you saying Travis Calhoun has been killed? He just took office."

"Yes."

"The Clintons?"

"No!" Kathleen said quickly. "It wasn't them."

"It was the same as them," Garrison said. "It was their hired gun."

"Their hired gun?"

"Jefferson Tyree," Garrison said. "Do you know him?"

Falcon nodded. "Yes," he said. "I know him. Tell me what happened."

Garrison told the story to Falcon as it was told to him by Harold Denham.

"Can a man really be that fast?" Garrison asked. "Everyone agrees that Travis already had his gun out and drawn, but Tyree just spun around and shot him."

"Yes, a man can be that fast," Falcon said. He sighed, and ran his hand through his hair. "You say Tyree is working for the Clintons now?"

"That's what I've heard," Garrison said. "And he was with them when this happened."

"If the Clintons actually have hired Jefferson Tyree, then they are as guilty of Travis's murder as he is."

"No!" Kathleen said.

"What do you mean no?" Garrison asked his daughter. "Think about it, Kathleen. You know that is true."

"It might be true about the rest of the Clintons, but not about Billy. I know that he wouldn't have anything to do with something like this. You don't know Billy the way I do."

"Are you sure that you know him that well?" Garrison asked.

"Yes, I'm positive. What are you trying to say, Papa? Are you saying that you think Billy is like his brothers or his father? Because I know that he is not."

"And yet, he stays with them, does he not?"

"It's more complicated than that," Kathleen said.

"Kathleen, I think you should listen to your father," Falcon said. "I know men like this. I have known them for my entire life."

"You, too? But you met him on the train. And you saw how he was at the dance. You know he was different from the others."

"He behaves differently, now that is true," Falcon said. "But the very thing that makes him a good man is his sense of honor. And if that sense of honor is misplaced, it's also going to doom him."

"What do you mean, misplaced?"

"I mean that when it comes right down to it, if Billy is forced into choosing between his family and outsiders, Billy is going to choose his family," Falcon said.

"No, never."

Falcon nodded. "I'm afraid he will have no choice. It

will be an act of honor—twisted honor to be sure, but its hold on him will not let him go."

Falcon attended the church part of Travis Calhoun's funeral, but as the funeral cortege moved slowly down Front Street toward the cemetery, Falcon saw Cletus and Ray Clinton going into the Hog Waller. Jefferson Tyree was with them.

"Corey," he said. "Give my apologies to Troy."

"What do you mean? You aren't going out to the cemetery?"

"I've got some business to attend to," Falcon said without further explanation.

Evidently, someone had said something very funny just before Falcon stepped in through the door, because everyone was laughing. But as they saw Falcon, the laughter stopped, not all at once, but in ragged spikes so that the last bit of laughter was Rosie's single cackle. Then, realizing she was laughing alone, she turned to see why.

"Well, now, if it ain't my old friend Falcon MacCallister," Tyree said. "My, my, look at you, all dressed up like that. You been to a wedding or something?"

"I've been to a funeral," Falcon replied.

"A funeral? Oh, yes, you must be talking about the marshal. I'm just real sorry 'bout that. All I saw was someone pointing a gun at me. Maybe if he had come in here and talked to me just right, I wouldn't have had to kill him. He was your friend, was he?"

"He was."

"Well, I tell you what. Just to show you that there's no

hard feelin's, how about steppin' up to the bar and havin' a drink with me. Bartender, give Mr. MacCallister anything he wants to drink, on me." A broad, arrogant smile spread across Tyree's face.

"I didn't come here to drink with you, Tyree. I came here to kill you."

Falcon spoke the sentence so calmly that, for a moment, those who heard him weren't sure what they heard. Then, as they repeated it to each other, and as they measured the cold set of Falcon's eyes, they realized what he had actually said.

"Hold on there, MacCallister," Cletus said. "You can't just come in here and—"

"Shut up, Clinton," Falcon said.

"You can't talk to me—"

Suddenly, Ray brought the back of his hand across Cletus's face, hitting him so hard that his lip began to bleed.

"Shut up, Cletus," Ray said. "This is between MacCallister and Tyree."

When Tyree saw that the Clinton brothers had just taken themselves out of it, and he was going to have to face Falcon alone, the smile on his face faded. He had thought that with the Clintons he had an edge. Now he saw that edge taken away. That left Tyree with self-doubt, and the self-doubt caused him to feel fear, perhaps for the first time in his life. And that fear was mirrored in his eyes and in the nervous tick on the side of his face. His tongue came out to lick his lips.

When he saw Tyree's fear begin to manifest itself, an easy grin spread across Falcon's face. Even that, the grin in the face of a life and death situation, seemed to unnerve Tyree.

Suddenly, Tyree's hand started for his gun. He was fast, but Falcon was just a heartbeat faster. Falcon fired, and Tyree caught the ball high in his chest. Dropping his gun, Tyree slapped his hand over his wound. He looked down in surprise as blood squirted through his fingers, turning his shirt bright red. He took two staggering steps toward Falcon, then fell to his knees. He looked up at Falcon.

"Son of a bitch," he said. He smiled, then coughed, and flecks of blood came from his mouth. He breathed hard a couple of times. "Son of a bitch, you're fast."

"No, you were just slow," Falcon said easily.

Tyree fell facedown, then lay still.

Cletus, seeing that Tyree was dead, held his hand out in front of him.

"I ain't goin' to draw on you," he said. "If you kill me, ever'one in here will be able to testify that you killed me in cold blood."

"Go home, both of you," Falcon said. "Tell your pa he has thirty days to sell his ranch and move out."

"What?" Cletus replied, practically shouting the word.

"You heard me," Falcon said. "You have thirty days to sell your ranch and move out of the state."

"What the hell! You can't order us out of the state!"

"I just did."

"And if we don't?" Cletus asked.

Falcon didn't say a word, but he smiled. It was the same smile he'd had just before he killed Tyree. The impact wasn't lost on either of the Clintons.

Chapter Twenty-one

J. Peerless Bixby, the Higbee undertaker, put Tyree's body in a wooden coffin, then stood him up in front of his establishment. One of Tyree's eyes was closed, the other was half open. His hands were crossed in front of his body, and he was holding his gun. A sign was pinned to his chest.

JEFFERSON TYREE

Noted Murderer And Outlaw

Killed in a <u>FAIR FIGHT</u>

by Falcon MacCallister

The Vermillion was decorated with black bunting around the windows and a black wreath on the door. It had been closed since Travis was killed, and had just re-opened for the first time tonight.

Rachael had accepted Falcon's invitation to dinner, and the two of them were sitting at a table at the back of the restaurant.

When the waiter came to the table, Rachael ordered baked chicken, green beans with mushrooms, and a salad. The waiter nodded, then started back to the kitchen with her order. He didn't ask Falcon what he wanted.

"Aren't you going to order?" Rachael asked.

"I don't need to," Falcon replied. "He knows what I want."

"And what would that be?"

"Steak and baked potato."

"You have the same thing every time?"

"Yes."

"Why?"

"I like it," Falcon said simply.

For a long moment, Falcon and Rachael sat in silence, a single candle lighting the distance between them. Finally, Falcon broke the silence.

"You're going back East," he said. It wasn't a question, it was a statement.

Rachael nodded, but said nothing.

"Edwin?"

"He wants me to come back and join him again for a series of performances."

"You should go back," Falcon said. "You are wasting your talent by playing piano in a saloon, even a saloon as nice as the Golden Nugget."

"That isn't the only reason I'm going back," Rachael said.

"Oh?"

"May I be frank with you, Falcon?"

"By all means."

"I have had romantic illusions about you, even before I met you, based in part on the way your brother and sister speak of you. Then, when I met you, I thought you were everything they said, maybe even more. But—"

"It's the *more,* isn't it?" Falcon asked.

Rachael nodded. "Yes, that's a good way of putting it. It's the *more.* Falcon, you are just too violent for me. No, wait, that isn't fair. It's this, this accursed West that is too violent for me. I had never known anyone who had been killed before. Since coming here, I have seen nothing but killing. And you—you are right in the middle of it. You killed the two men who killed the first Marshal Calhoun; then you killed the man who killed the second Marshal Calhoun."

"I didn't choose the life I live, Rachael, but I make no apologies for it. I've killed, yes, but I no longer kill anyone who doesn't need killing."

"You—you no longer kill anyone who doesn't need killing? What an odd thing to say."

"During the war, I killed men for no reason other than the fact that they were wearing a uniform different from my own. They were good men, with families that loved them. If I can kill such men during time of war, do you think I would hesitate for one minute to kill someone like the sorry example of humanity that J. Peerless Bixby is displaying in front of his mortuary right now?"

"I suppose there is some logic there somewhere," Rachael said. "But for the life of me, I can't see it."

"Mr. MacCallister?"

Looking up, Falcon saw Kathleen Garrison coming toward her. He stood quickly.

"Kathleen," he said. "Is something wrong? Is the general all right?"

"No, there's nothing wrong," Kathleen said. "No, wait, there is something wrong. It's Billy."

"Billy?"

"Billy is down at my house now, with my father. He asked me to come find you."

"All right," Falcon said. "Rachael, I'm sorry. I'm going to tell Troy to cancel my dinner. I have to—"

"There's no need to apologize," Rachael said. "You go ahead and do what you have to do."

When Falcon stepped into the parlor of Garrison's house, he saw Garrison sitting in a chair and Billy standing next to the fireplace.

"Billy, here's Mr. MacCallister," Kathleen said.

"Mr. MacCallister," Billy said, turning toward him and nodding.

"Hello, Billy. What's this about?"

"I came to warn you," he said.

"Oh?"

"Tomorrow, Pa, my brothers, and just about every rider we have will be coming into town. There will be at least twenty men, maybe more, and they are all coming after you, Mr. MacCallister. Pa has promised one hundred dollars to everyone who comes with him."

"I see," Falcon said.

"Billy, why are you telling us this?" Garrison asked.

"Because I don't want to see anyone else get killed," Billy said. "Mr. True was a good man. I remember going fishing with him once. And Travis Calhoun always treated me well when I came into the café." Billy looked at Falcon. "If you would leave town, there wouldn't be anything happening tomorrow."

"And you think my leaving town would end it?" Falcon asked.

"Yes, sir, I do, I truly do," Billy said.

"Would your pa drop his fight against the general building his railroad?" Falcon asked. "Because if your pa would do that, I would leave."

Billy glanced down toward the floor without answering Falcon's question.

"I didn't think he would," Falcon said, discerning the answer from Billy's reaction to his question.

"Mr. MacCallister, if Pa brings an army in here tomorrow, and he will, people are going to get killed. A lot of people. Maybe even—" He paused.

"Maybe even who, Billy? Kathleen?" Falcon asked.

Billy nodded, but didn't speak.

"General, it's up to you," Falcon said. "Do I leave, or stay?"

"Whether you leave or stay, I intend to see this railroad built," Garrison said. "And if that means an all-out war with Ike Clinton, then so be it."

"I thought you might feel that way," Falcon said. "I'm staying."

"Well, I tried," Billy said with a sigh. "I didn't think I could talk you into leaving, but I figured I had to try."

"Billy, does your pa know you came into town tonight?" Garrison asked.

"No, sir, he'd probably kill me if he knew."

"Isn't he going to wonder where you are?"

"I don't know. Maybe."

"Don't go back," Garrison said.

"I have to."

"Son, I'm going to ask you something. Do you love my daughter?"

"What?" Billy asked, surprised to hear this question from Garrison. "Yes, sir, I do. I reckon I love her more than anything in the world."

"And you, Kathleen, how do you feel about this boy?"

"I love him, Papa. You know that I love him."

Garrison sighed, and ran his hand through his hair. "I never thought I would hear myself say this. But I'm going to say it anyway. Billy, if you will take my daughter away from here, go someplace where neither your father nor your brothers can find you, I'll give you one thousand dollars. That should be enough for you and Kathleen to get married and start a life together somewhere. Then, when all this is over, maybe you could come back."

"Oh, Papa, thank you!" Kathleen said excitedly. "Billy, what do you think?"

When the three looked at Billy, Falcon thought he had never seen a more anguished face in his life.

"I can't," Billy said, barely able to say the words.

"What? Billy, didn't you hear what Papa said? He's given us his approval! We can go away somewhere and get married!"

Billy pinched the bridge of his nose and shook his head. "I can't," he said again. He started toward the door.

"Billy, no!" Kathleen screamed. She started after him, but Garrison reached out to stop her.

"No, darlin', let him go," he said.

With tears streaming down her face, Kathleen looked at Falcon. "You knew, didn't you?" she said. "You told me about his honor. You knew."

"I'm sorry," Falcon said.

When the eastern sky was laced by the first streaks of dawn, the town of Higbee was prepared for a siege. A barricade of wagons and barrels blocked the east end of Front Street, behind which stood at least two dozen armed men. There were also men on the roofs of the leather goods store and Moore's general store.

Every woman and child, plus the men who did not want to take part in the coming battle, had taken refuge in the church. The church was at the north end of town, set far enough off Front Street that it would be unlikely to catch any stray rounds.

General Garrison was in command of the men of the town, and he had strapped on his sword and put on his service hat.

"Where is Falcon?" Moore asked.

"Yes, where is MacCallister?" another wanted to know.

"Falcon should be here," still another added.

"Don't you folks be worrying about Falcon MacCallister," Garrison said. "All you have to worry about is keeping your head down and making every shot count when Clinton and his men get here."

In coordination with Garrison, Falcon was on a reconnoitering mission, having left town before dawn. He was actually on the Clinton ranch now, very close to the main house, and he lay flat on his stomach, looking through his binoculars at the activity below. Billy had said there might be as many as twenty riders come into town with them, but Falcon was surprised to see that there were at least twice as many.

From his position, he could not only watch them gather, he could hear them talking.

"Pa, we don't have to do this," he heard Billy say. "If we do this, a lot of innocent people could get killed."

"Boy, you are either with us or ag'in us," Ike said angrily. "Now I've put up with about as much pussyfooting from you as I can stomach. Make up your mind, and make it up now!"

"I'm coming with you," Billy said.

"Good boy," Ike said. "Lou?"

"Yeah, Boss."

"You take half the men and go through Elbow Pass. Go all the way around town and come in from the west. I'll take the rest with me and we'll come in from the east. That way, we'll have the town squeezed in between us."

"Let me take the other group, Pa," Ray said.

"No," Ike said. "I want you three boys with me."

As Ike and his men started saddling their horses, Falcon left.

Half an hour later, Falcon was sitting calmly on top of a large round rock watching as Lou and at least twenty riders approached Elbow Pass. The pass was so confined that they couldn't go through without squeezing into a single file. It was a place that no one with any tactical sense would use. But these were not men with a sense of tactics. These were cowboys, fired up by the prospect of one hundred dollars for going after Falcon. Because of that, they were men who could be easily lured into a trap.

Falcon stood up so he could clearly be seen against the skyline.

"I'll be damned! Look! There he is!" Lou shouted, pointing at Falcon.

"What's he doin' out here?"

"Who cares? Let's get him!"

The riders galloped through the draw, bent on capturing or killing Falcon MacCallister.

A couple of the men in front thought Falcon made an

easy target, so they pulled their pistols and began shooting up toward him as they rode. Falcon could see the flash of the gunshots, then the little puffs of dust as the bullets hit around him. The spent bullets whined as they ricocheted through the little draw, but none of them even came close enough to cause him to duck.

Falcon leaned over, almost casually, to light two fuses. A little starburst of sparks started at each fuse, then ran sputtering and snapping along the length of fuse for several feet alongside the draw. The first explosion went off about fifty yards in front of the lead rider, a heavy, stomach-shaking thump that filled the draw with smoke and dust, then brought a ton of rocks crashing down to close the draw so that the riders couldn't get through.

The second explosion, somewhat less powerful, was located behind the riders. It, too, brought rocks crashing down into the draw behind them, closing the passage off. All twenty men were now bottled up inside the pass, and it was going to take them at least a day, maybe two days, to dig their way out. They were no longer part of whatever might happen in Higbee.

Leaving the trapped cowboys behind him, Falcon leaped onto his horse and urged it into a gallop. When he came galloping into Higbee from the west end of town a few minutes later, he saw everyone in position behind the barricade, and he knew that he had arrived before Clinton and his men.

"Here's MacCallister!" someone said.

"Where've you been?" another asked.

"How did it go?" Garrison asked.

Only Garrison knew where Falcon had been, and why.

"I've got about twenty of them trapped in Elbow

Pass," Falcon said. "Another twenty will be coming from this direction. Is everything ready?"

"We're ready," Garrison said.

"Where's the breach?"

"Right there," Garrison said, pointing to a stack of barrels.

"You sure it's wide enough?"

"Major, you may have come up with the plan," Garrison said. "But I think I have the military experience to implement it."

Falcon chuckled. "I would never question you, General," he replied.

"They're comin'!" someone shouted down from the roof of Moore's general store.

"All right, men, get ready," Garrison said. Then, spotting Denham, he scolded him. "Mr. Denham, what are you doing up here? I said I wanted only young men who could run up here."

"I can get out in time," Denham said.

"Get back there now before I shoot you myself," Garrison said, pointing to the Golden Nugget.

"All right, all right, but don't think for a minute I'm not going to write an article about overbearing generals," he grumbled.

Falcon chuckled as he saw Denham moving back toward the Golden Nugget. Then, turning, he saw Garrison.

"General, you're no spring chicken," he said. "You need to get back there, too."

"Since when does a major give a general orders?" Garrison replied.

"Go," Falcon ordered.

"Hah!" Denham said as Garrison caught up with him.

The two men went about fifty yards down the road, then stepped in behind the Golden Nugget.

Falcon watched them until they disappeared. Then he stepped up to the barricade with his pistol in hand.

"Are you boys ready?" he asked.

"Bring 'em on," Tom said. Tom, Larry, and Frank, the three young men who had ridden as guards for the Thompson shipment of Garrison's depot material, were among the five who were waiting behind the barricade with Falcon.

"Hold it up, men, hold it up!" Ike Clinton said when he saw the barricade stretched across the street in front of them.

Suddenly, a ripple of gunfire came from the barricade. Ike and the others started shooting back.

"Pa, should we dismount?" Cletus asked.

"Yes, dismount and take cover on the side of the road," Ike replied.

Then a part of the barricade collapsed, and when it did, the shooting from the barricade stopped.

"Son of a bitch! Their barricade came down!" Ike said. "Mount up men! Mount up and charge! By God, we've got 'em now!"

"Now!" Falcon ordered. "Fall back!"

The five men with Falcon, all young, chosen for their youth and the ability to run fast, dashed down Front Street as fast as they could run. All five were faster than Falcon, who was considerably older than they were, and even before he got there, more wagons were being pulled into the street from alongside the buildings to form a second barricade. Falcon got there just in time to get behind the second barricade.

Behind them, Ike and his men, remounted now, thundered through the breach in the first barricade. No sooner had they passed through than another wagon was brought out behind them, resealing the breach. Dozens of the townsmen, who had been waiting behind the buildings, rushed out to man the second barricade.

Billy saw it first, and realized before anyone else that they had ridden into a trap. All twenty men were caught within a fifty-yard pen, with armed men behind barricades at each end.

"Pa, we're trapped!" Billy said.

"Shoot!" Ike replied. "Shoot the bastards!"

The men who had ridden in with the Clintons, suddenly realizing the hopelessness of their position, threw their guns down and started running to either side of the street with their hands up.

"Don't shoot, don't shoot!" they shouted.

"You cowardly bastards!" Cletus called toward them. He shot one of the fleeing men; then Cletus went down, shot by one of the defenders. Now, only Ike, Ray, and Billy were left, and the three men were shooting and getting shot at. Ray went down, then Ike, and Billy was alone.

"Billy, give it up!" Falcon said. "It's over!"

Billy pulled the trigger on an empty chamber. Then he picked up guns from both Cleetus and Ray and, with a gun in either hand, started firing again.

"Billy, no! It's over!" Kathleen shouted, suddenly darting through the barricade.

"Where did she come from?" Denham asked.

"Kathleen, get back here!"

Billy, who was firing both pistols wildly, suddenly saw a hole appear in Kathleen's forehead.

"No!" he cried in anguish. "Kathleen, no!"

"Give it up, Billy!" Falcon said. "It's over!

Falcon came out from behind the barricade then, and started toward Billy, who was now standing there, holding both guns down by his side, staring at Kathleen's body.

"Drop your guns, Billy," Falcon said as he approached him.

Billy looked up at Falcon. The expression on Billy's face was that of a wild man.

"No!" Billy shouted. Raising both guns, he began shooting at Falcon. One of his bullets nicked Falcon's arm and another took off Falcon's hat. Falcon had no choice but to return fire, and when he did so, Billy fell forward. Billy lay there for a second; then, wriggling forward on his stomach, he worked his way through the dirt of the street to Kathleen's body. Reaching out, he took her hand in his, squeezed it, then died.

One hour later, with the street cleaned up and with the bodies of the Clintons and Kathleen down at the undertaker's, the morning stage left for La Junta. Falcon saw it go by, saw Rachael looking through the window as it left. She didn't wave, and neither did Falcon.

Two months later

EPITAPH FOR HIGBEE.

This is the final issue of the HIGBEE JOURNAL. Should some future historian happen upon this journal, it might be of interest to know that only twenty-five copies of this issue will be printed. Only twenty-five copies, but this will be enough for every man, woman, and child remaining in Higbee.

Three months ago Higbee was a vibrant community, with the prospects of a railroad to be built by General Wade Garrison. That railroad, the Colorado, New Mexico, and Texas, would have connected our city to the rest of the country, indeed to the rest of the world. We had wonderful business enterprises. Moore's General Store was as fine a store as one could find this side of Denver. Moore's is no more. Our apothecary, leather goods store, hardware store, mortuary, all wonderful establishments of commerce, are gone, too. The Golden Nugget, where once we could gather in a convivial atmosphere and be entertained by the beautiful music of one of our nation's greatest musicians, is also gone, as is the Morning Star Hotel. Even the church closed its doors when the parson, Reverend E. D. Owen, found that he no longer had a flock to tend.

This all came about by the greed and evil machinations of one man, Ike Clinton. In this one man's twisted mind, the railroad, which would have guaranteed growth and prosperity for Higbee, was a threat, and he set about to stop it.

If a final score is somewhere being kept, let it be known that Ike Clinton succeeded in stopping the railroad, though not in the way he intended. Clinton's evil greed cost him his own life, as well as the life of his three sons. It also brought about the demise of Kathleen Garrison, a beautiful, innocent young lady who provided meaning to her father's life.

When Kathleen Garrison was killed, the spark which sustained General Wade Garrison was extinguished. Losing all reason to live, General Garrison stopped the building of the railroad. He left town, a broken and dispirited man, and at last report, was living the life of a recluse in a home for the mentally disturbed in Memphis, Tennessee.

Without the hope of a railroad, that which was sustaining the growth and vibrancy of Higbee, the town withered and died. And now, as I set the type that will reproduce these words, I can only hope that at least one of these journals will survive until some future time, one hundred, or maybe even one hundred fifty years from now. To you, dear reader in the future, I leave these final words. Our town, which will be but a faded shadow in your history, was once bright with hope and promise. And long after the last building has turned to dust, the spirits of such men as Norman True, Carl Moore, Titus, Travis, and Troy Calhoun, General Wade Garrison, Corey and Prentiss Hampton, and such women as the general's daughter Kathleen, the talented pianist Rachael Kirby, and yes, even the madam,

Maggie, will occupy this place until the entire planet returns to dust.

I am Harold Denham, editor and publisher of the Higbee Journal.

I bid thee all a final farewell.

Turn the page for an exciting preview of

SAVAGE GUNS
by William W. Johnstone
with J. A. Johnstone

Available wherever Pinnacle Books are sold.

Chapter One

I was mindin' my daily business in the two-holer when I got rudely interrupted. Now I like a little privacy, but this morning I got me a bullet instead. There I was, peacefully studying the female undies in the Montgomery Ward catalog, when this here slug slams through the door and exits through the rear, above my head.

"Hey!" I yelled, but no one said nothing.

"You out there. Don't you try nothing. This here's the law talking. I'm coming after you."

But I sure didn't know who or what was in the yard behind Belle's roomin' house. I thought maybe a horse was snorting or pawing clay, but I couldn't be sure of it. I wanted to see what was what, but the half-moon that let in fresh air was high up above me, and I had my business to look after just then. You can't do nothing in the middle of business.

I don't know about you, but I wear my hat when I'm in the two-holer, just on general principles. A man should wear a hat in the crapper. That's my motto. It was a peaceful enough morning in the town of Doubtful, in

Puma County, Wyoming, where I was sheriff, more or less. So that riled me some, that bullet that slapped through there knocking my good five-X gray felt beaver Stetson topper, which teetered on the other hole but did not drop. If it had dropped down there, I'd a been plumb peeved.

I thought for a moment I oughta follow that hat through the hole and get my bare bottom down there in the perfumed vault, but that was plum sickening, and besides, how could I slide a hundred fifty pounds of rank male through that little round hole? I don't need no more smell than I've already got. When I pull my boots off, people head for the doors holding their noses. It just wouldn't work. If someone was gonna kill me, they held all the aces.

The truth of it was that I wasn't finished with my business, and all I could do was sit there and finish up my private duties, and rip a page out of the Monkey Ward catalog, and get it over with. Like the rest of us who used the two-holer behind Belle's boardinghouse, I was inclined to study ladies' corsets and bloomers and garters for entertainment, saving the wipe-off for the pages brimming with one-bottom plows, buggy whips, and bedpans. Them others in Belle's boardinghouse, they felt like I did, and no female undie pages ever got torn out of the catalog. That sure beat corncobs, I'll tell you.

"Sheriff, you come outa there with your hands up and your pants down," someone yelled. I thought maybe I knew the feller doin' all that yelling, but it was hard to tell, sitting there with pages of chemises and petticoats on my lap.

"Hold your horses," I said. "I ain't done, and the

longer it takes, the better for you, because I'm likely to bust out of here with lead flying in all directions."

That fetched me a nasty laugh, and I knew that laugh, and I thought maybe I was in more of a jam than I'd imagined.

But no more bullets came sailing through, and I finished up, and ripped out a page of men's union suits, and another page of hay rakes and spades, and got it over with. I wasn't gonna bust out of there with my pants down, no matter what, so I stood, got myself arranged and buttoned up, drew out my service revolver, and with a violent shove, threw myself out the door and dodged to the left just to avoid any incoming lead.

It sure didn't do me no good. As my mama used to tell me, don't do nothing foolish.

Sure enough, there before me were eight, nine ratty-assed cowboys on horses, all of the lot waving black revolvers in my direction, just in case I got notions. And also a dude with a buckboard, holding some reins.

"I shoulda known," I said to the boss, who was the man I figgered it was.

"I told you to come out with your pants down, and you didn't. That's a hanging offense," the man said. "You do what I say, and when I say it."

"My pants is staying put, dammit," I replied.

I knew the joker, all right. I'd put his renegade boy in my jail a few months earlier, and now the punk was peering at the blue skies through iron bars. This feller on a shiny red horse waving nickel-plated Smith and Wesson at me was none other than Admiral Bragg. And the boy I was boardin' in my lockup, he was King Bragg, and his sister, she was Queen Bragg. Mighty strange names bloomed in that family, but who was I to howl? I sure didn't ask to have Cotton hung on me, and Pickens neither, but that's how I got stuck, and there wasn't nothing I could do about it except maybe move to Argentina or Bulgaria.

Them names weren't titles neither. Bragg's ma and pa, they stuck him with the name of Admiral. If he'd of been in the navy, he might have ended up Admiral Admiral Bragg. But the family stuck to its notions, and old Bragg, he named one child King and the other child Queen. It was King Bragg that got himself into big trouble, perforating a few fellers with his six-gun, so I caught him and he would soon pay for his killin' spree. I think the family was all cheaters. Name a boy Admiral, and the boy's got a head start, even if he ain't even close to being an admiral. Name a girl Queen, and she's got the world bowin' and scrapin' even if she ain't one.

I was a little nervous, standing there in front of his pa with seven or eight Bragg cowboys pointing their artillery at my chest. Makes a man cautious, I'd say.

"Drop the peashooter, Sheriff," Admiral Bragg ordered.

I thought maybe to lift it up and blow him away, which would have been my last earthy deed. It sure was temptin' and my old pa, he might've approved even as he lowered the coffin. Nothing like goin' out in style.

But there was about a thousand grains of lead pointing straight at me, and I chickened out, and set her down real slow, itching to pull a trick or two on these rannies. I sure was mad at myself for not spitting a few lead pills before I got turned into Swiss cheese. It just put me out of sorts, but I figured at least I was alive to get my revenge another day. So I set her down slow.

Now you get into the buckboard, Sheriff," said Admiral Bragg. "We're taking you for a little ride."

I got in, sat next to the old fart who held the reins. I knew the feller, old and daft, with a left-crick in his neck that some said was from a botched hanging. He spat, which I took for a welcome, so I settled in beside him. There was still about a thousand grains of lead aimed at me, so I sat there and smiled at these gents.

The old feller slapped rein over the croup of the dray, and we clopped away from there, heading down the two-rut road out of Doubtful in the general direction of the Bragg ranch. I sort of had a hunch what this was about, and it wasn't too comfortable thinkin' about it.

Bragg was one of the biggest stockmen around Doubtful, and had a spread up in the hills north of town that just didn't quit, and took a week with a couple of spare Sundays to ride across. He called it the Anchor Ranch, and it sure did anchor a lot of turf. He controlled as much public land as anyone in the West, and had an army of gunslicks to pin it all down, given that it wasn't his turf but belonged to Uncle Sam.

I guess that wasn't so bad; he raised a lot of beef and his men kept the saloons going in Doubtful. Admiral was a tough bird, all right, but I didn't have no occasion to throw him into the iron-barred cage in the sheriff office, so I pretty much ignored him and he ignored me until now.

I sort of didn't like the way this buckboard was surrounded by his gunslicks and we was headin' out of town, me a little bit against my will. But the bores of all them pieces aimed my way kept me from doing much complainin' about all that.

Old Admiral, perched on that shiny red horse, he ignored me, so I didn't have a notion what this was all about or how it would end. Or maybe I did. All this here stuff had to do with that scummy son of his, King Bragg, who grew up twisted and bad, and got himself into big trouble. From the moment King was big enough to wave a Colt six-gun around, he was doing it, shooting songbirds and bumblebees and gophers and snakes. It must have been a trial for old Admiral to keep that boy in cartridges, because that's about all that King did. He got mighty fine at it too, and could shoot better and faster than anyone, myself included. He could put a bullet through the edge of the ace of spades and cut that card in two.

Well, that kid, soon as he was big enough to ride into town on his own, without his ma or pa, was bent on showing the good citizens of Doubtful who was who. It wasn't lost on that boy that his pa was the biggest rancher in those parts, and maybe the biggest cattleman in the Territory, if not the whole bloomin' West.

He also was fast. Throw a bottle or a can or a silver dollar into the skies, and King would perforate it, or pretty near sign his name with bullet holes in a tomato can. I had to chase the kid out of a few saloons because he was only fifteen or so, and he didn't take kindly to it, but that was all the trouble I had, until the day he turned eighteen.

He come into Doubtful that day, few months ago, on his shiny black stallion, wearing a brace of double-action Colts, a birthday gift from his old man. I didn't pay no attention, but maybe I should have. I was busy with all that paperwork the Territory wants all the time, full of words I never heard tell of. I don't lay any claim to being more than fifth-grade schooled, so sometimes I got to get someone who's got more smarts to tell me what's what. But I make up for it by being friendly and enforcing the law pretty good.

Anyway, King Bragg tied his horse up on Saloon Row and wandered into the Last Chance wearing his new artillery. I wasn't aware of it, or I'd of kicked his ass out. He's too young to hoist a few shots of red-eye, and I'd of turned the brat over my knee and paddled his butt for pretendin' to be all growed up.

Well, next I knew, there was a ruckus, a bunch of shots to be exact, and I pop out of my office and hustle over to Saloon Row. There's a mess of shouting from the Last Chance, so I hurry over there and it was plain awful. There were three dead cowboys sprawled on the sawdust, leakin' blood. A few fellers were trying to stanch the flow some, but it was hopeless, and that threesome finished up their dying while I watched, and then people were just staring at one another. King Bragg was sitting in the sawdust, his emptied revolver in his hand. The barkeep, he was starin' over the bar, and them cowboys in there, they were staring at the dead ones, and there's me, law and order, staring at the whole lot, wondering who did what to who and why. It wasn't a very fine moment.

Well, I asked them cowboys a few questions and then pinched the kid, brought him in and locked him up, and got him tried by Judge Nippers, who told the jury the kid was guilty as hell, and sentenced him to hang by the neck until dead. And Doubtful, Wyoming, was going to see a hanging in just two weeks. In fact, I'd just hired

Lemuel Clegg and his boys to build me a gallows and charge it to Puma County. Meanwhile, the Bragg family lawyer was screechin' and hollerin', but it didn't do no good. That punk killer, King Bragg, was going to swing in a few days. Me, I'm all for justice, and with all them dead cowboys lying around, I'm thinkin' it ought to be sooner, but all that was up to Judge Nippers.

I sorta thought maybe this was connected to that, but I don't take no credit for smart thinking. Whatever the case, I was being transported by a rattling old buckboard out of town by some pretty mean-lookin' fellers with a lot of .45-caliber barrels poking straight at me, so I didn't feel none to comfortable.

"What's this here all about, Admiral?" I asked.

But that wax-haired, comb-bearded blue-eyed snake wasn't talking. He was just leading this here procession out of Doubtful, with me in the middle. I sure was getting curious. But I didn't have to wait too long. About two miles out of Doubtful, right where a bunch of cottonwoods crowded the creek, they were steering toward a big old tree, with a mighty thick limb pokin' straight out, and hanging from that limb was a noose.

Chapter Two

I sure didn't like the looks of that noose. That thing was just danglin' there, swaying in the breeze. That rope, it was thick as a hawser, and coiled around the way them hangmen do it. Like someone done it that had done it a few times and knew what to do.

Them cowboys and gunslicks was uncommon quiet as we rode toward that big cottonwood, which was in spring leaf and real pretty for May. But I wasn't paying attention to that. All I was seein' was that damned noose waiting there for some neck. I was starting to have a notion of whose neck it was waiting for, and that didn't sit well with my belly.

It got worse. That old goat driving the buckboard headed straight to that noose, and when it was plain dangling in my face, he whoaed the nag and there it was, that big hemp noose right there in front of me. None of them slicks was saying a word, and none of them had put away their artillery neither. I knew a few of them. There was Big Nose George, and Alvin Ream, and Smiley

Thistlethwaite, and Spitting Sam. They didn't think twice about putting a little lead into anything alive. You had to wonder why Bragg kept those gunmen around. Times were peaceful enough, at least until now.

"Admiral, this ain't a good idea," I said.

He laughed softly. You ever hear a man laugh like that, like he was enjoying my fate? Well, it's not something a person forgets.

"I'm the law, Admiral, and you'd better think twice."

I was thinkin' maybe I'd go down fighting, but before I could think longer, that old boy beside me wrapped his knobby old arm around me, and one of them slicks grabbed my hands, yanked them behind me, and wrapped them in thong until my arms were trussed up tighter than a fat lady's corset. Me, I'm not even thirty and had a lot of juice in me still, and I wrestled with them fellers, but it was like kicking a cast-iron stove. They knew what they was up to, and had me cold.

I began thinking that them spring leaves coming out on the cottonwood would be about the last pretty thing I'd ever see. I don't rightly know why I kept that sheriff job, but I had. I sorta liked the fun of it, and I was never one to dodge a little trouble. I kinda thought one of my deputies might be hunting for me now, but I was just being foolish. Them fellers slept late and played cribbage or euchre half the night in the jailhouse.

I didn't need any explanations. Admiral Bragg, he was getting even with me. Hang that boy, hang me. There wasn't no point in asking a bunch of questions, and no point in trying to talk him out of it. The hard, belly-grabbing truth was that this thing was gonna happen and there wasn't no way I could jabber and slobber my way out of it.

But I wasn't dwelling on it. I was eying the bright blue sky, and hearing some red-winged blackbirds making a racket down on the creek, and feeling good mountain air filling my lungs, and thinkin' of my ma and pa, and how they brought me into the world and raised me up.

I writhed some, but there was a passel of them around me in the buckboard, and strong hands pinning me while one of them slicks pulled off my five-X gray beaver hat and dropped that big, scratchy noose right over my neck. It was the first time I ever felt a noose and it wasn't a very good feeling. It was just a big, cold, scratchy twisted rope, and now it rested on my shoulders, and one of them slicks tugged it pretty tight, and tipped it off to the side a little so as to break my neck.

So I was standin' there in that buckboard with a noose drawn tight on my young neck, and all trussed up, and they all backed off and left me standing there, my knees knockin' and waiting for the final, entire, no-return end. I wondered if Admiral Bragg was gonna preach at me some, tell me this was his brand of justice, or whatnot, but he didn't. He just nodded.

That old knobby-armed geezer, he settled down in the wooden seat of the buckboard, me standing in the bed, and then he let loose with his whip, smacked the dray right across the croup, and away it went, jerking me plumb off my pins as the wagon got yanked out from under me. Then I tumbled past the wagon and started down, feelin' that hemp yank hard at my neck and jerk my head back, and then I felt myself topple to the ground, and couldn't figure what happened. I wasn't dead yet. Maybe this was just the last gasp. I bunged myself up some, hitting that dirt so hard, and landing on a cottonwood root too, so that I was really hurtin' and that noose was as tight as a necktie at a funeral, and pretty quick I was starin' up at the sky and seein' lots of blue, and the pale green of them cottonwood leaves.

"Now you know what a hanging is," Admiral said.

That was the dumbest thing ever got said to me.

They rolled me over and cut that thong that had me tied up like some beef basting on a spit. I felt some blood return to my wrists and hands, and I flexed my fingers, discovering they was alive, all ten or eleven, or whatever I got. And they loosened that scratchy hemp and pulled that thing loose and tossed it aside. One of them slicks even slapped my gray beaver Stetson down on my head. And then they let me stand up, even if my legs was trembling like a virgin in a cathouse.

I couldn't think of nothing to do, so I slugged Admiral, one gut-punch and a roundhouse to his jaw, and he staggered back as my boot landed on his shin.

That might not have been too smart, but it sure was satisfying. He let out a yelp and in about two seconds half of them slicks was pulling me off and holding me down. I figured they'd just string me up for certain, and make no mistakes this time, but Admiral, he got up, dusted off his hat, wiped some blood off his lip, and smiled.

This sure was getting strange.

All them slicks let go of me, and I was of a mind to arrest the bunch for manhandling a lawman, but the odds weren't good. I never got a handle on arithmetic, and took long division over a few times, but I know bad odds when I see them.

Admiral Bragg, he spat a little more blood and nodded.

That old knobby-armed geezer, he fetched that hemp rope and brought her over to me, but he wasn't showing me the noose end. I was more familiar with that end than I even wanted to be. No, he showed me the other end, which had been razored across, clean as can be, save for one little strand that sort of wobbled in the morning breeze. I hated that strand; it pretty near did me.

They'd cut that rope for this event, and I sure wondered why. This whole deal was to scare the bejabbers out of me, and it sure as hell did.

"King won't be so lucky," Admiral Bragg said.

"No, but neither was them three he killed."

"He didn't kill them."

"I saw them three lying in the sawdust. Every last one a cowboy with the T-Bar Ranch."

"And you jumped to conclusions."

"There was the barkeep and two others saying King Bragg done it, and they testified in court to it."

"You've got two weeks to prove that he didn't do it. Next time, the rope won't be cut."

"You tellin' me to undo justice?"

"I'm telling you, my boy didn't do it, and you're going to spring him."

"That boy's guilty as hell, and he's gonna pay for it."

Admiral Bragg, he sort of scowled. "I'm not going to argue with you. If you're too dumb to see it, then you'll hang."

Me, I just stared at the man. There was no talkin' to him.

"Get in the wagon or walk," Bragg said. "I'm done talking."

I favored the ride. I still was a little weak on my pins. So I got aboard, next to the geezer, and the buckboard rattled back to town, surrounded by Bragg and his gunslicks and cowboys. They took me straight to Belle's rooming house and I got out, and they rode off.

The morning was still young, and I'd already been hanged and told I'd be hanged again.

It sure was a tough start on a nice spring day.

I looked at them cottonwoods around town and saw that they were budding out. The town of Doubtful was about as quiet as little towns get. I didn't feel like doing nothing except go lie down, but instead, I made myself hike to the courthouse square, where the sheriff office was, along with the local lockup.

Bragg made me mad, tellin' me I was too dumb to see what was what.

It sure was a peaceful spring morning. Doubtful was doing its usual trade. There was a few ranch wagons parked at George Waller's emporium, and a few saddle horses tied to hitch rails. A playful little spring breeze, with an edge of cold on it, seemed to coil through town. It sure was nicer than the hot summers that sometimes roasted northern Wyoming. I was uncommonly glad to be alive, even if my knees wobbled a little. I smiled at folks and they smiled at me.

I got over to the courthouse, which baked in the sun, and made my way into the sheriff office. Sure enough, my undersheriff, Rusty, was parked there, his boots up on a desk.

"Where you been?" he asked.

"Getting myself hanged," I said.

Rusty, he smiled crookedly. "That's rich," he said.

I didn't argue. Rusty wouldn't believe it even if I swore to it on a stack of King James Bibles.

"You fed the prisoner?"

"Yeah, I picked up some flapjacks at Ma Ginger's. He complained some, but I suppose someone with two weeks on his string got a right to."

"What did he complain about?"

"The flapjacks wasn't cooked through, all dough."

"He's probably right," I said. "Ma Ginger gets it wrong most of the time."

"Serves him right," Rusty said.

"You empty his bucket?"

"You sure stick it to me, don't ya?"

"Somebody's got to do it. I'll do it."

Rusty smiled. "Knew you would if you got pushed into it."

I grabbed the big iron key off the peg and hung my gun belt on the same peg. It wasn't bright to go back there armed. King Bragg was the only prisoner we had at the moment, but I wasn't one to take chances. I opened up on the gloomy jail, lit only by a small barred window at the end of the front corridor. Three cells opened onto the corridor. King was kept in the farthest one.

He was lyin' on his bunk, which was a metal shelf with a blanket on it. The Puma County lockup wasn't no comfort palace. King's bucket stank.

"You want to push that through the food gate there?" I asked.

"Maybe I should just throw it in your face."

"I imagine you could do that."

He sprang off the metal bunk, grabbed the bucket, and eased it through the porthole, no trouble.

"I'll be back. I want to talk," I said.

"Sure, ease your conscience, hanging an innocent man."

I ignored him. He'd been saying that from the moment I nabbed him out at Anchor Ranch. I took his stinking bucket out to the crapper behind the jail, emptied it, pumped some well water into it and tossed that, and brought it back. It still stank; even the metal stinks after a while, and that's how it is in a jailhouse.

I opened the food gate and passed it through.

"Tell me again what happened," I said.

"Why bother?"

"Because your old man hanged me this morning. And it set me to wondering."

King Bragg wheezed, and then cackled. I sure didn't like him. He was a muscular punk, young and full of beans, deep-set eyes that seemed to mock. He was born to privilege, and he wore it in his manners, his face, his attitude, and his smirk.

"You don't look hanged," he said, getting smirky.

I sort of wanted to pulverize his smart-ass lips, but I didn't.

"Guess I'm lying to you about being hanged," I said. "So, go ahead and lie back. Start at the beginning."

The beginning was the middle of February, when King Bragg rode into Doubtful for some serious boozing, and alighted at Saloon Row, five drinkin' parlors side by side on the east end of town, catering to the cowboys, ranchers, and wanderers coming in on the pike heading toward Laramie.

"You parked that black horse in front of the Last Chance and wandered in," I said, trying to get him started.

"No, I went to the Stockman and then the Sampling

Room, and then the Last Chance. Only I don't remember any of that. Last I knew, I took a sip of red-eye at the Last Chance, Sammy the barkeep handed it to me, and I don't remember anything else. I couldn't even remember my own name when I came to."

Chapter Three

There's some folks you just don't like. It don't matter how they treat you. It don't matter if they tip their hat to you. If you don't like 'em, that's it. There's no sense gnawing on it. There was no sense dodging my dislike for King Bragg. I don't know where it come from. Maybe it was the way he kept himself groomed. Most fellers, they got two weeks to live, they don't care how they look. But King Bragg, he trimmed up his beard each morning, washed himself right smart, and even washed his duds and hung them to dry. That sure was a puzzle. The young man was keeping up appearances and it didn't make no sense. Not with the hourglass dribbling sand.

Now he stood quietly on the other side of them iron bars, telling me the same story I'd heard twenty times, and it didn't make any more sense now than the first time he spun it. It was just another yarn, maybe concocted with a little help from that lawyer, and it was his official alibi. Actually, it was more a crock than an alibi.

What King Bragg kept sayin' was that he had dozed through the killings, and when he woke up, he was holding his revolver and every shell had been fired. So he'd gotten awake after his siesta and got told he'd killed three men. And that was all he knew.

Well, that was a crock if ever I heard one.

"Maybe you got yourself liquored up real good, got crazy, picked a fight with them T-Bar cowboys, spilled a lot of blood, and got yourself charged with some killings."

That was the official version, the one that had convicted King Bragg of a triple murder. The one that was gonna pop his neck in a few days.

He stared. "I have nothing more to say about it," he said.

"Well I got nothing more to ask you," I said.

"Why are you asking? I've been sentenced, I'm going to hang. Why do you care?"

"Your pa, he asked me to look into it."

"Admiral Bragg doesn't ask anyone for anything. He orders."

"Well, now that's the truth. He sort of ordered me to."

"What did he say?"

"He didn't. He just hauled me out of Belle's crapper and hanged me."

"Now let me get this straight. My father—hanged you?"

"Noose and drop and all."

"I don't suppose you want to explain."

"It sure wasn't the way to make friends with the sheriff, boy."

"You calling me boy? You're hardly older than I am."

"I got the badge. I get to call old men boy if I feel like it."

"So my father, he hanged you?"

"Complete and total. And when I'm done here,

I'm gonna haul his ass to this here jail and throw away the key."

King Bragg laughed. "Good luck, pal."

He headed over to his sheet metal bunk, flopped down on it, and drew up that raggedy blanket. Me, I was satisfied. That feller wasn't gonna weasel out of a hanging with that cock-and-bull story. As for me, I was ready to hang him whether I liked him or not, because that was justice. A man shoots three fellers for no good reason, and he pays the price. I'd just have to deal with Admiral Bragg one way or the other. Now I'd talked with the boy to check his story and nothing had changed.

I didn't much like the thought of pulling the lever, but it would be my job to do it. They made me sheriff, and now I was stuck with it. I could quit and let someone else pull the lever that would drop King Bragg from this life. But I figure if a man's gonna be a man, he's got to do the hard things and not run away. So when the time comes, I'll pull the lever and watch King drop. Still, it sure made me wonder whether I wanted to be a lawman. It was more fun being young and getting into trouble. I was still young, but this wasn't the kind of trouble I was itching for. My ma used to warn me I had the trouble itch. If there was trouble somewhere, I'd be in the middle of it. Pa, he just said, keep your head down. Heads is what get shot.

I thought I'd ask a few more questions, just to satisfy myself that King Bragg done it and his ole man was being pigheaded, more than usual. Admiral Bragg was born pigheaded, and sometime it would do him in.

This sheriff business wasn't really up my alley. It would take someone with more upstairs than I ever had to ask the right questions. I could shoot fast and true, but that didn't mean my thinkin' was all that fast. There was a feller I wanted to jabber with about all this, the barkeep over to the Last Chance Saloon, Sammy Upward. That was his sworn-out legal monicker. Upward. It sure beat Downward.

The Last Chance was actually the first bar you hit coming into town, or the last one if you were ridin' out. That made it a little wilder than them other watering places. The rannies riding in, they headed for the first oasis they could find. It didn't matter none that it charged a nickel more for red-eye, fifteen cents instead of a dime, and two cents more, twelve in all, for a glass of Kessler's ale. It didn't matter none that some of them other joints had serving girls, some of them almost not bad lookin', if you didn't look too close. And it didn't matter none that the other joints were safer, because the managers made customers hang up their gun belts before they could get themselves served. No, the Last Chance was famous for rowdy, for rough, and for mean, and that's why young studs like King Bragg headed there itching for some kind of trouble to find him.

It wasn't yet noon, but maybe Upward would be pol-ishin' the spittoons or something, so I rattled the double door, found it unlocked, and found Upward sleeping on the bar. He lay there like a dead fish, but finally come around.

"We ain't open yet, Sheriff," he said.

"I ain't ordering a drink; I'm here for a visit."

"Visits cost same as a drink. Fifteen cents."

He hadn't yet stirred, and was peerin' up at me from atop the bar. That bar was sorta narrow, and he could fall off onto the brass rail in front, or off the back, where he usually worked, and where he had easy access to his sawed-off Greener.

"We're gonna visit, and maybe some day I'll buy one," I said.

"Someone get shot?"

"Not recently."

"I could arrange it if you get bored. If I say the word, someone usually gets shot in this here drinkin' parlor."

He peered up at me. He needed to trim the stubble on his chin, and maybe put on a new shirt, and maybe trade in that grimy bartender's apron for something that looked halfway washed.

"Tell me again what you told the court," I said.

"How many times we been through that, Sheriff? I'm tired of talking about it to people got wax in their ears."

"All right, pour me one."

"I knew you'd see it my way, Cotton."

The keep slid off the bar, examined a glass in the dim light, decided it wasn't no dirtier than the rest, and poured some red-eye in. The cheapskate poured about half a shot. I dug around in my britches for a dime and handed it to him.

"I owe you a nickel," I said. "Start with King Bragg coming in that night."

He didn't mind, or pretended he didn't.

"Oh, he come in here, and he was already loaded up. I could see by how he weaved when he walked."

"Why'd you serve him?"

"I make my living by quarters and dimes and nickels, damn you, and I'd serve a stumbling drunk if he had the right change. Hell, I'd even serve you, Cotton, even if it made my belly crawl. Just lay the change down, and I'll take it, and that's the whole story."

"You sure are touchy. How come?"

"I'll be just as touchy as I feel like, and I'm tired of telling you the story over and over. I ain't gonna tell it to you no more. You heard it, you've tried to pick it apart, and you can't. Now finish up and get out. I don't want you in this place. It's bad for business."

Upward was polishin' the bar so hard it was pulling the varnish off.

But I wasn't quitting. "What did King Bragg say to them T-Bar cowboys?"

"He said—oh, go to hell."

"That what he said?"

"No, that's what I'm telling you. I'm done yakking."

"How many T-Bar cowboys was in here?"

"I don't know. Just a few."

"Was Crayfish with the boys?"

"I don't remember. You want another drink? Fifteen cents on the barrelhead."

The man I was talkin' about owned the T-Bar, a few other ranches, and wanted Admiral Bragg's outfit too, just so he could piss on any tree in the county and call it his. His name was Crayfish Ruble. I don't know about that Crayfish part, but since I got Cotton hung on me, I don't ask no one about their first names. Not Crayfish, not Admiral. Crayfish Ruble had a Southern name, but I'd heard he was from Wisconsin, and who knows how he got a name like that. He come West with some coin in his jeans and bought a little spread, and then began muscling out the small-time settlers and farmers, paying about ten cents on the dollar, and pretty soon he was the biggest outfit in Puma County, and the T-Bar kept

Doubtful going. Without the T-Bar, Doubtful would be a ghost town, and no one would know Puma County from New York City.

I sorta liked Crayfish. He was honest in his crookedness. Ask Crayfish what he wanted from life, and he'd not mince any words. He wanted all of Puma County, as well as Sage County next door, and Bighorn County up above, and half the legislature of Wyoming, along with the judges and the tax assessor. I asked him, and that's what he told me. I also asked him what else he wanted, and he said he wanted half a dozen wives, or a good cathouse would do in a pinch, and his own railroad car and a mountain lion for a house pet. He got no children, so there ain't nothing he wants but land and cows and judges and women. You sorta had to like Catfish. He was a plain speaker, and he sure beat Admiral Bragg for entertainment. Catfish tried to buy out Admiral, but Admiral, he filed a claim on every water hole and creek in all the country, and that led to bad blood and they've been threatening to shoot the balls off each other ever since. There's no tellin' what gets into people, but I take it personal. I gotta keep order in this here Puma County, and I know from experience that when a few males got strange handles, like Admiral and Crayfish, or Cotton, there's trouble a percolatin' and no way of escaping it. The feller with the worst handle usually wins, and I've always figured Admiral is a worse name than Crayfish, and even worse than Cotton, though I'm not very happy with what got hung on me.

Well, I was gonna go talk to Crayfish again, for sure.

"Sammy, I think I asked you a question. Was Crayfish Ruble in here when the shooting started?"

Upward just polished the bar, like he didn't hear me.

"Who pays your wages, Sammy?"

I knew who. It was Crayfish. He owned the Last Chance, but didn't want no one to know it, so the name on the papers was Rosie, but she didn't have a dime more than she could make on her back, and someone put up a wad to buy this place, and it was Crayfish.

"I get my pay from Rosie," Sammy said.

I leaned across the bar and grabbed a handful of apron and pulled him tight. I seen his hands clawing for that Greener under the bar, so I just tugged him tighter.

"Don't," I said. "Who owns this joint?"

"Never did figure that out," he replied.

"You're a card, Upward. I think I'm going to look a lot closer at this here triple murder. Somebody shot three of Ruble's hands, and maybe it was King Bragg, just like the court says it was, but maybe it was someone else, you know who, and ain't saying. And I'm poking around a little more until I got a better handle on it. This ain't makin' me happy."

Upward, he didn't like that none.

THE LAST GUNFIGHTER SERIES BY
WILLIAM W. JOHNSTONE

THE MOUNTAIN MAN SERIES BY
WILLIAM W. JOHNSTONE